HEART OF A THUG
OMAR AND KEISHA'S TALE

KEELY

Wahida Clark Distribution

75 Washington St

PO Box 383

Fairburn GA 30213

1.866.910.6920

www.wclarkdistribution.com | www.wclarkpublishing.com

Copyright 2024 © Keely

All rights reserved. This book, or parts thereof, may not be reproduced in any form without permission. No part of this book may be reproduced in any form or by any electronic or mechanical means, including information storage and retrieval systems, without written permission from the author, except for the use of brief quotations in a book review.

Library of Congress Cataloging-In-Publication Data: Keely

Heart of A Thug: Omar and Keisha's Tale

ISBN: 978-1-957954-65-3 Hardcover

ISBN: 978-1-957954-63-9 Paperback

ISBN: 978-1-957954-64-6 eBook

1. Urban life fiction 2. Urban drama; Thug life; Love and redemption; Mental health in fiction; Trauma and recovery

Cover Design & Interior Layout by Nuance Art LLC

Printed in USA

DISCLAIMER

Fan fiction! To my girl and inspiration, Wahida, thank you. Thank you for waking up this desire and this hunger to want to write. I am twenty-seven years old and have been reading street lit since I was about eleven, and your *Thug Series*, Honey! I started reading this series when I was preparing for high school in the summer of eighth grade and I fell in love with every character. They were so real and relatable, I'm sure you hear that all the time.

After literally obsessing over what's to come with my "Thug Family," I grew an interest with other characters who didn't have big parts. The characters were Omar, Bo, Mel, Supreme, Shanna, Sannette and even some of the Santos clan. Omar, however, has been on my mind. He has some of Trae's blood running through him and I couldn't help but fantasize about giving him an "urban romance" tale with a modern take, a phase II, per se.

So, as your fan and someone who adores you and all of your books, I would like to give Omar a story; Over twenty years later! How crazy is that.

I want to put my pen to work, and you are the one I would like to do this for. This is my fan fiction piece, and I would love for you to consider this for publication.

I think readers will love this PHASE II of the Thug Series.

CHAPTER ONE

"MOMS! JORDAN!"

Fifteen-year-old Omar yelled out to his family as he walked through their townhome and sat his luggage by the kitchen table. His parents were divorced, and he'd just arrived back from a weekend with his father. He waited a few moments, and then heard tiny footsteps running toward him.

"Omar!" screamed Jordan, his four-year-old brother.

The two started play-fighting as laughter filled the kitchen. Upstairs, Olivia, Omar's mother, was applying make-up to her bruised and swollen face. She was once again on the opposing side of her boyfriend Victor's ass-whooping.

"Mom, why haven't you come down yet?"

Omar burst into her room and caught her sniffling while dabbing a makeup brush on her wounds.

"What happened to your face? That nigga hit you again?"

Omar walked toward her and yanked the make-up from her. His stomach turned while examining her black eyes, twisted nose, and busted lips.

"Baby, it's nothing. Don't speak about this while your brother is here," frowned Olivia as she looked at her two boys with tears forming in her eyes.

Omar stared down at his mother and told Jordan to go to his room.

"Every time I leave, this nigga finds a way to mess your face up! You need to stop putting up with this. I'm tired of it and Jordan don't need to be exposed to this! You endin' it with this punk-ass nigga, today!" Omar demanded.

His eyebrows were scrunched, breathing increased and he saw that she still had dried up blood along the crease of her lips.

"Baby, you're fifteen years old! I'm the parent! You don't make the rules on what I have going on. Let me handle my relationship. Okay?" Olivia yelled back. Omar was silent. "Your father stressed me out with his diabetes and the divorce. Victor is goin' through issues and our fights are just bad. Please, I don't need any more stress from the men in my life!" Salty tears dripped down her face and started stinging the wounds around her bruised lips.

"Pops doesn't have anything to do with this. He never hit you. Victor is a junkie! An abuser! And that pussy-ass nigga a freeloader. You've been doing everything on your own while he chasin' the next high!"

"Omar," she paused and collected her thoughts. "You're selling the drugs to him!" she scolded. Omar's heart stopped. "You didn't think I would find out, did you? *You*, Trae, Mel, Kaylin, Supreme, and Bo know better!" Her eyes filled with disappointment.

"I have to sell to help you! I can't sit back and watch my moms struggle to pay bills. Dad is struggling with his diabetes and medical bills. I have to do what I can to provide for y'all!"

She broke down crying. Every aspect of her life was stressful.

"You need to learn to stay out of your mama's business," chuckled Victor as he stumbled up the stairs.

He reeked of alcohol and was nodding off, drooling, and tripping over his two feet from the powder he just snorted.

"My mom is my business," Omar responded, throwing him a death stare.

"How about you go be a good li'l drug dealer and give me some free lines that's in that stash under your bed." Victor smirked, slurring his words. "I told your mama that I'll spare her from a few ass whoopins and I won't tell the police on you if you give me some of that dope," he mustered while laughing.

Omar immediately charged at him, punching him in his mouth. Blood leaked out from Victor's lip. He punched him again, this time in the eye and sent him crashing to the floor. He started stomping him in his stomach and Victor vomited on himself while Omar continued to beat the shit out of him.

Omar went into his room and grabbed his .9 mm from under his bed. He rushed back toward Victor and pointed the gun at his head. Victor's eyes opened wide as the cold steel pressed against his temple.

"Let me tell you somethin', bitch," Omar barked as he placed his finger on the trigger. "Put yo fuckin' hands on my mother again and I'ma turn your head into mush. You snort shit up your nose for a living. So snitch if you want to, and watch what happens to yo bitch-ass."

His mother ran over and grabbed his shirt. "Baby, no! Oh god, please put that gun away!"

Omar snapped out of it.

"Why do you have a gun in my house and you know your little brother lives here? Stop! First the drugs, now this!" She pointed to the gun. "You are gonna throw your whole life away," she cried.

Victor started coughing up blood and struggled to get off of the floor.

"Fuck you, bitch! You ain't got no control over that drug dealin' ass boy of yours! I'm out. You stupid bitch!" Victor yelled as he stumbled toward the steps.

Omar walked toward him, but his mother pulled him back. Jordan cracked his room door and saw his father leaving.

"Dad, where are you goin'?" Jordan innocently asked. "Dad?" His little eyes began welling with tears as he watched his father ignore him and walk out the door.

"I got us, mom. Forever. I promise. That nigga don't deserve y'all."

Omar looked at his mother and then at his little brother. Olivia knew she couldn't stand for anymore of the abuse with Victor. She had to be done because the last thing she wanted was for Omar to kill Victor and spend his life in jail. Her children came first, despite any bull shit she decided to put up with

CHAPTER TWO

TWO MONTHS LATER, Olivia was enjoying the summer and being free from the literal chokehold of Victor. She was in her kitchen making a phone call while Karyn White's, Superwoman was humming through the radio.

"Hey Sherry," stated Olivia while she looked out her window. "Can you give me a ride to Jordan's doctor appointment at two o'clock? Omar has my car and I'm sure his fresh behind is with a girl," she explained while helping Jordan get his shoes on.

"Let my godson live! He can legally drive, he doesn't bother anybody, and he knows how to defend himself," laughed Sherry. "I'm on my way."

She pulled up to the house and noticed the glow around Olivia. She was smiling more, and she had this aura about her that screamed she was at peace. *That's that fuck nigga free glow!*

"Look how happy leavin' Victor's ass has made you. It's only been a few months and here you go, looking like a glowing angel," smiled Sherry.

The women laughed. Olivia grabbed her house keys, put Jordan on her hip and they headed to the car. When they got outside, they were met by a drunken and deranged Victor.

"Olivia, where's your car?" He stumbled over to them. "You

lettin' that disrespectful-ass son of yours drive it?" Victor obnoxiously sniffled.

His facial hair was overly grown, he smelled like dog shit, and had white residue around his dripping nose.

"Your four-year-old son hasn't seen you in two months and when he does see you, you're worried about Omar? Please get away from my house," Olivia replied while they tried to brush past him. Jordan started crying and reaching for his dad.

"Bitch, who you talkin' to?" Victor pulled out a gun and pointed it at them. The women gasped and were frozen with shock as they stared at the gun. "You choose your criminal-ass son over me?" He dragged his words and loosely waved the gun.

"Oh my goodness! Victor! She's holding your child. Are you fuckin' serious?" Sherry yelled and stood in front of Olivia and Jordan.

She had no children of her own, but Omar and Jordan were her godsons and she loved Olivia like a sister. She would always be there to protect them.

"Get yo nosey ass out the way! Olivia can handle herself, bitch!" he stated as he kept pointing the gun. "Matter of fact, go in the house! Go 'head! All of y'all," he demanded, continuing to point the gun.

Their legs became Jell-O as they turned to walk toward the house. Sherry looked around to see if she could yell for help, but no one was around.

"Mommy, why does dad have a gun? You said those are dangerous," expressed Jordan who clung to his mother and watched his father yell insults to her.

"Shhh, baby. Just close your eyes," Olivia said. She unlocked her house door and they all filed into her living room.

"Olivia," Victor's high-ass smirked. "Let my son see this! Let him see how you allow niggas to have guns and sell drugs from your house! Dumb-ass!" His gun was aimed directly toward her while he continued to degrade her.

Olivia still kept her son's head turned away from everything and kept whispering for him to keep his eyes closed.

"You need to stop! You're scaring Jordan," panicked Sherry as she walked toward Victor with her hands up.

"Mind your business, bitch." Those were the last words Sherry heard before Victor fired off the gun striking Sherry in the head.

The bullet pierced through her forehead and killed her on impact. Blood leaked out of her lifeless body, making a thump sound as she hit the ground. Olivia started screaming and she held onto her son as she went to check Sherry's pulse.

When she looked up, she was met by a line of bullets that punctured her and Jordan, causing their bodies to jerk as they fell to the ground. The blood stained the hardwood floors and formed a puddle around Victor's foot. He looked at the four bullets in Jordan's head and chest. Then, he saw the two bullets in Olivia's head. He stood there in shock but then his coked-out mind had one thing on it, Omar's stash.

He darted to Omar's room and kicked the door until it flung open. He rummaged through his dressers and looked under the bed until he found a box that held packaged bags of cocaine. He took the entire box and headed toward the stairs. He was still drunk and high, so he tripped over his two feet and a few bags of cocaine dropped out. He picked up the ones he could see, then headed toward the dead bodies.

He stepped over Sherry's body and then went towards Olivia's purse that was around her neck. He ransacked it, searching her wallet for any cash. He went to the front door and closed it quietly behind him, smiling about his next high. He was on cloud nine and didn't give a fuck that he'd just killed his child, his child's mother, and a family friend.

CHAPTER
THREE

THAT SAME SUMMER DAY:

Omar was driving with his cousin Trae and longtime friends, Bo, Kaylin, Supreme, and Mel. They were all taking puffs from a blunt while Biggie's Ten Crack Commandments played through the car's speaker.

They were all getting a little bit of money and with money, came the bitches. Omar dropped them off at their destinations and went to meet up with a chick named Tanisha. He was sitting on her bed, and she was massaging his dick.

"You gon' pay for my nails to get done, Omar?" she asked as she kissed his neck.

He started chuckling in disbelief because Tanisha was trying to sell pussy already. They were only fifteen, and Omar thought that selling pussy was supposed to be for emergencies only.

Omar, however, didn't care to take any of these girls seriously because it was always the same thing, trickin' and fuckin'. They wanted the funds and all he wanted was a nut. Simple.

"Yeah. I got you," he told her.

She started rubbing up and down his dick and felt it grow. She got down on her knees, unzipped his jeans, and his massive third-leg was bulging through his boxers.

"Oh my god!" she was in shock as she stared down at the length of his dick.

She started sucking on the head and stroking the shaft up and down. She put more of his dick in her mouth and Omar grabbed her head. He started thrusting his hips and trying to get her to fit more of his dick in her mouth.

"My jaws gettin' tired," she complained after five minutes and opted to give him a hand-job.

Omar didn't say a word. *How you a bitch asking to get your nails done, initiating sucking dick but yet your jaws are tired, and you haven't did shit but suck the head?* If this was all the dating pool had to offer, he knew he would be single for life. She stroked him until she felt it pulsate and he shot his warm load over her boobs. Omar gave her the nail money and left the house. He made it to his mother's car and headed home.

WHEN HE PULLED *up to* his home, the lights beamed on the slightly cracked front door. Omar turned off the vehicle, got out of the car, and walked toward the front. The door creaked when he opened it and he almost slipped as he stepped inside a puddle of blood.

He was frozen like a statue while looking at the dead bodies sprawled out on the floor. He blinked his eyes a million times and his heart felt like it was ripping out of his chest. His mother was still holding onto Jordan while their blood mixed.

"Mom. Jordan. Aunt Sherry," his voice was shaky and cracking as he went toward their bodies.

Omar started throwing up as his tears poured out and mixed with the snot from his nose. He started dry heaving and shaking while he stared at the bodies of his loved ones.

"What the fuck!" he bent down to shake his mom's lifeless body.

He grabbed Jordan's small hand and bit down on his bottom lip when he felt how limp Jordan was. It was as if a dagger was placed through his heart while his body ran hot. Tears were steadily streaming but there was no sound.

Ten minutes passed, and Omar looked toward the stairwell and saw a bag of cocaine near the couch. His stomach was doing backflips as his nose flared. His thoughts were all over the place, and a lump had formed in his throat again. He stood up, closed his eyes while he deep sighed and went toward his room.

He saw his room door was kicked open and noticed his mattress was hanging off the bed frame. He looked under his bed and saw that his drug stash was gone; he already knew who did it. Omar started punching the walls as the tears continued to flow.

After about thirty minutes, he mustered up the strength to dial his father, but he could barely get any words out. His father, Carl, flew over to the home and held his hand over his mouth as he saw the terrible scene, tears streaming from his eyes as well.

He called the police, and the forensics team came to mark off the crime scene. Omar would never forget the sight of seeing those white blankets being thrown over his loved ones. The detectives came over to them and told Omar and his father that they were needed down at the station for a formal statement. Once at the station, the detective led them to his office.

"Sir, do you know anyone who could have done this? It'll help if you tell us everything," inquired Detective Creekmore to Omar from his desk.

Omar was in a trance as all the life drained from his body.

"Do you know of any drugs, previous violence, or any other issues your mother had going on?"

"What the fuck do you mean drugs! My mother wasn't a junkie!" Omar hollered at the officer as he became triggered by the drug accusations.

"I'm just asking a question. Calm down," stated the detective as he grabbed onto his holster.

"I'm not doing shit! My mother and brother were shot dead, and you worried about some fuckin' drugs. Did you check any fingerprints? Did you ask any neighbors what they heard? Or is this goin' to be another fuckin' cold case?" Omar stood up.

Other officers and detectives came over to deescalate the commotion.

"Sir, you have to calm down or we will have to arrest you!" yelled an officer as he grabbed Omar who was resisting.

"Omar, stop! Please! This day is already hard enough, son. Calm down!" begged Carl while he watched Omar yank away from the officers.

Omar made eye contact with him and saw his father's watery eyes. He stopped resisting and they sat him in a chair. The detective attempted to get Omar's statement again, but he blocked out his voice and refused to answer. He put his head down and darkness covered his thoughts. His mind was focused on doing treacherous acts to the motherfucker that did this.

He couldn't believe he took a piece of his heart away from him and had the trifling-ass nerve to steal from him after the murders were committed. Omar couldn't wait to get his hands on that nigga.

Two weeks later, Olivia, four-year-old Jordan, and innocent Sherry were laid to rest. Neither had any life insurance policies, so Carl had to use his savings to give his ex-wife and Jordan a proper burial service.

Omar stopped selling drugs completely and being that he was new to it, he didn't have any money put away to assist with the funeral arrangements, which further devastated him. All he wanted to do was provide for his loved ones and he failed to come through this time.

CHAPTER
FOUR

IT HAD BEEN several months since the awful murders and Omar still shed silent tears. He was lucky to have his father, but he missed seeing his mother's smile and her warm hugs. Despite everything, he knew she finally left Victor because she wanted to protect him.

He was emotionally traumatized by everything, but he had no time to grieve or understand his emotions because his father was struggling with his diabetes. The reason why his parents were divorced was because his father and his diabetes were too much to manage. He skipped out on his doctor appointments because he had to go to work in order to ensure a roof stayed over his son's head due to completely draining his accounts for the funerals.

Carl refused to speak up about any pain he felt in his kidneys and in his feet. Trae and Kaylin told Omar about an opportunity to sell more weight than what they were used to, and Omar was hesitant because he knew selling drugs upset his mother. Even though she wasn't alive, he still wanted to make decisions that would make her proud.

It was the day of Omar's sixteenth birthday, and he came into the house after playing basketball to get ready for dinner with his father. He walked toward the fridge and yelled out for his father.

"Pops, you said you were goin' to be ready when I got back!" Omar chuckled as he looked inside their fridge. His father didn't respond. "Pops! I know you ain't fall asleep when you the one who made the plans," he paused all his movements and again, no response.

The silence started to cause his heart rate to speed up. He went towards his father's bedroom, and saw Carl sitting on the ground turning his head side to side.

"Who you?" Carl asked through slurred words and then started laughing hysterically. "Agh!" he screamed. "Get out of my house if I don't know you muthafucka!" Carl let out a screeching laugh.

Omar stood there in a daze at his father in this state.

"Pops, where is your glucose monitor? Your sugar is too low, and you may be going into a diabetic shock."

Omar searched everywhere for the monitor, a piece of candy or something with sugar to get his vitals back right. He found a Snicker bar on the dresser and tried to feed it to Carl, but he smacked his hand away.

"Don't feed shit to me if I don't know you!" yelled Carl.

His sugar levels were plummeting, and he was extremely delusional. He tried to get up from off the floor, but he became dizzy and slouched back down.

"Eat this until I find your insulin!' Omar shoved a piece of the Snickers in his mouth and Carl chewed it.

He was still slurring his words and in a state of confusion but the sugar from the Snickers was starting to work.

"The monitor is on the TV stand," pointed Carl. His vision was becoming less blurry and Omar headed there to retrieve the items. He went over to Carl, pricked his finger, and the machine read fifty-eight which was deathly low. He called the ambulance, and the paramedics loaded him into the back of the truck. He was admitted to the hospital where they gave him a sugar drink and Carl's sugar levels were back to normal limits within a few hours.

"Mr. Carl Gaulding," the doctor called out as he checked over his chart.

"That's me," said Carl from the hospital bed with a lazy grin.

"I'm glad you're still with us. If your sugar would have dropped any lower, you would have had a seizure," the doctor explained as he walked closer to him.

"It won't get that low ever again," Omar reassured the doctor then glanced at Carl.

"I'm also sorry to tell you this but while doing your exam," he paused. "You had nerve damage so severe in two of your toes that we have to amputate them because of the poor blood circulation," he explained to Carl who was speechless. "You also are at the beginning stages of kidney disease but that can be reversed if you change a few daily habits."

The doctor told him that the surgery would be the next day, and it was for the better.

"The surgery is tomorrow? Don't I need time to prepare? Who's going to care for my son while I'm here? He's still a minor and I need to go to work to pay our bills!" Carl's blood pressure began to rise.

"You should be out of here in five days maximum," the doctor said to him as he walked to Carl and laid a hand on his shoulder. "Child Protective Services will also be coming to speak with you both to do a report. This is the sixth time in two months that you have been admitted due to low sugar levels. If this keeps up, you may lose custody of your son if they deem you unfit to care for him in this state," the doctor dropped a bomb on Carl, and he looked at Omar with worry in his eyes.

Omar had to leave the room and take a few deep breaths. The thought of having a meeting with CPS caused his breathing to increase but the thought of being away from his father, his only living parent, scared him.

He pulled his phone out and called up Trae. He told him he was all in to move weight for the Dons. His father had been working himself to the bone, but his health was deteriorating. He could not lose another fucking parent. He had to move weight so he could make sure his father focused only on his health. Omar would do all he could to take care of them.

CHAPTER FIVE

SIX MONTHS LATER, Victor was out begging some dealers for a fix. "Yo, you got twenty to spare for some white girl?"

Since the murders, he had been snorting powder at a ridiculous rate and had now added heroin into his drug rotation. He was so geeked up that he didn't even notice Bo approaching him. Bo examined Victor's bare feet, his thin, hundred pound body, and noticed that he was clinging to a bloody syringe needle.

"Yeah, I got you. It's back here. Follow me," said Bo. Victor followed him to a dark warehouse. "Just stay right here. I'll be back," he said and then left Victor there alone.

A few minutes went by before the lights from the warehouse flashed on, blinding him. He tried to block the bright lights with his hands, but it didn't help. He noticed a figure walking toward him and he started smiling with glee because he knew his next high was coming.

"You happy to see me like I'm happy to see you?" Omar asked.

Victor almost shit his pants. It was as if the devil himself came and summoned him to hell. The smile vanished from his thinly formed face, and he fell back on the ground while grabbing his chest.

"Omar," Victor paused and swallowed his spit. "What the fuck are you doing here?" he blurted out as he looked to see if anyone was around to help.

He spotted a door and tried to make a run for it. Omar pulled out a machete with a twenty-two-inch blade and whipped it across Victor's back. He let out an agonizing scream as he saw his blood splatter on the floor.

"Nigga, for what you did to my moms, my brother, and Aunt Sherry, you will die in this fucking warehouse tonight!"

"It was an accident! I swear!" Victor pleaded while flashbacks of the murders he committed flooded his mind.

"Shooting three people in the head was an accident?"

He lashed the sharp machete across Victor's hand and cleanly sliced off four of his fingers. Victor screamed like he was being cast for a horror film and his eyes bulged open as his fingers plopped to the ground.

"Please, Omar, please! Please!"

"Did you show my mom and brother any remorse before you shot them? Huh? Or how about when you kept putting your fuckin' hands on my mother?" he yelled as he chopped off Victor's hand. "You won't be able to use your hands for shit now, bitch!"

Victor began hallucinating as the blood gushed out of his wrist. His motionless hand was detached from his body and Victor swore he could hear his hands laughing at him. The hands that he used to beat on women with were now detached from his body.

"Omar, spare me. Please," Victor begged for his life while watching his blood spurt out.

"When my mother took her last fuckin' breath, you decided to go into her purse, steal her wallet and you decided to fuckin' rob me! You a bitch-ass nigga. I'll never spare a nigga like you," his voice was cold as he raised the machete and sliced off Victor's arm.

Blood was squirting out like someone stepped on a full

ketchup bottle. Omar stood there for ten minutes and watched him bleed out.

"I got the justice for y'all, mom," he said under his breath.

This was the first murder Omar committed, and it gave him a rush like never before. He felt a beast form inside him, and he enjoyed seeing Victor suffer. Omar was an observer and never did too much talking when it came to handling business.

He had been observing Victor's patterns for months, but he knew he had to plan this strategically. Murdering Victor didn't bring his mother back, but damn, he was finally able to get a piece of mind.

A FEW DAYS LATER, **Carl** was sitting on the couch checking his blood sugar. The six o'clock news was on and there was a gruesome story being explained.

"The head of an African American male was found along the outskirts of the city and it has been identified as Victor Portello," explained the news reporter. *"No suspects have been announced and this is a developing story."*

Carl's heart dropped and his stomach started to feel weak. His lips started quivering and his hands started shaking. A sweat bead formed across his forehead as the news anchor went on with the story.

As soon as he heard the victim's name, he knew this was his son. *Decapitating someone?* This was personal and the feeling of worry filled his entire body as he rushed up from the chair to dial Omar.

As soon as he grabbed the phone, Omar came through the front door and they stood there looking at each other as the news showed a family member of Victor's asking why this happened to him.

"Son," Carl swallowed his spit and turned the TV off. "What are you doing with your life? Finding someone's head is absolutely insane," he sincerely stated as he got up and hugged him.

Omar remained silent. "I love you. Don't throw your life away to these streets. He got what he deserved, but please control your emotions. Promise me you will just check in with me so I can know you are alive. We all we got, Omar," Carl's eyes welled up.

"I promise, pops. You gotta promise me you will take care of your health. I'll handle everything else," Omar spoke, embracing his father back.

"I don't agree with this lifestyle. The streets ain't nice to anybody," he explained as he hugged his son like it would be their last time.

CHAPTER SIX

AS TIME PASSED, Omar kept his promise to his father and remained safe and his father maintained his health. Carl's health was so good, that he found the courage and time to seek love again. He ended up marrying a woman named Michelle who was a school guidance counselor. Omar loved Michelle for his father, and she embraced Omar as if she birthed him. She couldn't have any children of her own, but her love was there.

Now let's fast forward to when that iconic book, *Every Thug Needs A Lady* was released. The year was 2002 and Omar was now twenty-five years old. He purchased himself a two bedroom home with three cars and even though the streets were ruthless, a nigga was out here getting major money.

He never quite settled down because ever since he started fucking, he just knew the selection of females wasn't worth settling down for. He felt they only wanted a guy for his material possessions, and he didn't mind fooling around with them with no commitment.

He was standing in his mirror listening to Roc the Mic by Freeway and Beanie Sigel while getting ready to head out for a booty call. He stood six feet tall and had dark chocolate skin. He had a six-pack and handsomely defined arms. He sported a low cut with deep waves, thick eyebrows, and dreamy bedroom eyes with long eyelashes. He had lips that any pussy would love to sit on and a medium muscular physique.

He reminded everyone of the rapper Loon that was in the song with Diddy and Usher called, I Need a Girl. To this new social media generation, gon' ahead and search in YouTube, Loon + I Need a Girl so you get the picture.

Omar's personality was always described as quiet but trust, he was never scared to get down when he had to. His phone rang and it was his childhood friend, Bo.

"Yo, nigga! What you gettin' into tonight?" yelled Bo through the phone.

"Nothing much. About to go slide in something," Omar chuckled as he slid his pants on.

"You always got somebody in the rotation with your quiet ass," laughed Bo.

"Nigga, that's you, or did you forget about Theresa and Miesha?" Omar joked as he headed downstairs.

"You got Lucille, Bria, Ava... Should I go on?"

"I ain't got nobody. I'm single. I'm getting tired of this shit though," Omar explained as he grabbed his keys.

"Go head and be a sucka like that nigga Trae. That just means it will be mo' pussy out here for me," both the men laughed. "Come meet up with us at the club after you finish creepin'," Bo joked and then the men hung up.

Omar grabbed his gun, keys, locked his house up and headed to this chick named Lucille's house. He had been fooling around with her whenever he felt like it. He pulled up to the house, locked his car, and knocked on her door. She opened it wearing a long robe and her hair was in a ponytail.

"Took you long enough. I called you two hours ago," Lucille hissed as she let him in.

"I know, ma. My fault," he subtly responded. She led them to the living room couch and the two sat in silence.

"So, I haven't spoken to you in about a week. You must've found yourself a girlfriend," Lucille said while rolling her eyes.

"Naw. I'ma single man. You know what me and you do. Let's not complicate shit."

He didn't want a relationship and he made that shit clear to her but for some reason that's the only conversation she wanted to have.

"You just had unprotected sex with me a month ago! You really ain't shit and keep playing these, 'I'm single', games," she screamed.

She felt like her heart was about to explode. She was so damn attracted to Omar, but he told her multiple times already that he was basically looking for a fuck buddy.

"That was a one-time slip up. But look, I'ma just leave. I told you I don't want anything complicated, and I don't want a relationship. You're getting emotional and I don't have time for that."

Omar got up to leave to avoid any escalation. He didn't like talking about his feelings, especially not with someone he wasn't emotionally invested in. She stopped him when he grabbed his keys.

"Okay, okay. Look, you're right," she said as she started rubbing on his dick.

She didn't want him to leave. So, she led him back to the chair and unzipped his pants to pull his dick out. "You got all this dick for all these bitches you deal with?" she teased. She began sucking on his thick dick head while she played around with his pre-cum.

"You worried about the wrong shit."

She continued to suck on the head and Omar put his hands on the back of her head, but she resisted.

"I told you I gag every time I try to deep throat. You know I don't even like suckin' dick," Lucille whined as she kept toying with it and stroking his dick up and down.

Once it was nice and hard, she stood up and opened her robe, revealing her naked light brown body. Omar stood up too and dropped his pants. He laid her down on the couch and put a condom on. He dropped some spit on her clit and tapped his dick on it while she moaned out his name.

He grabbed her by her waist and pushed his dick inside of her. He stroked in and out of her wetness and focused on getting his nut off. He pounded her until he felt her body tense up because of her orgasm. He kept going until he exploded. After he gathered his bearings, he tried to turn her around.

"No Omar, I told you I have to wait a few before the next round," she complained as she put her robe back on and stared at him.

She was too far gone thinking she could convince him to be emotionally attached to her or have emotions for her at all. He was detached from everything and only saw her as being beneficial for one thing, pussy. He pulled his pants up and got ready to head out.

"I'm pregnant, Omar," Lucille blurted out as she saw him leaving.

He stopped in his tracks and turned around.

"What? I fucked one time with no condom, and I pulled out," he explained, giving her his full attention.

His palms started to get sweaty and the embarrassment of having to explain how he got caught slippin' and impregnated this whore caused his anxiety to flare up. *Damn, this is the worst fucking slip up.*

"All it takes is one time and you can get pregnant with pre-cum," Lucille smirked from the chair.

She was going to trap his ass one way or another. He didn't want a relationship with her- okay, fine. In her mind, he would be forced to form a relationship with this baby.

"Look, okay," Omar rubbed his hands across his face. "I'll take accountability and if you keep the baby, I'ma do what I have to do. If you don't keep it, I'll pay for the price of that, too. But, I'ma get a test to be sure it's mine," he said and Lucille's heart sank.

"A test for what? This yo baby!" she screamed.

"Lucille, stop it. I fuck you, what? Maybe every other week. We're not together. It's only right I get a DNA test."

She started cussing Omar out about how stupid he was for wanting a test. He wasn't in the mood for the argument, so he turned around to leave while she was still fussing. He went to open the front door and was met by another man with his keys out. The men stared at each other. He was a few inches shorter than Omar, with curly hair, and golden colored skin.

"Who are you?" asked the unknown man.

"Who are you?" Omar shot back and reached toward his waist band for his gun, getting ready for whatever.

"This is my house and that's my wife. Who are you?" asked Sampson, Lucille's husband.

Omar was speechless. Here he was just being told that he was going to be a father and the whole time this bitch was married. He had no idea. Both of the men stared at Lucille whose mouth was to the floor. All Omar could do was shake his head. She specifically told him she was single.

"I'm out," stated Omar and he tried to move past Sampson.

"Please don't tell me my wife is having an affair," Sampson sobbed, tears running down his face.

He worked out of town and made enough for Lucille to be a stay-at-home wife. He desperately wanted children and this possibility crushed him.

"Lucille, are you carrying my baby or his?" Sampson almost threw up asking her that question.

Omar was silent at the fact she told him and her husband she was pregnant.

"Sampson, I am not having an affair!"

Lucille hurried up, pushed Omar out of the house, and closed the door.

"I gotta stop dealin' with these hoes and meetin' women at the club. All these muthafuckas do is lie!" Omar spoke out loud to himself while he started his car up and headed home.

What part of the fucking game was that. He wasn't even tripping because he gave no shits about Lucille. It's the fact that she lied about everything for no reason at all. She was grimy as hell. This bitch was cheating on her husband and letting however many other dudes fuck her raw. Disgusting. *The nerve of her trying to trap me with a baby.*

CHAPTER
SEVEN

SEVERAL WEEKS LATER, Lucille ended up getting an abortion because she did not know whose baby she was carrying. She called Omar every single day for months after that, but he refused to answer.

In the meantime, he found himself in another pregnancy scare with a trick named Bria. She also got an abortion because she, just like Lucille, did not know whose baby she was carrying and tried to pin it on him.

Omar was tired of living the bachelor life though. He didn't know if he was ready for a relationship, but he knew this ho life was at its end for him before he ended up putting a bullet in one of these grimey-ass females.

Other than all these "maybe babies," he was still heavy in the streets. His crew just got back from a successful drug drop, and they went to the club to celebrate. Omar saw Trae at the bar talking to a bartender and he went over to him. The music started to fade out the closer he got to the bar, and he was within earshot of their conversation.

"I'm giving you a family discount for this water bottle, my brother. Just keep treating my girl Roz aka Tasha right," stated Ke as she gave Trae his items.

"She ain't got nothing to worry about," Trae said to her and left her a hundred dollar tip.

Omar was checking out Ke's pretty brown skin and her plump lips. He said he was done meeting women at the club, but he couldn't resist. Trae left the bar area and Omar motioned for him to come to him.

"Yo, you know her?" questioned Omar to Trae as he nodded in the direction of Ke.

"Nigga," Trae chuckled. "Yeah, I know her. That's one of Tasha's friends."

"Tasha got a friend that is a bartender?"

"Why?" Trae asked.

"Introduce me to her. That's why."

"First Kay, now you," Trae laughed. "I ain't introducing you to shit if all you want to do is play. She ain't on them type of times O'," Trae warned his cousin.

"Nigga, I know the difference between someone who's trickin' and someone that can be wifey. Plus, you know I can do my dirty work myself with somebody that's trying to just play. I'm tired of playing. I want to be sprung and in love like you," Omar teased Trae. "I want to see what she about. So, introduce me."

"A'ight, come on," Trae led the way as he played match maker once again with one of his niggas and one of Tasha's friends. They both walked to the bar and Trae got Ke's attention.

"Trae you need something else?" Ke asked confused as she got her orders together.

"Naw, I just wanted to introduce you to my cousin, Omar," Trae stated. "This is Omar and Omar, this is Ke."

They exchanged greetings as Trae left. Omar noticed how pretty her teeth were. His eyes moved down to her petite frame with perky breasts and thick thighs. She turned around to take someone's credit card and he saw her round ass which sat perfectly in her jeans that was accompanied by hips that were spread like butter. He was completely turned on by her appearance.

Ke noticed his chocolate skin, low-cut with the waves, thick lips and dreamy eyes. His six-foot frame towered over her five foot four frame and she could tell he was cut underneath the sweatsuit he was wearing. Omar sparked up the conversation.

"Your name is Ke? You like working the bar? I see it's jumpin' in this shit tonight," Omar asked her and didn't give her much time to answer.

"Yes, that's my name and most weekends it's like this," she explained while handing the customer's receipt and card back.

"Are you here every weekend?"

"Just about," she responded while trying to get her other orders out.

Omar was observing her body language and her constant eye rolling. He also noticed that she had healed scars on her wrists which instantly intrigued him. He kept on with the conversation though.

"What do you do when you're not working here?" he questioned as he stood beside a bar stool.

She rudely smacked her lips and responded. "Why do you want to know?"

She was not trying to take this conversation any further.

"Because I want to take you out during your free time. Is that okay? " Omar stated with a sly smile while he licked his lips and made eye contact with her.

"Naw. I'm good," she stated matter-of-factly.

"Why not?" he pressed on.

This caught her off guard. Usually when she says she is not interested most men take the hint and leave her alone.

"Because I'm just not into dating right now."

"Let's exchange numbers," Omar pressed.

"I just said I'm good. I'm not giving my number out and my shift is about to end so can you wrap this up," she said in her sassy-ass tone as she continued to roll her eyes.

"Hmph, well I don't want to hold you up from ending your shift. We can just finish this convo tomorrow at your next shift," he stated back to her with a cocky smile. He then left her there speechless.

"Girl, who was that talking to you? He was fine as hell," asked Sarah, the other bartender. She handed Ke a customer's phone that was left at the bar. She labeled it and placed it in their lost phone bin.

"This guy my friend knows. Let's clean up. I'm ready to go and get in my bed."

They counted their tips and Ke had over seventeen hundred dollars for the night and Sarah had about twelve hundred. The girls high-fived each other and walked to their cars. In the parking lot, Ke saw Omar near a truck with a group of other dudes. The two locked eyes and he winked at her as she got in her car.

"Ugh, puhlease," she rolled her eyes and drove off.

CHAPTER EIGHT

HOLD ON NOW Y'ALL, *let's pause because who the hell is this "Ke" chick that's entering the Thug Series? Readers, hopeless romantics, and urban book lovers: don't y'all remember the vibe we used to get when we picked up an urban tale? Remember how every girl fantasized about a big dick dude who was all for them, protected them, and loved them? Remember how those books just gave us hope for Black love with somebody that was romantic, charismatic, and charming?*

I want us to get those vibes back and what better series to mix love and our modern issues of today with than the Thug Series. Sooo, Miss Ke is being placed in this series, but she fits the fucking script for my vision of this fan fiction piece. Let's check out who she is.

The next day, Ke was in her townhome listening to Mary J Blige's, No More Drama. That song spoke volumes to her because she indeed was living life drama free at the moment.

For the past year and a half, she worked on putting the pieces of her life back together after losing everything to a bad relationship. Her hips had started to spread again, ass was soft and had a nice jiggle, thighs matched the ass, and she had perky C cup breasts. She had smooth brown skin, almond shaped eyes and lips that were full and plump like a Bratz Doll. She wore her natural hair either straightened down her back or in a signature puff on the top of her head. She had a smile that would light up the room whenever she wasn't hiding behind her resting bitch face.

Okay, let me get dressed. After perusing the closet, she grabbed a pair of black leather pants, a snug fitting sweater, some knee length boots, and a black Chanel purse to match. She brushed her hair into a huge puff at the top of her head, applied some lip gloss, grabbed her keys and headed out to her car. She drove for fifteen minutes before arriving at her gynecologist appointment. She checked in and a few moments later, they called her to the back to check her weight.

"One hundred and twenty-seven pounds, Ms. Harris. Lookin 'good," the nurse told Ke. "Follow me to this back room and your doctor will be right in. Go ahead and undress and then lay on the table," she instructed before she exited the room.

Ke did what she was told, and laid on the table with a cloth covering her body.

Knock-knock!

In came the doctor. "How you doing, Keisha? How's this year been for you?" asked Doctor Greyson.

"Things have been well. I can't complain."

"Nice to hear that. I'm going to give you a pap smear and then check to see the progress of your tilted uterus."

She told Ke to spread her legs and then she began her examination. "Everything looks fine. Your uterus is still tilted due to the severe abuse but this will not hinder your fertility. You will still be able to have children. Would you like to consider any birth control options?" Doctor Greyson asked as she removed her gloves.

Ke wiped off the lubricant gel from between her legs. "No, I'm fine. I haven't been having sex and don't plan on having it ever again," Ke told her as they laughed. "I don't even want kids, Doc."

"Sex can help straighten out that uterus according to

research," teased the doctor. "You may change your mind about children."

They said their goodbyes and Dr. Greyson left the room with a smile.

Once Ke was dressed, she checked out of her appointment and headed to her car. Her phone rang just as she put her car in reverse. It was Kyra.

"Hey, girl! Are you still coming to the sleep study? I need you as my participant for this last internship so I can have research on those brain waves," Kyra explained over the phone.

"On the way to you now. Don't be scared about anything you see my brain waves do. You know a bitch ain't right in the head," she joked.

She told Kyra that she would see her in a few and when she pulled up to the psych institute, she sat in her car for a few moments. She raised the sleeves of her sweater to reveal the scars on her wrist and ran her fingers over them.

"You got this, Keisha." She took deep breaths and then got out of the car.

Chills ran through her body as she walked into the building. She went to the front desk and told them who she was there for. Kyra came around the corner with her four-month pregnant belly and greeted her.

"You ready?" she asked as they walked to the back.

"Yep!"

They entered an all-white room and Kyra gave her a hospital gown to change into. Then Ke went to lay on the bed while they stuck wires to her forehead. Kyra and the other psych students explained to her that she could listen to music while they gave her a sedative to help her fall asleep. Ke played *Eve's Love is Blind* on her Walkman, and that's when the flashbacks of her shitty-ass life began.

CHAPTER
NINE

KEISHA "KE" *Harris is the oldest of four siblings and is originally from Virginia. Her mother packed her and her siblings up and moved to New Jersey when they lost their father to mental illness. He was a retired Army Veteran and experienced serious PTSD from being in the field. There were times when Ke would recall her father just simply forgetting things, then the microwave would go off and he would lose it. He would start screaming, and even strangled her mother.*

Ke interfered one time and her dad, not in his right state of mind pushed her down like he was doing a combat drill. Her mother pleaded with her to never get involved again because their father was not well. She begged him to seek help, but he didn't want any help from, 'no head doctors because I ain't muthafuckin' mentally unstable', was what he always said. During those PTSD episodes, Ke would distract her brother and sisters so they wouldn't be frightened. Her dad would calm down and it was as if nothing ever happened until the next episode.

It was a cold December night and Ke remembered her mother cooking a real southern dinner of turkey wings, collard greens, baked mac and cheese, candied yams and some sweet honey cornbread. She was in the living room with her siblings going over their homework.

"Ke, can you help me with this math?" asked her younger sister, Brielle.

"Yeah, give me a sec."

A few moments later, they heard a loud bang at the door. It was their father having an episode trying to kick the door down. Her younger brother, Travon, went to open the door and their dad came in screaming while waving a gun saying that the enemies were near.

Ke's mother hollered for the children to go upstairs and not to come out until he calmed down. Ke already knew the routine, but this time, something felt different. As she was waving her siblings up the stairs, she heard a loud boom. She turned around and saw that their dad had fired into the ceiling.

"Oh my goodness, baby! Please put the gun down!" her mother screamed hysterically.

"Please, baby, please. Don't do this in front of the kids."

He put the gun down, dropped to his knees and cried.

He wept. "Baby, I cannot live like this anymore, I can't do it. I don't want to be here!"

He took a knife out of his pocket and slit his own throat, right in the middle of the kitchen floor. Ke's mother started screaming and yelling for 911 to be called.

He refused to seek help for his mental instability. His PTSD was "undocumented" according to the doctors and they could not receive any additional benefits. They were all traumatized living in a house and in the state that their father committed suicide in.

Their mother decided to move her family up north to Jersey for a fresh start. It was difficult because she had to work while supporting her children after being used to being a stay-at-home mother. But she was a strong woman, and she did what was necessary to provide for her kids.

CHAPTER
TEN

WHILE IN JERSEY, *Ke met a group of girls by the name of Kyra, Tasha, Angel, and Jazz. They were all cool through high school and then Ke met the worst thing that had ever happened to her, Sincere Washington. He was friends with Kyra's ex-boyfriend, Tyler and Ke met the narcissistic-ass nigga through her.*

Sincere was tall, had honey colored skin, a tapered fade and he played basketball. The first three years of their relationship were absolute bliss. This was the first and only man Ke had ever been with, and he was the man who she was head over heels for.

He felt the same way about her until he wanted some fast money.

Three years into the relationship, Sincere made thousands of dollars committing credit card fraud. He used that money to buy weight so he could start selling drugs. Ke was confused by his decision because he had a full ride from a basketball scholarship, and he chose to throw that away to be in the streets.

It never made sense to her why some niggas want that street life. Yes, the money is fast but if you had a free college education and a chance to go into the league, why would you jeopardize that for a life that seems to be glorified. Ke vocalized her concerns to Sincere, but he begged and pleaded with her to just stick by him.

A few months passed and Sincere started staying out all night and used hustlin 'as his excuse. One day Ke told him she was about to start bartending on the weekends at Diva Lounge for her own money.

"Why the fuck you tryna bartend? Is there another nigga you want to fuck that's at the club?" hollered Sincere.

"No! I just want a chance to make my own money! What the fuck is your problem?"

Sincere turned around and slapped the shit out of her, causing blood to drip from her nose. Ke held her throbbing face as she looked at him. Before she could muster any words, he grabbed her by her hair and dragged her into the bathroom. He forced her to get up and look in the mirror.

"Nobody will ever want a bitch like you! I'm the only nigga out here that's willing to deal with your whiny-ass shit. Don't no nigga want a bitch that gotta talk to a therapist every other month because she still losing her mind about her dead-ass daddy!" He threw Ke into the bathroom mirror, cracking it. "Your depression or whatever the fuck you want to call it has caused you to gain weight in your thighs. Lose some fuckin 'weight and then maybe niggas will want you!" Sincere continued to insult her.

Ke sat on the floor, crying from shock. Those words cut her deep and she had never been hit by a man.

Sincere ended up leaving the house and didn't come back until the next morning. He was out all night with some chicken while Ke was home alone distraught. The next morning, like the manipulator he was, he apologized to her and agreed she could work at the club on weekends, but she'd have to stop when he told her to.

Sincere knew Ke was the type of female niggas wanted. She was pretty, had an hourglass figure, goal driven, and didn't mind going to get her own money. But, he always tried to tear her *down mentally and throw blows to her self-esteem so she wouldn't get the courage to leave his no-good-ass.*

CHAPTER
ELEVEN

ON KE'S *third weekend at the club, a girl came up to her. "You a dumb bitch, I was just sucking your nigga's dick last night."*

"Come again?" *questioned Ke.*

"You heard me, bitch."

"Girl, so you know about me, then you know that's my nigga and you call yourself bragging on sucking his dick? Get a life bitch."

Ke was furious, but she was going to talk her shit.

As her shift ended, the bitch was waiting by her car and told her she was about to whoop her ass. Ke gave a deep sigh and the lady charged at her. She was quick on her feet though and was able to kick her in the stomach and that caught the lady off guard.

Next thing she knew, that mean right hook left hook combo came and Ke was whooping her ass. Club goers broke the fight up and the lady left with a bloody nose. Ke couldn't believe it. She was going to fuck Sincere up. How embarrassing. Bitches coming at her about her nigga at her job. When she pulled up to the apartment, she stormed inside.

"Sincere, where the fuck you at!"

"I'm right here. What are you yelling for?" Sincere asked, confused.

"So you got bitches sucking your dick while I'm at work?"

"What?" he said, trying to play it off. "I ain't been with nobody. You must be fuckin 'around and tryin' to flip it on me." He smirked as he watched her walk toward their bedroom closet.

Ke started grabbing her clothes and said she was out. When she turned around, he punched her in the mouth, drawing blood, and started choking her. This time, she wasn't laying down and getting her ass whooped. She dug her nails into his eyes so he could get his arms from around her neck. Then she started punching him in the face.

He was shocked and even lost his balance. He tried to lunge at her, but she kicked him in his balls and grabbed the TV remote and started going upside his head with it. He grabbed her arms and slammed her and then started laying slaps on her.

They were fighting like they were strangers. Even though Ke fought back, Sincere towered over her and his strength did prevail. He had her arms over her head and told her to stop tripping. She started crying and he began to unbutton her pants.

"Sincere, no! You just fucked a bitch yesterday. Get the fuck off me."

He had her pants and panties off and began rubbing her clit. He felt her clit start to swell and her pussy start to moisten. That shut her up, but the tears kept running down her face. He put his head in between her secret opening and began softly sucking on her clit. She moaned in ecstasy.

"Sincere. No. You can't just cheat on me, put your hands on me and then try to have sex with me. Stop," she said as her voice started trembling.

He ignored her and put his tongue in her pussy and started swirling and twirling it around. He was tongue fucking her pussy and slurping up all her juices. That turned her on so much although her mind kept racing. He went back to sucking on her clit softly and then started flickering it with the tip of his tongue, causing her to have a hollering orgasm. Sincere then pulled out his six-inch dick. He wasn't the biggest, but he was her only sex partner, and she was in love so that dick was humungous to her. He pushed the head of the dick in and climbed on top of her. "Baby, don't leave me," he pleaded.

Her pussy was tight, wet and warm. He couldn't imagine another nigga getting up in that because she was so sprung over him. He didn't know why he cheated, but he would lose it if she ever decided to leave and seek someone else.

"Ooo, Sincere, hit my spot, baby. Right there, yes!"

He began stroking his dick inside her tight walls and whispered all types of, 'I love you and don't leave me', in her ear.

He started sucking on her neck as he was pounding her pussy and that drove her up the walls. She started hollering and came all over his dick. After he came, Sincere planted kisses all over her face and promised he would never do that again.

She'd heard that shit before.

CHAPTER
TWELVE

THE NEXT YEAR *of her relationship with Sincere was filled with nothing but lies, cheating, abuse and control. Ke recalled Sincere being so controlling that whenever she went to hang with her friends, the nigga would throw a fit, as if she was the one known for cheating.*

She remembered one night, being out with her girls and just vibing with each other. She was shaking her ass, drinking, laughing and just enjoying being out the house.

Then a bitch stepped to her and what happened, they ended up fighting because of Sincere's ass. This time, Ke was arrested for going upside a hoes head with a bottle. Faheem bonded her out and she was so fucking mad when she saw Sincere that she swung on that nigga.

Since Faheem was there, he didn't want to hit her back. Sincere was one of them niggas that would hit a girl but scared as hell to fight a man. She ended up staying the night at Jaz and Faheem's house and Sincere called, begged and pleaded with her to come home but it was the same old song. She went back home, he ate her pussy good, fucked her, promised not to do it again just to do the shit again, niggas.

For some reason, Ke couldn't get rid of the hold the nigga had on her. She wondered if he practiced voodoo or some shit.

He was beating on her, constantly cheating on her and trying to control every aspect of her life. She was beginning to get depressed, and her mother became worried because of the struggle her father had with chronic mental illness.

Her mother was even more concerned when she noticed Keisha had fresh cuts on her wrist from when she attempted to commit suicide by slitting her wrists. She begged Ke to leave the relationship, but you know how that goes, people are only going to leave when they are ready.

Ke's last memory of this love is blind relationship was the one that brought tears to her eyes. She remembered feeling sick in her college class one day and threw up. She rushed home and peed on the pregnancy stick.

"Oh my gosh, I'm fucking pregnant!"

She didn't know how to feel. Her and Sincere's relationship wasn't the best but damn, could it really be possible that she is carrying and breeding a life? All she could think about was having a baby that truly loved her and having a human that she could give all of her love to.

The beginning stages of depression were beginning to sink in, but this pregnancy announcement actually had her... happy. Even though it's by an ain't-shit nigga. She scheduled a doctor's appointment to confirm the pregnancy. She was six weeks pregnant when she finally told Sincere.

"No way," he stated shockingly.

"Yes, I went to the doctor today and they confirmed it," she explained, handing him the documents.

"Damn, do you really think we are ready to be parents?"

"I don't think anyone is ever ready, but I mean, the baby is growing inside me," she responded.

"Damn, I really can't believe it. Guess we are having a baby."

Ke was excited to be pregnant for the sole reason of just feeling true love. But, she began to have mixed feelings. Sincere's reaction didn't seem like he was excited. He was not ready to be a father but having a baby by Ke could mean no one else would want her. He knew this would be the ultimate way to trap her.

Ke went upstairs to take a shower. After she got out of the shower, she got in bed. Sincere came up soon after and got in bed, too. He lifted up her nightgown and began fingering her pussy. She opened her legs up to give him as much access to her pussy as possible. He inserted one, then two fingers inside her and began massaging them inside her. He felt her juices trickle down his hand. He then went toward her pussy and began licking on her clit.

Even though he fucks with a lot of bitches, Ke's pussy was the only one he would eat. It was pretty, always bald from her Brazilian waxes, fat and juicy. She tasted good and felt so good. "Oh daddy, yes, keep doing my clit like that," she said.

He licked, sucked and rubbed on her clit. Then, he put a finger at the opening of her pussy while flicking his tongue over her clit. He had a nice rhythm of his finger going in and out her wet pussy and then his tongue performing its magic. She came all over his face.

He then laid down and Ke got on top of him and placed his dick right at her opening. She instructed him to grab her ankles while she slid down on it. He let out a deep moan. She had her feet planted near his hips and was riding his dick on her feet. This was her specialty move and Sincere always said this the move that's gone make a nigga keep her locked away because of how good she rides dick.

He held onto her ankles while she was bouncing up and down on his dick. The only sounds you could hear were their moans and her pussy gushing.

"Awe shit, you ridin' the fuck out my dick," Sincere moaned. "Ke, you feel so fucking good!" He grabbed her hips and began thrusting deeper inside of her until he came and she came quickly after.

She lay on his chest and these were the times where she felt that Sincere did care about her. But she knew it was only a matter of time before he had another cheating episode.

KEELY

Ke had been telling Sincere that they needed to get out of the house and spend some time together. So, because she kept telling him, he ended up booking them a hotel downtown and they were going to go out to eat at this new seafood restaurant and then to the Jagged Edge show. As soon as they got into the hotel room, Ke's phone rang.

"Hello?"

"Is Sincere with you? asked a female. Ke rolled her fucking eyes. You cannot be fucking serious, she thought.

"Umm, naw. Why the fuck you callin' me about my nigga?" Ke was so annoyed. Not again! She was pregnant and he still ain't doing shit to change.

"Look bitch, you can tell your nigga that he ain't got to answer my calls since he with you. I'll see him whenever he ready to fuck and give that money up again," the woman smirked.

This time, she was on speaker phone.

"She's a lying bitch. I don't even know who that is!" screamed Sincere.

'Oh, I'm lying? Nigga, you was just calling me last night saying you was gon' be with her until Sunday."

Sincere ended up hanging up on the woman. He found himself in the position again of being caught cheating. Ke didn't even cry this time. She was tired and over it. Tired of fist fighting him, tired of fighting bitches, and tired of this nigga lying to her. She deserved better. Her baby deserved better.

"Look, Sincere, I'm done. I'm not arguing. I'ma just walk away and you can go be with whoever you want. Me and my unborn don't deserve this shit. I go to school, I work, I cook, I clean and that shit ain't got me nowhere but pregnant and cheated on. I'm out."

As she walked away, he grabbed her by her neck from the back and slung her down. She was caught off guard but still tried to get up. As she was trying to gain her composure, Sincere grabbed her by her neck and dragged her across the floor.

"Stop! What the fuck are you doing. I'm pregnant!" she screamed.

He started smacking her to the point that her nose and lip were leaking blood. He threw her to the ground and started repeatedly kicking her in her stomach while she hollered out in pain.

"Leave me if you want to, bitch. Try it. I do the fucking leaving!" He continued to beat the shit out of Ke.

Sincere looked at Ke's body on the ground. She looked unresponsive. He began to panic and thought he had killed her. She had blood leaking from her head, and it looked like she was bleeding from her vagina. Sincere froze. He then left her there to bleed out. He jumped in his car and drove with no destination, as his mind began to think that he really overdid it with the abuse this time.

Knock! Knock!

"Is anybody here?" questioned a maid.

"I heard someone screaming, I'm going to open the door," said another maid.

When they opened the door, they gasped at the sight. There was a woman badly beaten to the point she appeared to be dead in a pool of blood. One maid immediately called the ambulance while the other checked for a pulse.

"Oh my gosh – she's breathing. Tell them to hurry!" she yelled. "Hold on, please hold on. Help is coming!"

The paramedics finally arrived and worked hard to keep Ke's weak pulse afloat. She was transported to the hospital where they cleaned her wounds and got the bleeding under control. Once Ke was aware and seemed to stabilize, the doctor came in.

"Hello, Keisha. I am Doctor Greyson. Nice to see you breathing," voiced the doctor.

"Hello. Thank you," Ke mustered.

Your bleeding has been stabilized and all your tests have come back normal. However, I am so sorry to inform you that you had a miscarriage. I am so sorry," stated the doctor. "Your uterus is shifted to the right, but it should not pose any additional problems,"

"What? My baby isn't growing inside of me?" Ke asked with tears streaming down her face. "Oh god, please, no."

She sobbed, absolutely devastated. Her unborn child's father beat her so badly that she ended up losing the baby. She promised that she was done with this shit. The police came and asked her what happened, but she told them she didn't remember. She just wanted to be done with this entire thing.

She spent the next three days in the hospital and her mother came to check on her. Her mother cried when she saw her swollen face and found out about the miscarriage. Ke was going through it and wanted to die. The baby she was growing, the one she would have been responsible for, she failed. She couldn't protect them.

She cried herself to sleep every night and was so disappointed in what her life had come to. She was always so full of life, always singing, dancing or helping others out and she couldn't believe how lifeless she had become because of what she allowed from Sincere. He didn't even check up on her one time while she was in the hospital.

They gave Ke her discharge papers and Roz was waiting for her in the car. She gave her the biggest hug.

"Ke, this has gone too far. I didn't know y'all fights were this bad. I am going to beat the shit out of him," Roz said, tears in her eyes.

"I'm done. Just take me to get my clothes and then take me to my mother's," Ke stated.

Roz went inside the gas station and Ke ended up calling Sincere. He answered.

"I'm just calling to let you know that I miscarried. I just want to come get my laptop and my clothes."

Ke held back her tears.

"You ain't getting shit that I paid for with my money," laughed Sincere.

"What? I just left the hospital and you talkin' 'bout, 'I'm not getting anything you paid for'? I could've paid for it myself if you weren't so controlling." She realized there was no point. "You know what, forget it. I'll be there to get my shit," Ke spoke before hanging up. She was at her boiling point.

When they pulled up to Sincere's apartment, their jaws dropped. Sincere got out of his car and went to the passenger side to help a woman out of the car. He then went to the back seat and pulled out newborn baby's car seat. As if this nigga couldn't destroy her heart anymore. Roz went to open her door to whoop this nigga's ass, but Ke told her to just get out of the car.

"What?" Roz asked.

"Get out the car. I just know this nigga ain't got a fucking newborn and this motherfucker got the nerve to be walking a bitch in the house!" Ke screamed. "Get out, Roz. I don't want you getting hurt," spat Ke with fire in her eyes.

"How I'ma..."

"Just get the fuck out!"

Roz got out of the car, confused as hell. Ke didn't seem like herself. When she closed the door to the car, Ke hopped in the driver's seat, put her car in drive, floored the gas pedal and ran straight through the home.

When she got through the door, there were dust particles everywhere. She went into her purse and grabbed her gun. Sincere came running down the stairs in a panic and the minute Ke saw him, she started shooting.

Bullets and screams were all that could be heard. He ended up jumping out of the window and his pussy-ass called the police on her. After all of the shit he did to her, when she finally snapped, he called the police.

Ke pointed the gun at the woman and the newborn baby. Her finger rested on the trigger as tears flowed down her face. She couldn't bring herself to do it. It wasn't this lady's fault at all that she was with a no-good-ass nigga.

The police burst through the door and Ke was apprehended. They were attempting to charge her with breaking and entering, *destruction of property and attempted murder. Things were not looking good for her, and she fell into a severe depression in jail.*

She refused to eat, refused to talk, and all she did was sleep. With the grace of God though, she ended up beating all her charges due to mental illness running in her family, postpartum depression of losing her child and her mother had records of the severe domestic violence. The judge ruled that she had experienced so much trauma that she snapped.

Thankfully no one was hurt but her mind plummeted. The judge sentenced her to undergo six to twelve months of medical, psychiatric, and psychological treatment. Her mother also wrote a letter to the board recommending Ke take some anger management courses and they sentenced her to those as well.

Her mother was happy because she tried to get their father in therapy, but he always refused. She didn't want to lose her baby girl. During that time, Ke didn't talk to any of her friends and wanted to be alone.

CHAPTER
THIRTEEN

(HER FRIENDS WERE WEATHERING *their own storms and if you are not familiar with them check out Wahida Clark's Thugs and the Women Who Love Them.)*

Ke had nothing. No clothes. Very little money. She was forced to go back home with her mother and three other siblings. Even though therapy seemed to work a little, she would still find her mind wandering back into a dark place.

She had a severe nervous breakdown one day in front of her mother. Ke wished death upon herself because her mind only thought about the negative things. Her mother called her therapist and psych ward to try again to get her out of this funk. She could not lose her baby to this shit.

Roz, Jaz, Angel and Kyra would send things to her mother's house to let her know that they love her, and are always praying for her. She never responded.

One day, she decided to finally get some sunlight after intense therapy and eight months of being in her room. She went to the store and ran it to Mrs. Smith, Angel's mom.

"Ke, baby, is that you? Oh God, how are you?" Mrs. Smith asked with open arms.

"I could be better, Mrs. Smith." Ke embraced her.

"Well, Ke, I tell you. These men these days really don't

deserve women like y'all. Do you know that Snake just disappeared out of Angel's life?" Mrs. Smith stated with tears in her eyes.

"What?" Ke asked as her eyes got wide.

"Angel hasn't come out of her room for a week. She won't eat and I don't know what to do."

Jazz is fighting that drug case. Kyra is back with that damn man who got her strung out. It's been a lot you've missed Ke and I'm sure they would all like to see you."

Ke soothed her and was seriously in shock. I mean damn, you got Kyra who was an ex-drug addict, Jazz was a damn drug cook, and Angel had a crazy-ass relationship with Snake. This made Ke realize that even though she was depressed, life went on.

Karma would tear Sincere up but now it was time for Ke to get back to herself and prove that this would not take her down. She decided to follow Mrs. Smith back to her house. She went in and knocked on Angel's door.

"Mommy, please, not now," Angel sobbed.

"Angel, it's me, Ke," she nervously stated.

Ke heard Angel jump up and open the door. Angel's jaw dropped.

"Oh my gosh, Ke! Ke... Oh my gosh!"

The girls hugged so long and so hard. They had a two hour conversation about Snake and Ke's mandatory therapy sessions. Tasha, Jaz and Kyra came over soon after and the girls all cried and talked for hours. Ke didn't know how to feel, but she knew right then and there that being with these strong-ass women made her so happy. She had to get back to her.

CHAPTER
FOURTEEN

TWO HOURS LATER, Ke finally woke up from the sleep study. She had tears in the corner of her eyes. Kyra helped her out of the machines, wires, and then told her to get dressed. When Ke came back, they went over all the data.

"Girl, your brain waves were all over the place," Kyra teased as she pointed to the graph. "What the world were you dreaming about?"

"My dad. The crazy ass mental institute my ass was in because I lost my mind. You know, the usual," Ke joked back with her.

Kyra finished up her research notes and then they headed out for a lunch date with their other friends. They went to sit down at a sushi restaurant and had some major girl talk.

"I ain't been in a relationship in almost two years. I am so damn traumatized from what I went through that I don't think I ever wanna be in one again," Ke said to Tasha. "I think I'm meant to be the fine auntie with no kids," she joked and looked at Jaz and Krya.

They all laughed.

"You might like a man that works with you at the school. A nice handsome teacher or even the principal," stated Angel. Tasha nodded her head in agreement.

"Bitch, I ain't ever dating anybody again. These niggas ain't shit and I'm not in the mood. I have to constantly tell the dudes at the club, with my stank-ass attitude, that I don't want your ass!" yelled Ke as they laughed.

"I went on a date with a teacher from my job and get this," Ke paused as she sipped her water. "He was not only married to a woman, but he was also an undercover gay man, the whole time. I didn't know any of this. The wife's sister came up to us during our date and exposed his ass," Ke explained. "I was so damn pissed and embarrassed. How you want a man and a woman? That's just plain fucking greedy!"

"Ke you are so anti-dating," laughed Kyra. "Let me ask you a question and no, I am not trying to be funny. But, do you still want to be with Sincere?" Kyra waited for her response.

"Hell no! Y'all, I swear I will never go back to that man. I am absolutely done with him. If he died today, I wouldn't shed a tear. I don't give a fuck about that nigga, but I am still dealing with the effects of how he treated me. I was mentally fucked up. I'd rather just be alone than deal with somebody who just wants to play games. That's it." Ke spoke honestly. She had no plans on ever going back to Sincere. Her therapist told her to never have any hate in heart. So she forgave him silently and forgave herself and decided to get her life back on track.

She ended up telling her girls how she was pregnant by Sincere, and how she ended up miscarrying that night because he beat her so badly.

"Now that makes perfect sense on why you drove the car through the house and started shootin' at folks. I get it!" stated Angel while she nodded her head.

"I see why your brain waves were going crazy. That's some serious-ass trauma!" stated Kyra. Ke chuckled. It was refreshing to share because talking about her abuse and miscarriage used to make her cry. She finally felt like she was moving on from that dark spot in her life.

"You know what, fuck y'all bitches. Like I said, I'm going to forever be the fine auntie with no kids," Ke reiterated. "Just get me a nice dildo for my birthday or something," she said. They cracked up.

She loved having these outings with her girls and it felt amazing to talk about the depressive state she was in once upon a time. They all said their "I love yous" and left the restaurant. Ke pulled up to her house, went in and took a shower, then called it a night.

Her bed did get lonely, but she has gotten comfortable with being alone.

CHAPTER FIFTEEN

THE NEXT DAY, Omar was at his mobile phone carrier, getting his number changed. Bria, Lucille, and the other chickens he used to deal with had been calling him non-stop for months.

"This shit is wild that these scandalous-ass chickens keep calling me. What part about *I don't fuck with you no more* do they not get!" he said to himself, getting aggravated as his phone rang again.

"Hello, Sir. How may I help you?" the front desk worker asked.

"Hey, I just need to get my number changed."

"Okay, not a problem. Let me get you set up. What's the name on the account and can I see your ID? Any specific reason you want your number changed?"

"Omar Gaulding and here go my ID. I want my number changed to stop... unwanted calls." She typed in his information and processed the number change.

"Okay, sir. Here's your new number," she said as she wrote it down and handed the paper to him. "Do you mind if I keep a copy for my own reasons? Can I be a *wanted* call?" The front desk worker was seriously shooting her shot.

"You may turn into an unwanted call," he replied and smiled.

It had been a while since Omar had a booty-call but that was because he had to slow his roll. Just then, her supervisor called her for something, and Omar left. I guess that was a sign from the Almighty telling him to not indulge in any of the temptations.

He dialed Trae and Kaylin to give them his new number. Then he dialed Bo.

"Who this?" Bo stated.

"It's me, nigga."

"Why you change your number, O?" Bo inquired, already knowing the answer.

"Nigga, you know why. Don't act like you ain't been around when Bria and Lucille called my shit at least twenty times before."

"You finally gave in and got a new number, my brotha," Bo laughed. "I'm about to take Shanna out on a date though. I'ma see you tomorrow at the lounge. I'ma make sure I give Bria and Lucille your number," Bo stated jokingly.

"You niggas always got jokes."

He hung the phone up and entered his driveway. He saw a few bags on his porch and was anxious to see what it was because not many people knew where he lived. He never even brought a female to his spot and he was glad because at the rate they were calling, ain't no telling how many times they would have popped up at his crib. He read the note attached to the bags.

You promised you would check in. Haven't heard from you in ten days, Omar! I'm sure you have no groceries. Hopefully these will get you through the next week, love you son.

-Dad and Michelle.

Omar couldn't do anything but smile. He was extremely lucky to have a nurturing father like Carl. A father, an active Black father, especially when you're grown is something that money could never buy.

CHAPTER
SIXTEEN

KE WOKE up the next morning and made a bowl of cereal. As soon as she got comfortable, her phone rang. It was her mother, Mrs. Harris.

"Hello," she stated in between her spoonful of cereal.

"Hey, Keisha. Just called to make sure you made it in from the club last night, girl," her mother stated. "How was your doctor's appointment? Have you visited your therapist, baby?"

"I made it in. Everything is fine," Ke explained as she rolled her eyes. She loved her mother but damn, she was always in her business. "What y'all getting into today?"

"Getting the house prepped for your granny to move up here," Mrs. Harris reminded her.

"Oh yes! I can't wait!"

"Yep! You know she's retiring and her retirement checks will help us out. Maybe you can finally stop working at the club. I can't stand how late you get off chil', and I think you are over-exerting yourself with school and working two jobs while living alone," she stated. "You need to start back enjoying your life while you got a second chance at it," she explained.

"Mama, you know the reason I'm at the club is to help you out with my siblings. I just want to do my part as the oldest," she deep sighed, getting annoyed.

She hated when her mother tried to tell her that she was overloading herself. She never wanted her siblings to ever feel like they needed anybody other than each other to make a way.

"Keisha! Okay. I did not call to go back and forth with you about this. This is your life, and I am going to let you live it. But you are my child and I know how stressful it can be to be working in the morning and overnight. But anyways, I am cooking tonight so come get you a plate before you go in for your shift. That's an order!" her mom demanded.

"Okay, fine," she replied as she hung up.

Once she finished her cereal, she headed upstairs to shower and get ready. She got dressed in a graphic sweatshirt, some jeans that hugged her curves and some converse. She locked up her home and got in her car to head to her mother's. Mrs. Harris stayed in a quiet neighborhood in Ewing, New Jersey. Ke pulled up and all of her siblings showered her with love.

"Where's Brielle?" Ke asked.

"She's upstairs with her girlfriend," said Travon.

He was fifteen, and the only boy of the tribe.

Ke headed for the stairs. When she burst through the door, her sister and her girlfriend of four years, Ashanti, were doing homework. Brielle had always been different and when she told everyone that she is a lesbian, all they could do was hug her because everyone already suspected it. The damn girl refused to wear dresses, sported a low cut, and had been crushing hard on Nia Long for years, they knew her ass was into girls.

Ashanti's parents, however, did not know that she is gay and Brielle made their mom promise not to "out" her until she Ashanti was ready. Their mother agreed. That's why Ke wanted to do all she could for her mother: she always made everyone feel welcomed. If it wasn't for her mother keeping record of some of the abuse, Ke may have not been found innocent in her case.

Ke also adored her mother because she knew there weren't many mothers like hers in the 'hood. Many people Ke's age truly had to just figure shit out on their own and were thrown to the wolves when they turned eighteen. Mrs. Harris always told her children that her house would always be open to them no matter the circumstances because she would never see her children outback.

"Hey y'all, y'all better not be up here eating nooo pussy," Ke joked. The girls burst out laughing.

"Girl, I wish you get laid soon so you can stop worrying about me," Brielle joked back.

"Honey, don't worry about what this pussy doin'."

They all laughed.

"But did y'all win the track meet?"

"Yep! I came first in the hundred-meter dash."

"That's my girl. I think the food 'bout ready too, y'all."

They all went downstairs and got ready to feast. Her mother made fried chicken smothered in gravy, homemade collard greens, macaroni and cheese and candy yams with a strawberry cake for dessert. The type of meal that gives you the itis, meaning you go straight to sleep when you finish. Ke helped their mother clean the kitchen then made her a plate to go because she had to get ready for her shift at the club.

"Keisha, about our conversation on the phone. I just want you to breathe and live your life. Go get laid or something, life is not all about working."

"Ma! Get laid? Really. I'm workin' so much to help you out and you're worrying about my vagina?" she laughed.

"I sure am. If your daddy was still alive, I'd probably have had four more children," her mother said as she put her hands on her hips. "But Keisha, we are okay. Save your extra money or get more ahead on your bills," her mother told her.

"Mmmhmm, I will. I love y'all. I'll call you tomorrow," Ke brushed the conversation off.

"I love you too! Go have sex!" her mother yelled as she watched her hop in her car and drive off.

CHAPTER
SEVENTEEN

TWO WEEKS LATER, Ke was at home listening to Missy Elliot's One Minute Man while getting dressed to go work her shift at the club. She always wore fitted jeans, tight fitted shirts and comfortable shoes. She hopped in her Lexus and began the thirty-minute commute to work. Once she arrived, she saw Sarah.
"We gettin' that money tonight!" Sarah yelled to her.
"Like we do every weekend!" Ke responded and they laughed.
"Lights on!" said Mr. Jose
"Showtime!" squealed the waitresses as they waltzed to their sections.
The bartenders were placing clean cups near their areas and the first guests began to walk in. DMX How's It Goin' Down was coming through the speakers and Ke was swaying her hips as she was swiping someone's card. When she turned around, Omar came walking up with a smile. The other bartenders were drooling over him.
"You can't speak?"
Ke looked at him with an evil stare and ignored him as she handed the customer their receipt and card back.
"That's the energy you give someone that walked all the way

through this crowd to come speak to you?" Omar pressed her. "I've been making sure to come and speak to you for the past couple weeks and I see you don't appreciate that," he teased.

"I didn't ask you to come speak to me. This the energy I give a man that walked all the way over here to *bother* me," she shot back and smacked her lips.

"You got a nasty attitude," he said while smiling. "What else nasty 'bout you?" he grinned.

"Um, excuse me? You and the rest of these niggas in here will never find out," she cocked her head to the side.

"Don't put me in a category with these lames. You know I ain't them. I'm the only nigga that can tame that attitude. Watch."

"Come again? You gone tame what?"

"That attitude," he repeated cooly. They just stared at each other. She decided to taunt him.

"Well, how are you gonna fix my attitude when you can't even get my number?"

Sarah walked up behind Ke and laughed at her question.

"You clownin' me in front of everybody, Ma?" Omar asked while laughing.

He never had much time to converse with her because he always had to leave to handle business. But he was enjoying this conversation and her sassy ass comebacks.

"Well, answer. You've been asking me all these questions. How you gonna fix my attitude Mr. Omar?"

"Well, for starters when you see me walking up you need to fix your face and greet me with a nice smile. None of that eye rolling shit."

"Okay, so you want me to stop making my money, stop tending to my customers just to personally greet you and then say what? All hail, King Omar?" she bucked back.

"Yeah. Say exactly that."

They both burst out laughing. She had the brightest smile he had ever seen, and it was very warming considering she had been mean as hell.

"You got a pretty smile. That's the type of smile you give someone who went out of his way to come and see you," he sarcastically stated.

She ignored his comment and went back to tending the bar.

"Where you from? When you talk, I'm hearing a southern accent."

"I'm from Virginia. Are you going to ask me a million questions tonight?"

"Pretty much. I'ma be asking questions and staring at you for the remainder of the night."

"That's not creepy at all. Damn, who said I wanted you to talk to me and stare at me?"

"Yo, that mouth is wild. I can't wait to get that under control," he said while laughing.

Ke ignored him yet again but that didn't matter because Omar was back to asking her where in Virginia she was from, where else did she work, her favorite color and all. She couldn't believe he was asking her all of this at the bar and she couldn't believe herself for even entertaining him and answering them. The way he looked at her with that, "I want you" stare made her nervous and she honestly couldn't take the heat.

"Omar, it has been an hour. I'm trying to tend to these customers and you are not allowing me the time I need to get their orders right. In fact, you're kinda messing up my tips for the night."

"Okay, I don't wanna mess up your money. Let me order a bottle of water and tell everyone at the bar their rounds on me for the rest of the night," he stated.

"Okay. You serious?" she grabbed him a bottle of water.

"Yeah."

She told everyone that their rounds for the next thirty minutes were on Omar and everyone sitting at the bar started high-fiving each other. His tab came up to eight hundred and thirty three dollars.

"Here's your total and the water bottle is on the house. All that talking you've been doing, I'm sure you could use some water," she joked.

He peeled off eighteen one hundred dollar bills.

"Have you been drinking? This is too much," she stated as she tried to give him the excess money back.

"Pay for the liquor and then you keep the change for your tip since I've been *bothering* you all night," he responded, putting his wallet back in his pocket.

"You don't have to leave this much in tips," Ke tried to push the money back.

"It's cool. I was distracting you a little and I ain't trying to come in between you and your money."

This was very generous, and she had suspicions about his line of work. Sincere had traumatized her and she refused to deal with any scammers, thugs, or drug dealers because they came with too much drama. All men are capable of having drama, but those in particular were a hell-to-the-got-damn-no for her. Omar eventually made her take the excess cash and she gave three hundred dollars to her girl Sarah and pocketed the rest. That was a boss move that he made by paying for everybody's drinks for the final hour and he was *cute* for leaving her a tip. But, mmm-mmm, she was not falling for it.

The people at the bar were finishing up their drinks and they all thanked Omar. The bartenders wiped down the bar and Ke walked over to the area Sarah was in.

"Girl, why you being so mean to that fine-ass man down there?" Sarah asked.

"You know I have boundaries set up and I refuse to take them away just because a nigga is interested in me," Ke stated. "Plus, I'm not being mean. He talkin' just as much shit as me."

"No, he's not. You told the man, 'how can he fix your attitude when he can't even get the number'! Ke, you are crazy. I see him posted up in the back with the other ballers all the time," Sarah's nosey ass stated.

"Girl, all these niggas just want some pussy that I'm not giving up. He seems like a nice guy, but you know like I know that all them niggas who be posted up back there doin' some shit that comes with consequences. I told you what I went through with my ex who was living a small-time life like that. I ain't going back. My girl Mary J. Blige said, 'No more drama in my life,' she sang, "and I'm staying true to that." Sarah laughed.

"Well, look. If you don't want his fine ass, send him my way. But he's into you. It looks like he is still waiting for you."

Ke left Sarah and went back to clock-out.

"You're going to walk out of here when you know we still have things to talk about?" asked Omar.

"What else could you possibly want to talk about? You talked all shift, Omar."

Just as he was fixing to say something, Bo called his name and Omar went toward him. She clocked out, grabbed her purse, and proceeded to walk out with the other bartenders. It was something they always did for safety in numbers because some of the men get a little creepy and aggressive when they've been drinking. She was pushing the unlock button to her car keys when she heard his voice.

"Yo, Ke wait. We still have to talk." He smirked.

"Talking to you messed up my tips."

"I ended up fixing your tips, ma." He smiled. "But I see you like to play crazy, so I'll give you a rundown," he said as he licked his lips. "You can't just leave without giving me a proper exit."

"Okay, so now I gotta greet you a certain way and have a proper farewell? You are something else, Omar." She started shaking her head. "I'm sure whatever girl you dealin' with do not want to be demanded all the time," she teased.

"When you finally let a nigga take you out or get the number, I'll put you on game to all my demands. You gon' listen too," he smiled at her.

"For the millionth time, I'm not going out with you," she stated matter-of-factly.

"Why not? Why you being like this to me?"

"I told you. I'm just not into dating right now."

"We don't have to date just yet, but you don't even want to give me your number."

"Nope."

"Can I know why?"

He looked her dead in her eyes when he asked her this. She glanced from him to the ground as her heartbeat sped up and hesitation consumed her.

"Even though you've been stand-offish to me, you've been talking back to me," he paused. "You say you're not interested but your actions show otherwise."

"It's not personal with you. I'm just not ready to get into anything yet. I've answered every question you've asked me. Can I please get a pass on this one?"

"Okay. I'll give you a pass. This time," he chuckled. "How come you work at the school, the club, and you're in college? You don't be tired?"

"I'm a little tired but only because certain men keep me at my car beyond the time I'm supposed to be at the club," she sarcastically stated. He laughed at her. "However, if you must know, I work both jobs because teaching is my career path so I am getting as much hands-on employment in that area as I can. As far as the club, when y'all ballers, shot callers and flossers come in there on the weekends, y'all are fairly generous with the tips and I use that extra money to take care of things and help my mother and siblings out."

"I understand. Whatchu mean by *y'all* ballers being generous? You know something about me?" he asked cooly with his signature grin.

"Oh please, Omar. Not everyone can leave a nine hundred dollar tip and pay for everyone's drinks for an hour. Now, I'm not judging you for your career path but I'm not naive. Matter-of-fact, let me ask you a question?"

"Oh, you finally got a question for me?"

"Sure do. How come you choose to you know... do that? This is a judgment free zone. If I can remember, you said your dad had connections with decent jobs, so why this?"

"Well... I didn't just up and choose this," he looked at the ground because was about to tell her some shit he never told any female. He enjoyed talking to her and felt safe communicating with her. "My mom, four-year-old brother and godmom got killed when I was fifteen. My dad ended up getting full custody of me, but he started struggling with diabetes and that caused him to miss out on work and CPS had to get involved. We were making it, he did what he could to keep a roof over our heads, but it was at the cost of his health. I felt desperate in a way and couldn't lose another parent. So I was presented with the idea of slangin' and I couldn't pass it up. It ain't the path I want to be on forever, but this shit has helped me provide for my dad and take the stress off him," he honestly replied. "I know many folks live long and healthy with diabetes but he's the type that would really ignore the pain he's in because he couldn't afford to miss work."

When he told her that, she started to look at Omar in a different light. As he was talking, she observed his confident demeanor, the sincerity in his voice when he spoke about his father and the honest necessity of having to move weight to be a provider. Her eyes also traveled from his sexy lips, to his sculpted arms, and then her gaze stopped right at his thick dick print. A bitch was stunned about that nine and a half inch third leg that was greeting her through his pants. She had to blink twice to make sure she was seeing things correctly.

"Wow. Okay. That was a lot. I know how it is to try to provide for your family and I am sorry about those deaths you've experienced. I know how it is to lose a parent as well," she sincerely stated.

"Your father passed away? I know you said you helped your mom out, so your dad is gone?"

"Yep, when I was fifteen too. He was a retired army Vet and he experienced extreme PTSD. He ended up slitting his own throat right in front of all of us in our house in Virginia," she stated while taking a deep breath.

She didn't like talking about this but how could she not share this when he just shared something deep with her.

"Damn, that's wild. You seem to be strong mentally. I think I would have still been torn up seeing one of my parents commit suicide. My mother and brother were shot in the head by my mom's boyfriend and that shit still controls my thoughts some days."

"Shot in the head by her boyfriend? OMG, that is horrible," she gasped. He nodded in agreement while she finished up her story.

"Honestly, I struggled a lot mentally, but my mom sent us all to therapy to cope with everything. Mental instability is the reason we had to move because my father never went to seek help for his PTSD so his illness was undocumented according to the army and we couldn't get any supplemental financial help. My mom used the money from his life insurance policy to move and start fresh here." She complained to him about how the government works sometimes. "I work these jobs to just make sure we ain't never put in the situation where we were stressing about money ever again."

She didn't want to tell him about Sincere and how he took everything from her.

"I never went to therapy for my mom's death so I'm glad it worked for y'all. But you would think that somebody who fought in the war would be set for life in this country," Omar stated.

"It's never too late to seek therapy. You should do it," she stated as she looked into his eyes. Therapy was difficult but that shit has really saved her. "But on another note, it's very technical about who gets military benefits for life and what doesn't," Ke explained.

"I didn't know that about the military," he expressed as he shook his head. "But back to the therapy conversation, I'ma have to pass on that. I don't really like talking to people."

"You don't like talking to people?" she yelled and gave him the side eye. "Omar, you just talked me to death for my entire work shift and more."

"I'm usually quiet and straight to the point with everything and everyone. I'm talking to you because I like you and I'm trying to get to know you. I don't know if I could open up to a therapist. I am not against it, but everything is not for everybody."

Ke had to agree with him on that.

"You can be my therapist, can't you? That's why I need your number, so you can give me advice," he joked as he looked at her. "Give me a kiss, Ke," he demanded.

"No, Omar."

She shook her head. He grabbed her by her neck and placed his lips on hers. Ke gave in to his irresistible-ass and kissed him back. He started sucking on her bottom lip and she opened her mouth so he could slip his tongue in. Their tongues moved in sync while trying to become acquainted with each other. It felt like fireworks were going off and both of them were tingling with emotion. Her nipples started to get hard, and that's when she stopped their lip locking session.

"I like the way your lips taste. I hope I get to kiss on the other lips you got. I know that pussy taste phenomenal," he stated as he grabbed her by her waist, making her pussy twitch.

"I was supposed to go home after work. Not kiss you," she said as she tried to get out of his embrace. His arms felt so good around her.

"Unexpected shit happens all the time. Give me your number," he pulled out his phone.

She gave a nervous stare but eventually gave in. He promised to call her when he thought she made it home. He gave her another peck on the lips and let her go.

He walked towards his Cadillac truck, and she started up her car. Keisha's mind was racing. She could not let another man take her to that dark place again. But, it had been a while since she just "talked" to a man with no strings attached and he was making her create a pivotal relationship foundation: communication. She pushed all the thoughts of Omar out of her head. Once she got home, she sat at her kitchen table. Omar had her mind gone.

"Fucking great," she deep sighed. "Lord, get this man out of my head!" she yelled as she went upstairs.

She took her clothes off, hopped in the shower and started imagining how Omar's lips would feel on her pussy. He told her he hoped he could taste the lips between her legs and the bitch almost came on herself at the thought of that.

Maybe I do need to listen to my mama and just get laid. She hadn't had sex of any kind in two years. Shit, it'd been two years since she'd even gave a nigga a kiss on the damn cheek.

"But, nope! This pussy is too fat, too wet, and to muthafuckin' good to be just giving this shit out. I'll get fucked when I'm ready. My mom needs to mind her damn business," she vented; annoyed with herself that she was even fantasizing about him.

Omar pulled up in his driveway and was happy with how the night played out. When he first saw Ke, it was for sure a lust thing. He thought he was going to be back on his bullshit and revert back to that wild whoring life he was living. But, tonight when he found out about her family history that shit made him even more attracted to her. It was so weird because he never spoke much about his mother and the murders since they occurred, but he was comfortable being vulnerable with her.

CHAPTER EIGHTEEN

KE WAS DONE with her shower and turned her TV on while she relaxed on her couch. She was in college to be a certified Special Education teacher and had to get three research portfolios together to submit before the end of the semester. She was filling out her checklist for her portfolios when her phone rang.

"Hello?"

"What's up, Ma. You make it safe?" Omar asked.

She melted when she heard his deep voice. "Yes. I made it in. Are you settled?"

"Yep, when are you free for a date?"

"You asked for my number to talk, not to plan dates. You don't think this is too soon?" she asked.

"Hell no. You know I want you. Plus, I can't stop thinking about how you were sucking on my tongue. I'ma suck on your clit, just like that."

Her pussy started to throb at the reminder of their kiss.

"I see you don't know what to say out your mouth," she grinned. "Well, there won't be any of that going on with us. I'm sorry. I told you already, I'm enjoying being by myself," she stated.

"Remember, you said no to your number, and I finally got that," he said while smiling.

They spent the next four hours talking about everything under the sun. Omar asked her what her dream vacation was and she told him she always wanted to go to Egypt and see the pyramids. She asked him what his aspirations were, and he told her he wanted to eventually get into real estate.

"Omar, I have not been to sleep yet and the crack of dawn is here."

"I won't be at the club tonight. I'ma be out of town for a few days, but I'll be back sometime next week."

"Thanks for letting me know. Finally, my ears will be able to rest," she teased.

"Since you will be my woman soon, we gotta get in the habit of letting each other know stuff. That's another thing I'll handle when you stop playing with a nigga," he replied.

"You really have your own fantasy world. You're nuts," she laughed.

"I'm not nuts. I know what I'm talkin about. Ima try to call you sometime later. I need to be getting some rest too."

"I may be a little busy because I am helping my grandmother move up here and I have important schoolwork to do. But I'll return your call."

"A'ight, cool. Good night."

"Goodnight."

She hung the phone up and then headed up the stairs and got in her bed.

Do not fall for him, Keisha! She thought to herself as she went to sleep.

CHAPTER NINETEEN

OMAR PULLED up to an abandoned warehouse with Bo. Supreme and Mel had this dude named Terrel tied to a chair, and when Omar walked up, he ripped the tape off Terrel's mouth.

"Speak, nigga," Omar firmly stated.

"Yo, Yo, Yo, O, don't hurt me man, please. Please, I'll tell you whatever you need to know." Terrel was released from jail the month before. The nigga was facing fifty years for conspiracy and all of a sudden, he's out free. Any time that happened, a nigga was snitching or gave the feds a lead on something. Omar had to make sure he and his crew weren't under the feds radar.

"Nigga, cut to the fucking chase!" Omar barked, getting aggravated.

"O, please, please!" he begged.

Omar responded by punching him in the mouth. "Talk!"

"I didn't snitch on y'all, I swear. That nigga Tee get out soon. You know he run with Nikayah and word around the cell block is them niggas been running their mouths," Terrell cried as he spit out blood. "They said Nikayah in his feelings because Trae slid on his lady. You know I don't have any beef with y'all! The nigga I got beef with is Rayzo and he gon' get his."

It all became clear to Omar. Rayzo just got locked up the other day and it had to be because of Terrel. He may not be snitching on any of them, but nevertheless, he was snitching. Plus, word around town was that nigga Rayzo was working with the feds, too.

"Nigga, so you did snitch." Omar raised his gun to Terrel head.

"Not on y'all, O! Please!" Terrel pleaded.

"Once a snitch, always a snitch. You can't be trusted. You moved weight with that nigga Nikayah and you know how this shit go when it comes to my family," Omar started connecting the dots.

He pulled the trigger, putting a bullet through Terrel's head and then his chest.

"These niggas talk to fucking much," Omar said to Bo.

"Damn right. He been a rat," Bo responded.

"He had to go," he said in agreement. "Bo, call the Haitian boys to clean this up. Make sure Supreme good since he had to leave right when we got here. I'ma put Trae on game to this shit, even though he might already know."

"I'm on it."

Omar dialed Trae's number while leaving the warehouse.

"Yo where you at?"

"Tasha crib, where you?"

"I'm about to stop over there, it's urgent. Come down."

"A'ight," Trae replied as he put his pants on.

He got the call that Omar was outside and went downstairs.

"What's up, nigga? You good?"

Trae was always the concerned big cousin. Omar didn't do too much talking so when he said he needed to discuss things, Trae knew it was important.

"Me and Bo was at the warehouse with that nigga Terrel," Omar said while sparking his blunt. He inhaled it and passed it to Trae.

"The snitch?" Trae asked before he hit the blunt.

"Yes. Long story short, he says that he was the one who told on Rayzo and that's why he ain't doing that time for conspiracy."

"Damn, that makes sense because Rayzo just got locked up. But they say Rayzo has been working with the police, too," Trae responded.

"I heard he was an informant but there ain't no proof, so that's something we'd have to look more into," Omar stated trying to stay on track. "Get this. He goes and says Nikayah and Tee in there snitching. Nikayah in his feelings about how you slid on Tasha."

"Hmm. The nigga just called her phone yesterday and I had to tell him don't call her because he ain't got no pussy here. But he snitching?"

"Yeah, that's the word. I ain't know how to take it because Terrel a snitch and here he was trying to expose other rats."

"True. Well, I'ma see how this shit plays out before I make a move. It's all business to me. What's Terrel's status?"

"You know I handled that," Omar stated.

"Didn't I tell you that's my job to handle shit, li'l nigga?"

"Nigga, gon' 'head with that shit."

They both laughed. Although Trae was only older by a few months, they always joked about it.

"You know it's all love."

Trae went to open the car door. Omar stopped him. "Wait, nigga."

"What?"

"What's up with Ke? Does she have a man or something?"

That shit with Lucille had him thinking all these females could possibly be married or have something extra going on.

"Nigga, what?" Trae said, settling back in the car.

"What's good with Ke? I was chopping it up with her and the vibes were there. But she hesitant as fuck with me."

"Figure it out yourself what's good with her, dawg," Trae chuckled. "She cool peoples though, but I heard she was a li'l crazy," Trae explained as he got out of the car.

"You can't throw a nigga an assist? That's fucked up." Omar laughed and started his car.

"I introduced you. Now let's see if you can really handle being sprung like me," Trae joked.

The men parted ways.

For the next few days, Omar tried to call Ke but she didn't answer. It was frustrating him because he was never on the receiving end of someone being nonchalant or simply just ignoring him. He was the nonchalant one.

CHAPTER
TWENTY

FOR THE PAST week and a half, Ke had turned off her phone, took off from work, and got into her focused zone so she could knock out her portfolios about bringing awareness to Special Education.

The day came for her projects to be submitted and she felt like a weight had been lifted off her shoulders. College was hard work but damn, it was rewarding. She had been extremely stressed this past week and wanted some drinks, so she turned her phone back on to call her girls and see what their plans were for the night.

She saw countless missed calls from Omar and being that it had been several days, she was too embarrassed to call him back. She dialed up Angel.

"Hello?"

"Hey girl. Are you getting into anything tonight?" Ke asked as she downed a bottle of water.

"Oh bitch, you finally decided to crawl from under that damn rock," Angel joked. "I'm going to assume the portfolio submission went well," Angel went on. "But we're going to a block party so Shanna can go see Bo and then we're going to the bar for drinks. Come with us. I'll tell Sanette come get you!"

"Okay, I'm down," Ke said. "But I'm driving my own car.

You bitches don't know how to leave and I ain't got time to be stuck waiting on y'all asses." The girls promised to meet up within the next two hours.

Ke hopped in the shower and scrubbed her body. Once she got out, she lotioned her body down in Cocoa Butter. She then sprayed her Coco Mademoiselle Chanel perfume over her entire body. She decided to wear a red leather one piece shorts style jumpsuit. It was long sleeved, cinched at the waist and hugged every curve. It accentuated her wider hips and plump ass. The outfit stopped right over the cuff of her ass and her perky breast stood up in it.

Ke paired the outfit with a pair of thigh high red leather boots. She combed her hair down, put her lip gloss on and grabbed her car keys so she could head out to the address Angel gave her for the block party.

She headed out to her car and drove to the destination. Everything was smooth sailing until her phone vibrated and dropped on the ground. She took her eyes off the road for literally one second to grab the phone and lightly tapped the back of a Cadillac truck.

"Fuck!" she screamed as she pulled over.

She grabbed her insurance card out of her glove compartment and exited her vehicle. The driver of the other car got out of their vehicle, put his hands in the pockets of his hoodie, and grinned when he saw her.

"Well, well, well," smiled Omar. "You can't return my phone calls *and* you don't know how to give a safe following distance either," he joked. She just shook her head.

"You of all people is who I rear end," she laughed. "I'm sorry about that. Are you okay?"

She looked at the damage to the cars. He had a few scratches on his back bumper and the grill to her car was slightly dented.

"I'm good. Why haven't you been returning my calls? You scared? I don't bite," he challenged as he licked his lips.

"I told you I had stuff to do for school. I had these big assignments that I finally submitted," she explained while putting her hands on her hips. "And what I gotta be scared of you for? You ain't nobody." She cocked her neck to the side and was screaming on the inside about how fine this nigga was.

"You love talking shit," he said to her as he checked out her outfit and his eyes roamed her body. "Why you got on them fuck me "thigh high boots"? You plan on bein' in somebody bed tonight?" he smirked as he grabbed her hand.

"It ain't your bed. So why you worried?" she shot back. The two stared at each other.

"It'll be my bed in due time," he responded. She decided to keep quiet. "What're you getting into tonight? Your hair looks nice and you look pretty. I hope this little accident didn't mess up your plans. My car is fine. It ain't nothin' but a few scratches to fix," he stated as he grabbed her by her waist. He ran his fingers through her bone straight hair.

"As long as the car can drive, it won't ruin my night. I'm going out for drinks with a few friends, though. I was supposed to meet them at this block party but I'ma just go to the bar and wait for them instead." She got goosebumps while he rubbed up and down her back.

"How much money do you need to enjoy yourself tonight?" He reached into his pocket for his cash.

"Nigga, I don't need your money. I have my own." She rolled her eyes as she watched him peel six hundred dollar bills off his wad.

"Stop having this wall up with me." He wrapped his arms around her waist and placed the money into her back pocket.

"It's nothing personal with you. I told you that."

Ke broke their embrace.

"What is it then?"

"I don't want to talk about it," she said as she took a deep breath. "I have to get goin' though, Omar." She tried to walk away from him.

"Okay. Well I'm proud of you for getting your work submitted. I'm calling you tonight. So answer. Give me a kiss before you go."

He grabbed her hand and pulled her back in. She wrapped her arms around his neck and their tongues intertwined once again. He was gripping her ass and pressed her all up on his dick. She started sucking on his tongue and felt his big-ass dick start to grow. The two stopped kissing when Ke's phone rang.

"You always get saved by the bell," he chuckled as he planted soft kisses on her neck.

She answered the phone and it was Angel telling her that they were heading to the bar.

"Okay, I really have to go this time," she laughed as she broke their embrace again.

"Write this address down and take your car to them in the morning. They'll fix it for you. Tell them to charge it to me."

He gave her the address to this car shop. The two went their separate ways and she double checked that her phone's volume was on the loudest setting it could go to. A bitch didn't plan on missing anymore of his calls.

CHAPTER
TWENTY-ONE

KE WAS BACK HOME from getting drinks with her girls. She showered and as promised, Omar called her phone.

"Hello?"

She crawled under her covers.

"You really been frontin' on a nigga for damn near two weeks. That's fucked up," Omar teased. "How do you plan on paying up for duckin' me? You know you owe me right?"

"I don't owe you shit," she laughed.

"You owe me a date and next week I'm taking you to my house for a few days. I'm ready for us to just vibe and have some more face-to-face time."

"I'll go on a date with you. That's fair. But I am not spending the night with you."

"We'll see about that," he chuckled. "I'm picking you up for dinner tomorrow at five. I need your address."

She gave it to him along with explicit directions on how to get to her home.

"Omar, like I said, I'm not spending the night with you. What I look like spending the night with you and we ain't together. You must really think I'm one of these weak-ass bitches that do whatever a nigga say because he got a few dollars. Well, I'm not.

You need to pump the brakes," she bucked with her slick ass mouth.

"Like I said, I'ma handle that mouth of yours," he laughed. "I know you ain't weak. I don't invite females to my house. Can't no female I ever dealt with tell you where I live. I told you I want you. I like you. I like talking to you. I like what we doing and I'm ready to move forward. What we waiting for?"

He waited for her response but the phone grew silent. She was shaking her head no because she didn't know if she was up for this. "You the reason why we ain't officially together. You scared of being with me?" He waited for her response.

"I just do things at my pace. Damn, what you going to do, tie my ass up and force me to be with you?" she joked.

"I mean… I can tie you up and force you if that's what you want me to do." They laughed. "But I won't have to do that. You want me, too. Stop playing with a nigga, Ke. Be ready tomorrow night. Do you need any more money to handle anything?"

"No. I'm fine, Omar. I'll be ready," she told him and the two hung up.

CHAPTER
TWENTY-TWO

IT WAS ALMOST three o'clock the next day and Omar was driving home from the barbershop listening to Bobby Brown's, Rock Wit'cha to get himself in a sensual mood for his date with Ke. He called her during his drive to make sure she took her car to his peoples and got her front bumper fixed.

He pulled up to his home, hopped in the shower, and began getting ready. He gave himself the once over in the mirror before he left out and was proud of what he saw. He dabbed on his Dior cologne, went downstairs and grabbed the keys to his Audi Coupe. He started the engine and he headed to pick up his date.

Ke was putting the finishing touches on her outfit. She decided to wear this one shoulder black dress that hugged her curves. She paired her dress with a pair of black opened toed stiletto heels that had diamond accents on the foot straps. She put on her Chanel earrings and combed down her bone-straight hair. She sprayed her Chanel Mademoiselle perfume all over her body and checked the time. It was almost five, so she put a piece of gum in her mouth and went downstairs to wait for Omar. The doorbell rang, and Ke took a deep breath to calm her nerves as she opened the door.

"What's up, Ma?"

He smiled and handed her a beautiful bouquet of white roses. She allowed him to come in while she sat the roses down.

"I like the way that dress looks on you and I see you like Chanel."

He glanced at her earrings and saw her purse with the double C's embellishment. He made a mental note to ask her about the scars on her wrists from when she was inflicting self-harm. He noticed them before, but now he *had* to know why she wanted to hurt herself.

"You look pretty," he added. She couldn't help but smile.

"Thank you. You look kind of nice yourself," she teased. They both laughed.

He had on a black tuxedo which was perfectly tailored to fit his frame. He had on a white dress shirt underneath that was adorned by diamond cufflinks, and a black handkerchief. He had a fresh cut and both his ears were laced with diamond earrings. Her eyes went to his Cuban link necklace and glistening pinky ring.

"I like that you have both of your ears pierced. It brings out those long ass eyelashes you have. Do people ever tell you that you favor the rapper Loon?" she asked.

"All the time. I tell them that nigga favor me. Can't nobody be me."

"No fa'real. I didn't see it before but damn, you might need to see if that man is your brother. Y'all got the same chocolate skin, same build, same damn goatee and same low-cut with the waves."

"So what that mean, Ke? You want him to be the one taking you out on the date?" he asked while putting his lips on her neck. That gave her goosebumps.

"You know what. Let's just go. Dinner is at six, right?"

"Yep, you ready?"

"Yeah, let me grab my purse."

She turned off her lights and locked her door. She was expecting to see Omar's truck but she was met with his coupe instead. He explained that he only pulled the coupe out for special occasions. She blushed while they hopped in the car to head to their destination.

They pulled up to a beautiful yacht on the harbor. There was a line of cars waiting to be checked in by the valet. Every luxury car you could think of was in the lineup and everyone was dressed elegantly.

"We're having dinner on the yacht?" she questioned as she soaked in the scenery.

"Yeah. And sorry to break it to you, but they don't have fried cabbage or turkey wings here." He jokingly stated as he made fun of her favorite cuisine: soul food.

"Oh, whatever Omar. I told you the soul food here ain't got nothing on the soul food from my hometown."

Omar's car was checked in by the valet and a hostess walked them to their seats. Ke was blown away by the decor. There were chandeliers hanging from the ceilings. Each table had a thick white tablecloth on it with gold plates and gold napkins that held the silverware. The chairs were also gold and had a plush cushion for comfort. The lights were dim, and someone was playing a harp. Their table was seated in the corner and right next to a circular window that had a great view of the water. The sun was setting and the rays reflected off of the water.

"Wow, this yacht is beautiful," she stated in awe as she watched the sunset.

"Yeah, it is. This my first time here. My dad and stepmom had their wedding anniversary here and kept saying I need to find a lady I really like and bring her here. So yeah," he said while grinning and grabbing her hand.

"You probably bring plenty of women here. Who do you think you're fooling?"

"I haven't. I promise. I ain't been into nothing serious to bring anyone here."

"Mmm-hmm."

The waiter came over and placed a bucket of vintage Dom Perignon on their table. He asked her if she wanted a glass, but she declined.

"Did you want another kind of champagne or wine?" Omar asked, handing her the drink menu.

"No alcohol for me tonight. I have to work tomorrow and I need to be on my Ps and Qs when dealing with you," she said and shot him a look.

"I'm always on my best behavior with you!" he stated while laughing. "I haven't put the pressure on you just yet. Trust me, I have a lot of plans for you," he said while smiling at her.

"You get into the habit of asking me a million questions *and* you always making slick comments."

"I'm asking all these questions because I want to know everything about you. I wish you would stop second guessing me and see that. You gone be weak in the knees for a nigga. I'm already getting a little weak in the knees for you."

"Oh, whatever Omar. You tryna see how I taste between my legs already and all you got was a kiss from me. You're more than a little weak in the knees," she teased back at him.

The waiter came back and they proceeded with their orders. She ordered the lump crab cake that was topped with a lobster and shrimp cream sauce with asparagus and truffled mashed potatoes. Omar opted for the honey glazed salmon with broccolini and truffled mac and cheese. They enjoyed their food, and he handled the dinner bill.

"I got you a slice of their cheesecake to go. Are you ready?" he asked.

"You northerners and y'all cheesecake," she joked. "But I'll be ready after I use the ladies room." She washed her hands, and checked her reflection in the mirror while she applied more lip gloss. She gave herself the once over and walked out. Omar was waiting for her and held his hand out so they could walk out together hand in hand.

As they headed to the car, they were stopped by a woman who was working valet. She wanted to speak directly to Omar. He told the valet woman to hold on as he opened the door to help Ke get into the passenger seat.

"This won't take long, Ma," he stated as he approached the other lady.

Ke cracked her window and folded her arms. She had to hear what the fuck this conversation was about. He wasn't her man so she couldn't wild out but what bitch was going to approach a man holding hands with another woman? Unless that bitch was somebody he deals with.

"*Hmph, just when I thought I could make it work with this nigga. He got bitches approaching him needing to talk. Typical! And I got the nerve to like his ass a li'l bit,*" Ke thought to herself. "I'm so over these niggas!" she barked.

Omar was now face to face with the other woman and Ke was tapping her foot on the floor of the car because she was anxious about the conversation.

CHAPTER
TWENTY-THREE

"WHAT'S UP, PATRICE?" Omar confusingly asked while shrugging his shoulders and scrunching up his eyebrows.

"You ain't shit. Why haven't you been returning Lucille's calls yet you holding hands with somebody?" she inquired while putting her hands on her hips and glancing over at Ke in the car.

"Why does this concern you?" he glared at her with a death stare.

The nerve of this bitch to question him about her lying-ass homegirl.

"This concerns me because my friend said you made her get an abortion!" Patrice screamed, throwing her arms in the air. "And she said you ghosted her after she gave you the news about the baby. You fucked up for that,"

"That has nothing to do with you. She knows exactly why I don't fuck with her," he firmly stated as he turned away from her.

Other valet workers were walking past them. He started biting on his bottom lip as his heartbeat rose while people witnessed this conversation. He hated the feeling of embarrassment, and this caused his anxiety to flare up.

"I'm going to tell her that I saw you with someone," she blurted out while watching him walk away.

"I don't give a fuck. Make sure you let her husband know she's still callin' me. That bitch knew from jump what she was there to do," he said as he left Patrice standing there.

He hopped back in the car and apologized to Ke for leaving her while he addressed that.

"Oh, you ain't gotta apologize but you can explain. You had a baby? Do you have a girlfriend? Who was she?" Ke asked as she watched him start the car up.

"No, no, and no to all those questions. Her name Patrice and she's a friend of this broad I used to meet up with here and there," he explained while driving.

"What do you mean? Like y'all was fucking?" Ke cut to the chase.

"Pretty much. I was dealing with this girl named Lucille a few months ago and she did some shiesty shit so now we don't deal with each other anymore," Omar shrugged. "I charged it to the game."

"Well what did she do? And why did Miss Patrice mention something about a baby or an abortion you made Lucille have?"

He took a deep breath because Lucille really was a bitch that he acted like didn't exist.

"Up until a few months ago, I was living a wild life. I was with different women and some of the decisions ended up catching up with me," he said while looking at her. "I don't really like having uncomfortable conversations and this shit don't feel good Ke," he confessed.

"That's your anxiety talking," she explained to him while watching him survey his surroundings as he drove. "But you gotta understand where I'm coming from. You been kissing all on me and telling me you only want me. You keep asking me questions. Now it's your turn to be in the hot seat. These were choices you made, so don't be scared to talk about them. You want me to be your therapist, right? Well, this is our first session. Gon' 'head and talk," she responded while cocking her neck.

He hated when all of the attention was on him and he hated giving old shit his attention again. He tried to avoid it at all cost, because this was a coping mechanism for his *undiagnosed* social anxiety. But, he explained to her the situation with Lucille, how they were just fuck buddies and how she had a husband the entire time. He also told her about the pregnancy, his decision to want a DNA test and how Lucille's trifling-ass had him and her husband thinking they were both the father.

"Oh my gosh. That poor man is who I feel so bad for. Muthafuckas cheat and can never own up to the shit," she expressed while frowning her lips and shaking her head. "But, Lucille was married, creeping, and then fucking you with no protection?" Ke asked.

"She told me she was single and I didn't care enough to confirm the shit. And as far as condoms go, that was a one-time thing when I didn't strap up."

"No, I'm saying," she paused and explained, "she was fucking you and her husband raw. It could've been more than a baby that transpired between that."

He agreed with her and explained that he was thankful he never caught anything because he stayed on top of his checkups. He also explained that Patrice was addressing him off the strength of Lucille lying about what happened. He told her about how he had to get his number changed because Lucille kept calling him.

"Are there any other females or possible babies I should know about?"

"There's one other girl named Bria who got pregnant. She wasn't married though," he tried to make a joke.

"What happened with her?"

"I met her in the club, too."

She interrupted. "Oh, so you just love meeting women in the club, don't you. I work at the club. Hmmm, how convenient," she sarcastically stated.

"No, No. It's not like that. I used to spend most of my time there due to the fellas wanting to go there. But Ke, please don't make it seem like females ain't going to the club with the hopes of scoring a nigga with money. Come on, Ma, don't act like that," he challenged.

"I'm not acting like that. I'm saying you clearly enjoy meeting women at the club. Please don't try and act like y'all niggas ain't going to the club looking for y'all next booty call," she said matter-of-factly.

"It's crazy because I actually hate all the club shit. It's too many people and something pops off the majority of the time. I especially can't stand when females get to fighting and then all the attention be on the nigga that they dealing with," Omar went on.

"Key phrase, the nigga they dealing with," she shot back.

"Lord, okay. Let me just get back to explaining this story," he chuckled. "I met Bria at the club. That night we fucked and all that. I would call her whenever I was in the mood for a booty call. She would answer. Then, about a month later she got pregnant."

"Oh my god. Omar, wrap it up."

"Like I said, other than pregnancies I am grateful for not catching a disease. I basically asked her the same thing as Lucille, 'What you going to do?' I told her if she keeps it, I'ma make sure she straight and if she doesn't, that was cool too. I told my pops and he wanted me to get a DNA test. I was going to do that anyway."

"He was right for telling you to get a test. I mean damn, Omar. You told the man about two kids in a matter of months."

"I know. Bria ended up getting an abortion without me knowing, and she was kicking it to me like she was still pregnant. One of her old friends showed me the paperwork of her abortion because the two of them started beefing and exposing each other's business," he said as he shook his head. "Women can be so grimy. Bria was going to play like she miscarried because she still wanted me to make sure she was straight. She knew having a kid by me was the only way she could've solidified that," Omar expressed. "I was so confused on why she snuck and got an abortion when all she had to say was she ain't want the baby. We weren't together. Just fucking. I could care less if she kept the baby or not. I was just goin' to own up to my shit since I did have sex with her with no rubber."

"Wait. An abortion without you knowing?"

"Yep. When she first gave me the news, she basically said she didn't want to give up drinking and partying. I told her that's fine but then she told me she was keeping it," he said as he shrugged. "It was also talk that it could've been another nigga's baby but I don't know and I don't care. I told you, we were just fucking."

He didn't understand females like Bria's logic. Omar was out doing his dirt and he was transparent about it. These bitches really just lie about everything and it made his skin crawl because of how conniving they were.

"What did you expect? You said you met her at the club, you said women in the club looking for niggas with money and you said all y'all did was have sex with no real connections. You put yourself in this position."

Ke wasn't trying to defend the women, but he was to blame for some of it. Just because his goal was to be out here fucking gives him no right to place majority of the blame on the females.

"Why have unprotected sex with women you ain't even in a relationship with or want anything long-term with?"

"I don't know. Us niggas do dumb shit. But, like I said, I was living wild so please don't judge me. Both those situations opened my eyes and I just stopped being a bachelor for a while. I realized that if they would've kept them babies, I potentially could've had two kids by two different women," he shook his head. "I had to get my shit together. That is not the life I want for myself. My dad told me I needed to be more careful because he ain't raise me to be irresponsible like that. Then, Lucille and Bria got to fighting in the club," he said.

"Oh lord, Omar," she said, rubbing her forehead.

"I cannot stand a lot of attention being on me. They realized I was dealing with them around the same time. That shouldn't matter because I wasn't in a relationship with either of them," he explained. "That night pissed me the fuck off. For them to be fighting was insane because I was done dealing with both of them during that time," he said.

"You need to be more careful. Just like your dad said." Then she followed up with, "You seem to be so chill and laid back, but I should've known that was a front. You got women out here acting crazy just like all the rest of these men," she said while shaking her head. "Everything ain't always Omar's way and you need to understand that. Your intent was just to fuck, but clearly these women wanted something more," she hissed.

"I know it ain't always my way. But if we first meet and I'm telling you this shit just sex and a female agrees to that, why am I the bad guy?" he challenged. She just deep sighed. "I'm not living like that anymore though."

"Mmmhmm, sure you're not. Was that hard for you to express?" She noticed his demeanor became relaxed.

"It's not that it was hard to express. On some real shit, Ke, I use to tell my mom all the time to leave the nigga that was abusing her. She never left until it was too late. So I just decided to not express myself because what's the use. My moms used to express to that nigga how she ain't like being abused or she ain't like his drug use and what happened, he still fucking killed her. So there's no point to express myself about some shit when them bitches gon' tell the story they want to tell anyway," he vented.

Ke really had a deeper level of understanding about him now. They pulled up to her house and she was about to open the car door to go inside. She had a lot to soak in with him.

"Wait, Ke. I just answered this mess about my past with you and shared a lot of my deep emotions. I really hope you can see that I'm not that person anymore. But can you tell me why you are so hesitant with me? Why don't you want any relationships? Tell a nigga what's up," he pleaded.

"Omar. I'll tell you another time."

"Tell me now," he demanded.

She took a deep breath. She couldn't believe she was about to tell him about Sincere and all the shit that happened.

"Omar. Look, I was really not trying to get into this with you. The stuff you told me got me considering if I even want to move forward with you because it reminds me of the same shit that I said I would never put up with again."

"Tell me."

She looked at him and told her story.

"Two years ago, I was in a relationship with a guy named Sincere from age sixteen to twenty-three. The first part of our relationship was good. Then, he earned a scholarship to play basketball but decided not to take it because he wanted to scam and sell drugs. Why he would throw away a damn scholarship, I don't know. But, anyways, he ended up hitting a big scam, got us an apartment, and a car. I wanted to start working to earn my own money. Long story short, there was an argument about me working and it got so bad that he started putting his hands on me."

"He hit you?" Omar asked and he immediately thought back to his mother.

"Yep. I know I shouldn't have let it slide but love really makes you blind to so much. He was my first love. The first and only man I ever was with. I had it bad for him. It was embarrassing all the fights I got in behind bitches stepping to me about him," she expressed. "Whenever I addressed him about the other females, we would fight. I let the hits slide one time but after that, I started fighting back," she paused. "I'm not letting nobody beat on me and then you cheating and fucking lying. Every time I tried to leave, he would do all he could to make me come back. So stupid!"

"Wow. No Fucking words."

"One time, well two times I went to jail because of the shit," she said as she held up two fingers.

"Damn, you were his woman and you going to jail behind that dumb shit?" Omar said as he shook his head.

She nodded and went on. "I ended up getting pregnant by him and a girl called my phone one day. That was the last straw for me," Ke said.

She explained to him how Sincere beat her to the point she

was unconscious, had a miscarriage and he called the police on her after she drove into his apartment.

"Damn," he said as his heart went out to her.

"I was fighting an attempted murder case, but I beat it because there was so much proof of me being a battered woman. Also, my mom advocated for mental illness and showed that we have a family history of it with my father," she explained and he nodded his head. "They placed me into a mental asylum for mild disorders for a few weeks because I got very depressed and started trying to commit suicide," she confessed.

She showed Omar her scars. His heart was fluttering at how she was opening up to him. "I had to go to intense therapy sessions because they said I had PTSD from the trauma, postpartum depression from the miscarriage, coping issues and anger issues," she chuckled because one thing the world was going to do was diagnose a muthafucka.

"Damn, ma. That's deep. That shit doesn't make any sense that a man cheats constantly like that but doesn't want to let the woman go that he's hurting. That's how you really ruin somebody. I'm so glad you seem to have overcome all that. That's some major time you could have faced and it wasn't even your fault. You were acting off what somebody else did to you over the years," Omar said.

"I hate that I lost myself. Depression is a muthafucka. I'll never go back or let somebody take me there again," she said. "That's why I'm hesitant with you," she looked at him and explained. "It's not you personally but from my experience, relationships these days come with too much disloyal and toxic shit. I can't do that to myself again," she sat there shaking her head.

"That nigga a lame. When I was doing what I was doing, I ain't never put my hands on any woman and I never cheated on anybody. I tried to discuss things with them even though they weren't my woman. And, I told you my mom was in an abusive relationship. I'd never do no shit like that," Omar sincerely stated.

"Yes. You told me. And it's not that I don't believe you. I'm dealing with the after effects of that shit. I would never go back to him or any nigga like him. It's been two fucking years and I'm still scared to jump out there because niggas really ain't shit," she stated. "I went on a date a few months ago with a teacher I work with and whole time the nigga was married and I didn't know! I would never do no shit like that to another woman. So, it's not just you. It's all you niggas. Y'all just ain't shit."

"Other than Patrice addressing me about Lucille, which ain't even valid. I never gave you a reason to think that about me. Plus, you are the only female with this number and the only one I want. I can handle you the right way if you just let me."

Ke just looked at him. The long conversation had worn her down. She believed that Omar wasn't out there wilding anymore, but the insecurities she had as a result of Sincere just wouldn't let her avoid her overthinking. She needed to get in her house and be alone.

"Have you enjoyed being alone for two years?"

"Yup. I have. Two years is a long time without any male companionship, but I had to get my life on track. All I make time for is myself and it feels good to finally be happy and somewhat healed."

"That's dope that you chose your happiness and got yourself back right," he replied. "I respect that you know how to be alone and put yourself first. A lot of people don't know how to do that."

"There's a lot of girls out here putting themselves first and doing the damn thing. Don't you want to go bother them instead of bothering me all day, everyday?" she teased, smiling at him.

"Naw. I want you." The two just stared at each other. "Let me put my face all in that pussy, Ke," Omar stated.

"What? No," she was caught off guard by this. "You wanna put your face in between everybody's legs that you take on a date?"

"Trust me. My face only wanna be in between yours. One thing I ain't doing is sticking my tongue in everything. I can promise you that," he said. "Let me taste it."

"No."

"Okay, well give me a kiss. You owe me at least that for going missing for almost two weeks. I ain't forget."

"No. I'm not kissing you anymore. Matter-of-fact, whatever we got goin' on needs to stop right here. I need time and space to process this long ass conversation," she told him.

He wasn't trying to hear any of that shit. He grabbed her by her neck and placed his lips onto hers. He started nibbling on her bottom lip and she couldn't help but to slip her tongue into his mouth.

Omar slid his hand between the split of her dress and started caressing her soft ass. He then moved his hand towards her pussy and started rubbing her clit through her thong, causing her whole body to tingle. That scared the shit out of her. She couldn't believe how good he was making her pussy feel.

"Omar, please don't make me cum," she moaned as he put his lips on her neck and moved her panties to the side.

He started lightly sucking on her neck and rubbing his thumb in a circular motion over her clit. He pressed on her clit and her pussy started gushing out her juices. He felt her clit start to swell and he circled a finger around her warm opening. She placed her hands over his and tried to stop the motion because she was fucking terrified. Omar moved her hand from off of his and placed it on his rock-hard dick. She moved her hand up and down his length while he continued to play with her pussy.

"I wanna make you cum all on my face. My mouth a seat just for you," he said, enjoying how wet and soft her pussy was.

He turned her legs towards him and pulled her thong off. Her body was on fire as goosebumps covered her. He slowly pushed her back toward his car window and spread her legs as far as they could go. He stared face to face with her fat, bald, and juicy pussy.

"This pussy pretty as fuck," he admired her while he flicked his wet tongue over her clit.

"Mmmm! Oh my God!" she gasped and her body flinched from the stimulation.

"I see this clit sensitive to the touch."

He put his entire mouth over her swollen clit and began tongue kissing it while her legs started trembling. He sucked on her clit while simultaneously darting his tongue on it. Then he started teasing her again by placing soft kisses around her pussy opening.

"Omar!" she cried out.

She was in disbelief that he had his head between her legs. She fantasized about this. He moved his head up and twirled her clit in between his tongue while massaging her nipples through her dress. He stuck his tongue inside of her opening and she started grinding on it.

"You taste so fucking good, Ke," he said as he kept tongue fucking her while catching all her juices with his mouth. "You said it's been two years? This pussy ready to start back talkin'," Omar said as he slipped a finger inside of her opening.

He pushed his finger in and out while sucking on her clit. Her juices were dripping down his hand and towards her ass. He spread her ass cheeks and started licking up and down her ass crack. He then stuck his tongue inside of her asshole and Ke started quivering.

"What the fuck!" she hollered.

She couldn't describe how amazing it felt to have his tongue in her ass. While keeping his rhythm, he fingered her with one hand, rubbed her clit with the other hand, and tongue fucked her asshole.

"Oh shit, Omar, wait! Baby, wait!" she yelled because she felt like she was about to pee on herself.

She knew it had been a while since she had an orgasm, but it felt like her spirit had left her body. Her toes were tingling and her mouth was wide open. Her heart was pounding and she was trying to rise up and move away from his lethal ass tongue. He kept thrusting his finger in and out of her while putting pressure on her G-spot. His warm mouth made its way back to her clit and when he released his finger, Ke hollered in pure ecstasy as she squirted out an overflow of pussy juices over his seats, all over his face, and her thighs were covered in her juices.

"Fuck! Oh my gosh! What the fuck!" she screamed.

Her legs were still shaking and Omar was in heaven seeing her pussy release like that.

"Damn, Ke. You a squirter," Omar said as her juices dripped down from his goatee while he watched her try to get her bearings together.

She didn't want to look him in his face. Her eyes were wide and her lips were trembling. She never squirted before a day in her life and here her pussy goes acting like it had no home training and showing off for Omar.

"I didn't know I was. I didn't know I could do that," her voice was shaky as she controlled her breathing. "Omar, I can't do this. How did a date end up with me squirting in your car. What the fuck," Ke closed her legs and just sat there. The bitch was shook and embarrassed about the mean-ass mouth piece he just put on her. He grabbed a small towel from his glove compartment and dried his face off.

"Why can't you do it? Stop fighting it. You deserve to cum hard like that every night. Every part of your body and soul deserves attention. You deserve this dick I'ma give you too. I promise you my dick will stay harder than any terrible thing you've ever been through in life," Omar smiled at her, grabbed her wrist, and rubbed her scars.

She was about to cum on herself again from his words.

"But fuck all that sex shit. I'ma make it so you won't ever have to hurt again. Let me love and protect you. You won't regret it. I told you, don't put me in a category with no lame ass nigga," he continued to rub on her scars.

"I have to go," she told him as she opened the car door and headed to her front door.

She didn't even give a fuck that half her ass was hanging out because she didn't pull her dress down. Omar followed behind her and she walked inside of her house.

"You're still coming to my house this week. I'm picking you

up when I get back. I'm aiming for Friday but whenever I get back, I'm going to call you. Your spring break is the same week and it's going to be perfect for us to keep spending time together."

"I told you I'm not staying," she said as she put her purse on the table.

"It's been two long years. You gotta start letting them walls down. I'm the one to do it with. I wouldn't lead you on if I was trying to just play. I'm serious about you," he said in her ear while he embraced her.

"I still need time to heal, Omar," she tried to push him off her.

"Heal with me," he shot back as he kissed her neck. "I'm bringing you to my house whether you're packed or not. I gotta go," he kissed her neck one last time. "Your pussy tastes good, smells good, and it feels good. Did you like what my tongue made you do? You almost drowned a nigga back there." He smirked and she couldn't help but to blush. "I can't wait to make you squirt on my dick," Omar said as he headed to the front door, leaving her speechless as usual.

An hour later, she put Xscape's, *Do You Want To* on repeat while she grabbed her suitcase and began packing for her stay at Omar's. Yes, she was packing a week early. Wouldn't you if a muthafucka just ate you from your "rooter" to your "tooter"?

CHAPTER TWENTY-FOUR

IT WAS Wednesday of the following week and Ke just pulled up to the Pink Pussycat Boutique: a sex store in Manhattan, New York. She got out of her car and entered the shop. Her nose was immediately attacked by the smell of leather, and she noticed that the left side was dedicated to female sex items and the right side for male sex items. She was looking around at the variety of kinky things from whips, whipped cream, butt plugs, lubricants, strap-ons and even silicone vaginas.

"You are not the person I expected to see in here," smiled her co-worker from the bar, Sarah looking at her from behind the counter. She put down some boxes and walked over to Ke.

"Girl, you and me both," Ke smirked but she started to get embarrassed.

"Anything specific you lookin' for?" Sarah asked while she stared at Ke looking at the store's entrance. Ke hesitated to answer, but then just blurted it out.

"I'm looking for a dildo. It's been a while since I've had sex, and I don't want to be too tight. So, I'm looking for something to just open me up a little. I don't know. I feel dumb," Ke explained and both women cracked up laughing.

"I know Ms. I Have Boundaries is not tryin' to open her legs up," Sarah taunted.

"My boundaries are still up," Ke explained. "I just need to get back into learning the inside of my body," she kept going as she had flashbacks of squirting on Omar's tongue.

She didn't know she could do that and just wanted to see what else her pussy could do just in case she gave that pussy up to him. "So can you help me find a nice size dildo or something?" and both the women started chuckling. "I don't get how you can work here. This shit is so fuckin' awkward," Ke said while still laughing.

"It's easy. Most people know what they come into these types of stores for," Sarah explained and directed her to a huge wall of dildos.

They were every size, every shape, every color, and some of them came with a vibrating feature. Ke went toward a brown six-inch basic dildo with girth.

"This one should do," said Ke as she grabbed the package and was about to head to the register.

"Oh no, ma'am!" Sarah yelled and stopped her. "This is the one you need right here! Something that's gone hit every cobweb you got down there," she teased again as she showed her a ten-inch, black dildo with veins popping out of it. It was one of the toys that had the vibrating feature and spurted out some type of lubricant gel.

"Bitch, I am not taking all that," Ke gasped as she stared at the massive toy. "Big dicks are not my thing. Seriously," she deep sighed as she once again thought back to Omar.

She didn't want things to be embarrassing if they ever had sex because she hadn't been penetrated in two years and what if he couldn't open her up. She was worried.

"A whole baby can come out of a vagina! We can take any dick as long as we're turned on," Sarah expressed. "Just try it! Get both of them and see which one you like. I bet twenty dollars you're going to be obsessed with this anaconda sized one," she joked as they went to the register.

Sarah gave Ke her discount code for both dildos and she headed home. She was looking forward to playing with her toys.

CHAPTER
TWENTY-FIVE

KE WAS BACK HOME from her sex store mission and was about to set the mood for an erotic night by herself. She placed the dildos on the couch and ran upstairs to make sure she had a few necessary items.

"Okay, got me some candles, got my bubble bath, got my two dicks downstairs, and now all I need is some food and Keith Sweat's beggin'-ass voice to have me bustin' like a water gun," she chuckled while she checked off all the things she had.

She went downstairs and started preparing her dinner of baked chicken with a Tuscan cream sauce over mashed potatoes and string beans. She was making her homemade sauce when her cell rang.

"Hello?"

"What's up, Ma?"

"Nothing much, sir. Just finished cooking."

"Whatchu makin'? I'm on the way to come get you," he anxiously stated.

She froze up and was silent for a few moments.

"Omar, you said Friday. It's only Wednesday!" she frantically stated as she thought about her plans for her solo night. She needed those extra days to get her nerves, mind, and body together.

"I finished a little quicker than expected. Plus, I said the minute I got back I was coming to get you," he stated. He was not trying to have her back out. "Ke, if I know you and how scared you are of me. You're most likely already packed," he teased.

She held the phone to her ear and awkwardly looked at her suitcase by the living room chair.

"Can you please come Friday? Please!" she pleaded.

"I'm almost there. Put me a plate up," then he hung up. Not giving her any space to protest.

"Oh my god! I am not prepared for this shit!" she yelled as she rubbed her hands over her face.

She quickly finished her sauce and tasted it at least twenty times. He told her to make him a plate and now she was thinking about how he might not like her food.

"My goodness. This nigga just thinks he can push his way right in my life. What the fuck," she stressed as she made both of their plates and Omar was knocking on her door.

"What's up, Ma?"

She ignored him. Her mind was trying to get itself right for being with him for a whole week.

"I thought we already had a talk about how you supposed to greet a nigga." He grinned.

"Omar... You told me Friday and you know I have work the rest of the week," she stated. "Did you want me to follow you in my car? Have you been to your house yet? Are you sure you are ready for me today?" She took deep breaths as she asked all these questions because of her anxiety.

He grabbed her shoulders and started laughing. "Calm down," he looked at her bags on the floor by the living room chair. "I knew you would already be packed," he smirked. "My house is waiting for you, Ma. It's been waiting for you since I made that pussy squirt everywhere," he joked. She rolled her eyes. "Did you make me a plate? Want to eat right now?"

"I'm just... Just caught off guard," she said as she walked away to turn the oven off. "Yes, we can eat now."

"Okay, and you gon' be ready after?"

She just looked at him. They sat at her kitchen table to eat and Omar told her everything was delicious. She washed the dishes, bleached down her countertops and turned the lights off. Omar grabbed her suitcase from off the floor by the couch and he noticed two packages on the chair with a handwritten note that read:

Have fun! I hope this helps to open that pussy up for your boo!

"You didn't want me to come today because you had plans with those?" he laughed and pointed to the dildos. All the blood drained from her body and it felt like her heart had stopped. She had completely forgotten to put them away.

"Oh my gosh," she went to grab the dildos and put them in her room. She came back down and Omar's eyes were glued to her.

"You might as well throw them away. I don't need any help opening that pussy back up," he motioned for her to come on.

"Again. You don't know what to say out your mouth," she said and he started laughing.

"Do you want me to follow you in my car? I have work tomorrow."

"No. You can drive one of my cars to work or I can take you."

He looked her in her eyes. She broke their gaze and Omar smiled to himself. He got a kick out of her nervousness. It made his heart smile because he knew she was trying not to catch feelings for him, but each encounter made her fall for him a little more.

"Okay."

She grabbed her purse, locked up her house and Omar put her bags in the backseat and then opened her door.

"Let's go," he said with a big smile.

She could tell he was happy and despite all her nerves, she was happy, too.

"Why you got that big smile?" she asked as she buckled her seatbelt.

"Because I get you all to myself for a week. I have a lot planned for us."

"Hopefully you don't plan on touching my vagina with your mouth or fingers while I'm there," she replied and instantly regretted letting that slip. She was only supposed to think that. He looked at her and smirked.

"I planned on touching that sensitive-ass pussy with my dick. I made her squirt everywhere and I can't wait until my dick gets blessed with that. Like I told you back there, I'ma show you that I don't need any help from a sex toy."

"Whatever, Omar. I'm not fucking you," she firmly stated.

"I know. I'ma be the one fucking you, ma," he countered while laughing. "Or would you rather have the dildo?" he asked, not letting that go.

"You like to play all the damn time," she stated and shook her head.

"Okay, okay. But can a nigga at least taste it again?"

He really wasn't focused on fucking Ke. He wanted all of *her.* He knew the pussy would come eventually and he was genuinely trying to spend time with her this week. If they ended up fucking, then great and if they didn't that's fine, too. He was a real nigga first and he knew she wasn't on no 'just fucking' type of shit. He knew that pussy ready to play though.

"No. You already got a taste last time," she said while looking at him. "That's all you getting from me." She sat back and let that marinate with him.

"I ain't handle it how I really wanted to. I wanted to make you cum on my face again, but I know you scared of what I can do to that pussy," he teased.

He couldn't get it out of his mind how good her clit felt when it swelled up or how good her pussy juices smelled and tasted. It was turning him on. Ke was the one who started this conversation, and he was going to finish this muthafucka.

"Whatever, Omar. I'm done speakin' about my pussy with you," she stated. "Are we almost to your house?"

"Eventually you and everything that comes with you will be mine. So you might as well get used to me speaking on it." She ignored that last comment and he grinned. "And yeah, we'll be there in about ten minutes," he told her as he directed his attention to the road.

He pulled up to his home. "We're home."

He opened her car door to let her out and then opened the back door to grab her luggage. He checked his mailbox and then stuck his key in the door. His home opened up to a spotless kitchen with a marble table set. From the kitchen, you could see the all-black living room.

"Omar, do you have any water?" she asked as she looked around at his navy blue and cream marble kitchen decor.

"Yeah. Look in the fridge."

She opened the fridge and freezer, noticing he didn't have any damn food. There was only water, lunch meat, and a frozen pizza in there.

"How are you going to invite someone over with no damn food? See, I told you, you should have waited 'til Friday," she deep sighed as she folded her arms and scrunched up her eyebrows.

"This grocery mess is an issue I deal with on a daily. I really don't be havin' time," he laughed. "You want to go grocery shopping with me tomorrow when you get off?"

"Nooo. You said you were ready for me to come. You gon' make me starve over here."

"Pretty please. You're able to work, go to school and find time to cook and clean. That's why we make a good team. You gon' teach a nigga how to manage all that," he stated as he wrapped his arms around her.

"I'm glad we ate before we got here. It's getting kinda late and I need to get ready for bed," she stated as she pushed out of his embrace. "Where did you put my things?"

"Upstairs in my room. I'll show you."

He grabbed her hand and led her up the stairs to his master bedroom. His king size bed frame was black with a red, black and white comforter set. He had a huge black dresser, a walk-in closet and a flat screen in his room. He also had a small section on his dresser that was designated to his smell goods: all his cologne, lotion and a brush for his waves. He had black and red curtains hung up over the windows and a white sheer curtain over top. His bathroom was decorated with the same red, black and white color scheme and it complimented his room very well.

"Who decorated for you?"

"My stepmom. When you move in, we can change it up if you want," he said as he looked at her. "I'm rarely home, believe it or not. If you noticed, I don't even keep much food in here," he said as they laughed.

"It's decorated nicely."

"Thank you. Are you sleeping beside me tonight?" he asked while playing in her hair.

"I don't know. You keep talking shit to me and I don't have time for that when it's time for bed," she said.

He laughed and she went to get her night clothes out. He gave her a towel and two washcloths. She went to the bathroom, undressed and turned the shower on. She washed her body, face, and let the soap run down her body. She rinsed off and allowed the water pellets to soothe her. She grabbed her towel, dried off and began her nighttime routine. She lotioned her body in cocoa butter. She then grabbed one of her favorite scents, Victoria Secret Love Spell and sprayed that over her. She put on her pajama short set and some long socks. She went downstairs because that's where she heard Omar watching TV.

"You smell good, Ke," he complimented as she came to sit beside him.

"Thank you. Do you like the color black?" she pointed to his black leather couch and observed the decor.

"I love it. It's my favorite color," he replied while staring at her.

He admired her fresh face and smooth skin. He started

rubbing on her smooth brown thighs and told her how soft she was. He tugged at the elastic waist of her pajama shorts then reached around and softly gripped her ass.

"Here you go starting up again."

"What? I like rubbing on you," he smirked as he inhaled the scent of her neck and kept caressing her ass. He tried to reach around to rub her pussy, but she stopped him.

"It's getting late. I'm going to bed. I told you I'm not doing anything with you."

"We ain't did nothing. Let a nigga show you some affection," he said while sucking on her neck.

Her body was tingling but she managed to get away from his soft lips and headed to the guest room. She got under the covers, set her alarm, and was fast asleep.

Omar went upstairs after the game highlights went off. He took a shower and went to the guest bedroom also. He got in the bed and cuddled up against her. After doing drops for the week, he felt so peaceful in her presence and fell asleep.

A few hours later, Ke's alarm went off and she began getting ready for work. She softly tapped Omar on his shoulder.

"Good morning to the most worrisome man who was supposed to had slept in his own bed," she teased and he cracked a smile. "Where are your car keys? I need to get goin'." She stood there while he rubbed his eyes.

"Kitchen table. Make sure you come back here. You know how nervous you get and probably making a plan right now to avoid being here with me," he joked with her and put the covers over his head.

She smacked her lips. "Nigga, please. Ain't nobody nervous or scared of being around you," she lied.

He chuckled. "You think you will remember how to get here? I can drive you if you need me to," he mumbled from under the covers.

"I should be good. I'll call you when I get off," she told him as she headed down the steps.

She grabbed the car keys off the table, locked the door, and headed to work. The work day was easy and they told her she could take a half day the next day since there was early release due to spring break. As she was clocking out, she pulled her phone out to dial Omar but he was already calling her. She answered the phone:

"What time you get off," he said, still sounding sleepy.

"Well hello to you too. Is that a New York or northern thing to never say hello when you call someone? You just jump right into the convo?" she laughed while pushing the button to unlock the car door. "And didn't I say I would call you when I got off?"

"Is it a Virginia thing or southern thing to have a smart-ass mouth to everything I say?" he countered.

She laughed. "My mouth ain't smart. You're the one always talking crazy." She giggled as she started the car up and headed back to his place. "But I just got off. I should be at your house in like twenty-five minutes. Is everything okay?"

"Yeah. I'm about to get up so we can go grocery shopping."

"Okay. I didn't agree at all to any grocery shopping."

"You didn't agree to squirt in my car either, but it happened. That was great southern hospitality by the way. I loved it."

"Fuck you, Omar!" She grinned and he burst out laughing as they hung the phones up.

He was ready when she got there and they picked up food for the week. Once they got back home, Ke started preparing dinner of pan seared salmon, seasoned broccoli, and rice for them. Omar made a few calls while she was getting herself together for work tomorrow. Once it was time for bed, he talked Ke into sleeping with him in the master bedroom. She couldn't resist and they found themselves cuddled up in bed again.

CHAPTER
TWENTY-SIX

"KE, I have something fun planned for us." Omar beamed as she walked through the door from her last work shift before break.

"Ok, what is it," she said, putting her purse down.

"I know you said you wanted to go sky diving. I got us tickets to go indoor skydiving at Fly zone down in times square."

"OMG, really?"

Ke lit up. She was the ultimate daredevil. Omar was happy to take her there, even though he was terrified. He wasn't into stuff like that, but she said it was something she wanted to do.

"Our appointment is in an hour so let's head out."

"Okay!"

They got to the appointment and Ke could sense Omar getting quiet. He was never quiet around her. She asked him what was up, and he told her

"It's too many people in here and skydiving ain't on my bucket list," he admitted. Ke burst out laughing.

She watched as the people went as high as eight hundred feet and she couldn't wait. She dragged Omar to put his equipment on and he took five deep breaths.

"Ma'am, when we let you go, the air will soar you to a height of eight hundred feet. You ready?"

"Yesss!"

"Sir, are you ready?" the attendant asked Omar. He shook his head no.

"I like being on the ground but I'ma G. I got this."

Ke grabbed his hand, looked at him and they leaped. It was so empowering. They both screamed and she even spun backwards. She was enjoying herself and he was squeezing her hand so tight, but he made it through.

"Ke, we never doing that again." He was relieved when they finally were finished. "That was crazy. You're a thrill seeker."

"That was fun. You've been quiet the entire time we were here, and I could use the silence," she teased.

"Next time we do it, I'ma be back to talking. Don't worry."

He drove them back to his place where he told her to get ready because they had dinner reservations at the Grand Center Oyster bar. She took a shower and picked out her outfit. She decided to wear a black leather miniskirt and a low-cut white blouse with puffer sleeves. She wore some red strap heels and paired that with her red Gucci purse and red Dior shades. She had on a tennis bracelet and her Chanel earrings. He had on a Gucci pullover sweater, black pants and Gucci loafers. He had on his signature Cuban link and pinkie ring.

"We can stay here and I have you for dinner," he couldn't stop staring at her thighs.

"Sorry, Sir, I am not on the menu," she shot.

"Oh, you know you can be," he shot back as she blushed. "You ready?"

"Yup!" They walked out of his house to the car, and headed to the restaurant. It was slam packed, but they had reservations.

"Hey, Omar," smiled Jamie, one of Lucille's friends. She was a hostess. "Checking in for two?" she asked then glanced at Ke.

"Yeah," he responded and put his arm around Ke's waist.

"Okay. Your server will be right out to get you seated," stated Jamie as she checked off his name and reservation time.

They waited for a few moments and made small talk until their server came over to introduce herself. She escorted them to their table and Omar grabbed Ke's hand so they could follow. She led them to a table, smack dab in the center of the restaurant under a chandelier. Omar's heartbeat sped up and he was squeezing her hand as he tensed up. The feeling of all eyes being on them made him uncomfortable.

"Okay, here's you guys' table," said the cheerful server.

Omar was silent as he looked around and gripped Ke's hand even tighter. Social anxiety at play again.

"Is there any way we can sit at that table back there in the corner next to the window?" Ke asked as she stepped in to try to calm his tension.

"Yes, ma'am! No problem! Follow me."

The server picked up their menus and led them to the corner spot that was a little more private. Omar loosened his grip on her hand and she put their menus in front of them.

"Thanks, Ke," he whispered and she started giggling.

"Mmmhmmm. You need to put me on payroll as your therapist. This anxiety is really somethin'," she laughed.

"So you trying to say I have anxiety because I like to be a little private with things? Nope. I'm not convinced. Just know that when it come time to fuck, this anxiety or whatever is out the window. I let it all out."

He chuckled as his nerves calmed down and he was back to his slick mouth self. She started laughing and that caused Lucille, who was at dinner with her husband, to look toward them. Lucille had a fire burning in her stomach as she watched the two interact as if they were the only ones in the building.

"Lucille, what are you looking at?" asked Sampson as he watched her appear to be in a trance. "Lucille!" he yelled and she directed her energy toward him.

"I'm ready to go! You always pick the worst fuckin' places. Damn, why would I ever marry you!" she screamed to him as she stormed toward the hostess area. "Where's Jamie?" she rudely asked one of the workers. They told her she was in the back and then went to get her. Jamie walked out with wide eyes as she rushed to her.

"What's wrong?" Jamie asked as she hugged her.

"Omar is here with some bitch and got the nerve to make me get an abortion," Lucille explained. Jamie was confused.

"I thought you were here with Sampson though," Jamie stopped hugging her.

"Jamie! That abortion mentally affected me and you're going to allow someone to just ghost me? You know Patrice saw him last week and she stood up for me! Why can't you do the same?" she played reverse psychology on Jamie's weak-ass.

"I always stand up for you," she spoke up. "Didn't you say his number was out of service? I got the reservation book and this number has to be in service for us to confirm it. Let me give you his contact info and then maybe he will talk to you," Jamie stated as she tried to win Lucille back.

She reached for the book and gave Lucille Omar's new number while Sampson was occupied with paying the bill. Right after Jamie gave Lucille Omar's new contact information, Sampson walked up and Lucille stormed off to the car, annoyed by his presence.

On the flip side, Omar and Ke were enjoying their dinner and each other's company. Omar kept telling her how this was the most at peace he'd been at in years. She couldn't stop smiling. If he wasn't telling her how pretty she was, he was telling her how sexy she was, if he wasn't saying that, he was saying how happy her vibe made him and when he wasn't saying that, he was telling her how bad he wanted to eat her pussy.

Anxiety and all, he was a character. Ke excused herself to go to the bathroom and when she came back, Omar paid the check and they headed to the car. Jamie noticed them leaving and rushed to the bathroom and dialed Lucille.

"What Jamie?" asked Lucille with a rude tone.

"Omar and his girl just left. You should be all clear," Jamie explained. Lucille perked up. She hung up the phone and quickly dialed the number Jamie gave her.

"LET ME ANSWER THIS, Ke. I don't recognize the number and they've called six times," he told her as he stopped their small talk and picked up the phone. "Yo," he spoke into the receiver.

"Oh, I see you too busy with other bitches to talk to someone that was carrying your child," Lucille yelled in the phone from her front porch.

"How the fuck did you get this number?"

"Nigga, don't worry about it. You're a piece of shit," she stated.

Omar hung up. His eyebrows were scrunched up and his nose was flared up. He was sick of this shit and irritated about how delusional she was being about what transpired between them. Her and her friends were purposely trying to damage whatever he had going on with Ke and that made his blood boil.

"Seems to me you have a lot going on," Ke said as she watched him put his phone away and shook her head. She started regretting letting her guard with him.

"I promise you I don't," he said as he calmed down and pulled into his driveway. He wanted to put a bullet through Lucille's lying ass.

CHAPTER
TWENTY-SEVEN

"OMAR, I'll just call a cab or something to go home. You specifically told me none of your exes or whatever have your number," she stated trying to keep her cool. "I'm not dealing with extra drama or bitches. I told you that," she expressed as he opened the door to his house. She walked toward the stairs.

"I already told you what it was. Her friend was the hostess at the restaurant and I'm sure that's how she got my number," he honestly stated while grabbing her waist and trying to plead his case. He did not want her to leave. These bitches sure knew how to ruin shit.

"I let the first time slide with her other friend but I'm not letting this time slide with her calling a brand new number. This shit ain't okay," she said.

"I wouldn't be trying to make you my woman if I had some other shit going on. I'm straight forward about everything," he explained.

He was pulling her in close and she turned her head to the side and tried to push him off her. He didn't budge and started placing soft kisses on her neck.

"Omar. No. Get off me. I'm going home."

She was so busy trying to push him off her, she didn't even notice his strong hands rubbing up her thigh. He found her pussy and started rubbing it through her panties while sucking on her neck with his soft lips.

"Omar. Stop," she whispered.

Her pussy was soaking wet, and her body started to tremble. He eased her to the couch and kept rubbing on her through her panties. He moved her panties to the side and found that sensitive-ass clit that he couldn't stop thinking about. He pressed on her clit, and she let out a moan. He began caressing it in a circular motion and his fingers became moist with her juices. He eased up off her clit and put his tongue in her mouth. She sucked all over his tongue as they kissed.

"I'm not ready," she moaned.

He ignored her and laid her down on the couch and slid her thong and skirt off. He put his face near her pussy.

"I don't give a fuck about no other females, okay? The only thing that's been on my mind is you and the way this pussy tastes."

He blew on her clit and she arched her back. He ran his tongue up and down the opening of her pussy and went to her swollen clit. He licked her clit and Ke's moans got louder. He alternated between sucking and licking while she threw her pussy to his face. He lifted his head up and dropped a little bit of spit right inside her pussy and licked it up.

"Oh god!" she screamed.

He stuck his tongue inside of her pussy and she gyrated her pussy up and down it.

"I told you I wanted my face all in this pretty pussy," he continued to pleasure her with his tongue. She was moaning and he started putting pressure on her clit with his tongue.

"This pussy wanna talk to me again?"

"Yes, baby. Yes. Make it talk to you!"

He dropped some spit right on her clit and was getting that pussy all wet and messy. He zoned in on it and started sucking it again and she was hollering and screaming as her climax built up.

"Oh, oh, yes! I'm cumming! Ugh!" she cried as her legs started shaking.

She was trying to catch her breath. He eased her shirt over her head and started caressing her perky breasts. He then rubbed on one nipple while he put the other in his mouth.

"Omar," she whimpered.

He spread her legs open and went back to eating her pussy. She grabbed onto the back of his head. Her mouth was wide open as she watched his tongue go to work on her pussy. He was lapping up all her juices and was about to make her cum again. He stopped eating and spread her pussy lips so he could suck all over her pearl. He then slipped a finger in her pussy and pressed on her g-spot while sucking on her clit and looking in her eyes.

"Oh shit, Daddy!"

She was screaming in pure ecstasy as she had a gut wrenching squirt session. Her juices leaked out over his couch and Omar licked her thighs so he wouldn't miss any of her sweet juices. She held on to his head as her body calmed down. He stood up and started undressing. She sat up and when he pulled his boxers down, she saw his big-ass black dick sprang out, resembling that big ass dildo with the veins she purchased.

"I don't think I can take that," she shamefully admitted as she closed her legs.

It was thick, long, and chocolate brown in color just like him. The head was oozing precum and it hooked to the left. His dick was absolutely gorgeous.

"Yes, you can. You ain't even know you were a squirter," he watched her admire his dick and that gave him the greenlight.

Her pussy tasted so good that he had to feel the intensity of her orgasms on his dick. He placed the condom on, and he saw her tense up.

He started sucking on her neck and moved up to her lips. She licked and sucked off her own juices that were on his lips. His fingers started playing in her wetness which caused her to moan. He laid her back on the couch and spread her legs so she could make room for his body to be on top of hers. He got on top of

HEART OF A THUG

her and put the head of his dick right on her clit and started to make circular motions while she grinded her pussy on the head. He moved the head of his dick towards her opening.

She started breathing heavily but her juicy pussy was telling his dick to bring it on. He thrusted his dick inside of her tight pussy and tried to force himself not to cum. He couldn't describe how good this first encounter felt.

"Got-damn, Ke! Yo pussy feel so good on my dick," he moaned as he stroked the first half of it inside of her. She was moaning and with each moan she was letting him slide more of his dick in.

"Omar, oh my god!" she screamed in bliss.

He was stretching her pussy to fit his member and it felt wonderful to her. She was in disbelief that she was taking all this dick.

"This pussy so fucking tight and wet," he said while still holding his nut back. The whole thing wasn't even inside of her, but her pussy grip had his dick in a vicious choke hold. He pushed more of his dick inside of her until she let most of it fill her up.

"Open that pussy up for daddy," Omar whispered as he nibbled on her ear. That drove her up the walls.

"Omar, ugh! I feel it in my stomach!"

She moaned as she just laid there and gave herself to him. Omar started kissing her while he simultaneously pushed her legs back and laid down his pipe game, missionary style. He pulled his whole dick out, squeezed it to stop from cumming and immediately slid it back in. Her gushy walls covered his dick. He put one of her legs over his shoulder and started stroking toward the left of her pussy. He felt her G-spot on his dick and her pussy started contracting as he pounded her spot.

"My spot! My spot!" she hollered as she grabbed onto his shoulders.

"Cum all on my dick," Omar said as he talked her through her orgasms. "I thought you said you couldn't take it."

Her legs started shaking and her body started trembling. Her orgasm came through like a wave and her entire body started convulsing. He was hitting her G-spot, kissing on her and talking that shit to her. She had no control. He told her to cum all over his dick and she did. Omar took a few more strokes and then he came, too.

"Damn, Ke!" he said as the last of his cum dripped in the condom. He was still laying in between her legs telling her how good her pussy was.

"It had my dick in a vice grip. I couldn't get out of it, Ma! You tryna make a nigga lose his mind! That pussy ain't got no business being that good."

She was still laying there quiet and in shock. Did she really just give the pussy to Omar. Did she really just take his big-ass dick. Did she really cum three times and this nigga dick was back hard. She was through.

She had no words as she collected her clothes and headed to the shower. Her heart was still pounding and her pussy was throbbing. Omar was on the couch grinning while he watched her try to process their first encounter. He heard her turn the shower water on and he headed in that direction. He cracked the door open, steam seeped out and she peeked from the side of the curtain.

"Get out, Omar. I'm done with you and your dick for the night," she said as she placed the washcloth over her recently stuffed pussy.

"We ain't done with you," he told her as he hopped in the shower with her. "You're everything I want and need in a woman. I never felt so damn soft and vulnerable with anyone."

He chuckled as he grabbed her washcloth and went to soap her up.

"You just saying that because you got the pussy," she stated while he scrubbed up and down her body.

"You know that ain't true. Stop making things up in your head. I'm one nigga that's gon' let you know what it is upfront," he told her as she grabbed a washcloth and began washing him up. "That pussy top tier though."

She blushed. They got out of the shower and dried off in the middle of the bathroom floor. Omar grabbed her by the waist and started planting hickeys on her neck. He bent down to suck on her nipples while he rubbed on her clit. It swelled between his fingers and started wetting up.

"No more tonight, Omar," she moaned as she rubbed up and down his arms.

He pulled her towel off and placed her on the sink. He spread her legs wider, inserted two fingers inside of her and pressed on her clit with his other hand.

"This pussy knows me already. I know you about to cum," he pushed his fingers in and out of her until he found her G-spot.

"Oh shit!" she yelled as she came all over his fingers moments later. When her body calmed down, he lightly grabbed her by her neck.

"Open your mouth," he firmly stated in his sexy deep voice.

She did what she was told and he put two fingers in her mouth and she sucked off her pussy juices. He then leaned in for a kiss and their tongues danced.

He still had a hand over her neck and he grabbed his dick to slide it in while she was still sitting on the sink with her legs open. His knees buckled as her pussy wrapped around him. She took a deep breath while his raw dick made its way through her fleshy walls.

"Get a condom," she whined and tried to gently push him out of her, but it was too late.

Omar got a feel for her with no protection, and he knew he fucked up because he didn't want to get out of the pussy. It was hot, wet, tight, and he wanted all of it. He kept stroking and then lifted her legs up. Her toes were pointed, and he started sucking on them while he was dicking her down. He rubbed on her clit, and he felt her flex her pussy muscles against his dick.

"This pussy all mine," he started kissing on her neck. "Tell me you're my woman while I'm stretching these walls out," he moaned.

"I'm yours, Omar! All yours!" she hollered. The way he

talked to her while they were fucking sent her overboard. "I'm cumin' all over yo big dick," she moaned as her pussy clenched down and she rode her orgasm.

Her walls sucked him in and he couldn't help but to release himself too. They both were breathing hard from those intense orgasms.

"That's your last time fucking me with no protection. I don't want any children any time soon!" she scolded as he slid out and helped her off of the sink. Her legs felt like Jello while she went to freshen up.

"I thought I could manage but by the time I attempted to pull out, the contractions from your pussy pulled my dick in," he explained while they walked into the bedroom. "You mine now," he firmly stated as he looked into her eyes. She didn't say anything. "I like hearing you scream when you cumin'."

She blushed and told him condoms every time from here on out or she would cancel this shit. Raw sex is a dangerous game, and she did not want to play with it.

CHAPTER
TWENTY-EIGHT

THE NEXT MORNING, Omar woke up before Ke and went downstairs. He chuckled to himself because she put it on him so good that he wanted to prepare breakfast for them. Omar pulled out his toaster, some eggs, and started cooking. Ke woke up to the smell of bacon. She threw on her robe and went downstairs to make sure she wasn't tripping. She saw Omar down there in his boxers and his back muscles were flexing with every move he made. He turned around and the two made eye contact.

"Good morning, Ma."

"Good morning. I didn't know you knew how to cook. You've been making me cook for you and you could cook the whole time," she scolded while cocking her neck to the side.

"I mean, I can make toast, eggs, and throw some bacon in the oven. That's about it. I hope I don't ruin this meal for us," he said as they both laughed.

"You need my help?" she asked.

"No, I'm almost done. Grab our plates."

She went to grab the plates out of the cabinets and gave each of them a slice of buttered toast. Omar scooped the eggs onto their plates and then placed the bacon on there. He remembered that she liked apple juice, so he poured her some and himself orange juice.

"Okay. God, please don't let Omar get us sick with his cooking. Amen," she teased.

"Amen," he laughed.

Everything was good and she told him that he makes eggs the way she likes them: nice and fluffy.

"Now hopefully we won't have any stomach pains later!" she joked and prepared to wash the dishes. "Maybe next time I'll make some pancakes. You like pancakes?"

"Yeah, pancakes and French toast are actually my favorite."

"Okay. I'll make those for you next time."

She went towards the sink and ran some water for the dishes and poured a cap full of bleach in the water. Omar questioned her about that.

"Adding a li'l bit of bleach to your dishwater just gives it a little razzle dazzle. This an unspoken rule in all Black households," she laughed because he was looking confused. "My grandma does it, my mom does it and here I am doing it. Let me handle this please because you really missing out."

"Are you trying to kill me? Bleach in the dishwater? I think that must be just a southern thing," he teased. "I'm going upstairs to shower," he said as he kissed her cheek.

He had never heard of the bleach in the dishwater thing. He couldn't recall either of his parents doing that. Ke finished the dishes, bleached the counters and wiped down his marble kitchen table. She then swept the floor and lit one of her Strawberry Pound Cake bath and body works candles she brung over. It had his house smelling good. She went upstairs to shower and that's where Omar was. It was pouring rain, so she assumed they would be chilling in the house. His phone rang and it was Trae.

"What's up, li'l nigga?"

"You always gotta go there," Omar laughed.

Just then, Ke got out of the shower and she asked Omar if she could use his washer and dryer for her dirty clothes that had accumulated.

"Yeah. You know where it's at?" he asked then directed his attention back to Trae.

"Sounds like you busy. Must be Ke."

"Yeah, that's her, nigga. I told you I was feeling her."

"I taught you everything you know," Trae laughed. "I'll catch you later tonight," and they hung up. Ke came back up the stairs and Omar told her to come here.

"Did you figure out how to work the machines?" he asked.

"Yes. I do know how to wash clothes, Omar," she sarcastically stated.

"I'ma fix that smart-ass mouth," he said while grabbing her by her waist.

He leaned in for a kiss and she started sucking on his lips. He took her robe off and admired her body. He guided her to bend over and felt her tense up. Before she could protest, he stuck his tongue in her pussy from the back.

"Mmm, daddy," Ke moaned as he thrusted his tongue in and out of her pussy.

He reached around the front and started rubbing her clit while he devoured her. His tongue was so far in her pussy that his nose was in the crack of her ass. She started throwing it back on his tongue while he put pressure on her clit. He inserted two fingers inside of her and her walls gripped his fingers. He went to suck on her clit and her legs began to get weak.

"Cum all on daddy's face," he said as he smacked her ass.

She started shaking and her orgasm shot out.

"Oh shit," she cried as she felt her juices trickle down her thighs. "What the fuck are you doing to me!" she quivered. Her heart rate was through the damn roof.

"I'm breaking this pussy in," he responded and was still in shock by her overflow of juices. He guided her to stay bent over because he had to tear her ass up doggystyle.

"Omar wait," she panicked and tried to get out of the position.

"Don't even start, Ke. Look at what I've been making that pussy do," he said as he placed her on all fours and guided her to arch her back.

He slapped her ass and rubbed his dick along the opening of

her moist pussy. He used one hand to grab her waist and the other hand to slowly guide his dick inside of her. She kept her arch and that shit turned him on big time.

"Omar, ugh!"

He pushed his dick further inside until he hit up against her walls. She gasped as his dick filled her up. He then put both hands on her small waist and began stroking in and out of her gushiness. He was loving the view of her round ass jiggling with each stroke. He started pulling her hair and she began creaming. His dick went in the chocolate color of his skin and came out white because of her creamy pussy. He then spread her ass cheeks, dropped some spit in her asshole, then put the tip of his thumb in her ass as he pounded her pussy from the back.

"You like that?" he taunted as he kept knocking against her walls, causing her titties to bounce with each thrust.

"Yes daddy, I do," she cooed.

She started throwing that pussy back at him and their strokes were in sync. All you heard was her pussy smacking and their moans.

"Throw that tight ass pussy on my dick," he moaned while he slapped her ass. "I'ma have this pussy trained. You feel so good, baby," he said as he found her spot with his dick and hammered at it.

"I'm about to cum! Omar, make me cum! Yes! Yes! Right there!" she yelled as she climaxed.

When he felt her pussy contract, he pulled out and shot his load on her ass. He used his dick head to rub his seeds onto her ass cheeks.

"I need a nap," she giggled as she collapsed on the bed.

"You can nap in a few. Come ride my dick first," he demanded.

She looked at him in disbelief that his dick was back hard. Since the night before, she had been squirting and skeeting on that dick non-stop. He was tearing her pussy up and she had to get used to his stamina. But the way he commanded her to come ride his dick turned her on and she slid her fat pussy on his pole, reverse cowgirl style.

She braced herself to fit all of him inside of her and slid all the way down to the base and came back up to the tip. She did this a few times and planted her feet next to his hips while her hands held on to his knees.

"Hold my ankles, daddy," she seductively stated as she balanced herself.

"Hold your ankles?" he questioned and she nodded her head.

He did what he was told and enjoyed the show. She began bouncing up and down his dick on her feet while he kept her planted. She was making her ass cheeks clap and moving in a circle while she teased the tip. Then she glided all the way down so he could feel her gorilla grip. She had her back arched while practicing Kegels on his dick head.

"Agh, fuck, Ke! I love this pussy," Omar moaned while watching her take all of him.

Her juices traveled down his dick and she started massaging his balls. His toes curled as he grabbed her hips to slow her down because he was about to explode. He lifted her legs up a little, leaned her back toward him, and started rubbing her bulging clit while he pounded her pussy from underneath. Ke hollered and that feeling of an intense orgasm was returning.

"Omar! Take your dick out, take it out! Please!" she screamed.

He put a hand around her neck and increased his pace as he rubbed her clit.

"You mine forever, Ke," he staked his claim and put two fingers in her mouth.

She sucked on them and he went back to circling her clit. "Can I make this pussy cum again?" he asked and she couldn't take it anymore.

"Baby," she quivered and tried to move his hand because her soul was leaving her body. She was about to erupt like a volcano. Her body was shaking and her pussy felt like something was about to come out of it. She lifted up and half of his dick came out.

"Oh fuck! Oh shit!" she screamed in ecstasy as her stomach caved in like an empty Capri Sun while she squirted all over his dick.

There was a downpour stream of pussy juices that soaked his dick, the side of his body and the bed. It was like ocean waves crashing on him as her pussy wet his dick up. Omar was moaning her name and exploded right after her.

He was in shock watching her pussy drown everything. When he got done releasing himself, she was still on top of him trembling and trying to control her breathing. He rubbed the head of his dick onto her clit and she gushed out more pussy juices. He tapped at her delicate clit, she had tears in the corner of her eyes, and homegirl passed out. *That dick knocked her out.*

CHAPTER
TWENTY-NINE

OMAR CARRIED Ke to the guest room while she was asleep and washed the sheets to the master bedroom. After he replaced the sheets, he hopped in the shower. Once he finished, he tapped her lightly on the shoulder to tell her that he was leaving out.

"Okay. Be safe," she said as she went back to sleep.

"Be in the master bedroom when I get back. The sheets cleaned so you don't have to worry about sleepin' in the wet spot," he teased.

"Omar, leave me alone. I know I've earned at least a few hours of rest, your highness," she grinned while rolling her eyes. "Besides, nigga, you would've been sleeping in that wet spot. Not me."

"Without a doubt I would've slept in it," he admitted and they laughed. "Where I tell you to be at when I get back?" he asked.

"In the master. I heard you and I'll be in there. There's nothing wrong with my hearing," she stated as she went back to sleep.

"That mouth, Ke," he laughed.

He left her to rest and grabbed the keys to his Expedition and headed to the warehouse. At the warehouse Trae told them that their next drop would be in Miami and they might be gone for as long as two weeks due to having to move extra careful because of all this talk about folks snitching.

"Damn, two weeks?" Bo questioned.

"Yeah, y'all know we're getting closer to the end with this shit. Gotta start taking bigger and longer risks," Kaylin explained.

"These niggas better not be on no bullshit," Bo said. Omar was standing around and observing.

"Oh yeah, O. Word around town is that nigga Rayzo is out," Trae confirmed.

"What? He was just facing sixty-seven years on drug charges," Mel barked.

"That nigga snitching," Omar replied.

When a nigga gets out of jail with that much time, they in there talking. That just confirmed his suspicions of Rayzo.

"Exactly. That's another reason why the drops have to start being longer. We don't know who fucking watching or telling." Trae vented getting annoyed. "So sick of these talking-ass niggas, yo."

"Omar, they said that nigga Sincere that Ke use to deal with out of jail, too," added Supreme. Everybody directed their attention to him. When Ke explained to him the bull shit that happened with her and Sincere, he started digging up information on the nigga.

"Word is that nigga snitching, too!" Supreme followed up. Omar was still quiet and soaking in the information. "He supposedly lives in Rhode Island now and was trying to move weight there but niggas said he on paper work and got the proof he was trying to set them up."

"I can believe it," Omar said while flaring his nose up. "Any nigga that can beat on a girl and call the police on somebody you been in a relationship with for four to five years will snitch on a nigga in a heartbeat," he went on. "I'ma handle that nigga if I ever see him."

"Chill, O'. He got his ass whooped and is fighting for his life. So niggas already handled it up there," Supreme said.

"I don't care. If that nigga even step to Ke, I'm putting a fucking bullet through him," Omar voiced and everybody nodded their heads.

"What Ke over there doing to you boy? You trying to put bullets in niggas already," joked Mel.

Everyone snickered. They went over everything they needed for the upcoming drop and headed home.

CHAPTER
THIRTY

KE FINALLY GOT herself together and downed two bottles of water. All that squirting had a chick dehydrated. She grabbed her cell phone and checked her missed calls. She noticed that Kyra, Angel, Tasha, and Jazz all had been trying to reach her, so she called them back and they put each other on four-way.

"Bitch, are you dating Omar? Trae told me a few weeks ago he asked about you!" Tasha asked through the receiver and the other girls laughed.

"Girl. He my man now. I done gave the pussy up to him!"

They were all screaming, cheering and parading. Kyra's ass even pulled out the blow horn.

"Y'all ain't shit for that!" Ke laughed as she yawned.

"He over there wearin' yo ass out. This ho sounds tired as hell!" said Jaz and they all laughed.

"Fuck y'all. I'm so damn worn out that I'm just really waking up from a session we had earlier today," Ke said as she heard Omar coming through the front door and then he called her name.

"Yes Omar, I'm up! she yelled so he could hear her. "Okay y'all, my husband back home and he wants me. I gotta go," Ke joked.

"Ke! Come downstairs!"

"Okay, I'm coming."

He had gone and got some takeout for them from this late-night soul food spot called Mitchell's. He got the turkey wings for them both. The turkey wings were good, but Ke said she had to let him taste hers. He also got her a new Gucci laptop bag for her computer. It was tan with the classic Gucci logo. It was embroidered on the inside to say, *Stay focused my super soaker*. She couldn't help but smile. They went upstairs, she showered and then put on her night clothes.

"Since you passed out from squirting earlier, I'ma give you a night off to recuperate," Omar smirked as he got in the bed and pulled her close to him.

"Oh whatever. It's been a while, but I've been hangin' in there and takin' that dick like the champ I am."

She laughed as he wrapped his arms around her and started playing with her fingers. She forgot how good it felt to have a man's arms around her.

"Come take it again," he challenged.

"I got you tomorrow," she replied and they both laughed.

He had been beating her pussy out the frame. She loved it but girlfriend had to ease into this consistent dick shit. She went from getting no dick, no fingers, no tongue to having someone who can't keep his hands off of her.

THE NEXT FEW days were filled with nothing but fun, bliss and connections. They talked, they fucked, and they did more adventurous activities. They went indoor paintball shooting, painting, parasailing which Omar was terrified of and he even took her to the gun range. He reminded Ke that if she aimed a gun at someone, she is telling that person that she wants them dead and she needs to follow through with threats like that or people can retaliate. She aimed the gun at Sincere and because of principle, she was supposed to kill him to eliminate any options of him retaliating against her.

That's just the street code. Never make threats you can't stand on and never point a gun you don't plan on using.

They went shopping and he bought her two extra robes and clothes to have at his house. She displayed some of her cooking skills and showed Omar that she threw down in the kitchen.

The entire week, his belly was full, balls were empty, and he was enjoying having Ke all to himself. Even though, she was ready to go home to her bed. She was going to miss Omar when he went out of town.

It was crazy because she wanted nothing to do with him at first, and now he is her man.

CHAPTER
THIRTY-ONE

"I'M all packed and ready, Omar," she told him from the living room.

"Just stay here at my house and wait for me to get back," he said while walking up to her.

He knew they both had things to do but he wasn't ready for her to leave. These had been the best ten days in years for him.

"I don't have any more clean clothes and I need to get back home."

"You don't need clothes. We just bought you a few things. So now what's your excuse for leaving?"

"You ain't tired of fucking yet?" she teased.

"Hell no! The way your pussy been gripping and squirting on my dick, you got a nigga obsessed. And you told me it's all mine," he sang. "Didn't I tell you in due time, you was going to be all mine?"

"Oh please, you made me say that!" she yelled as she hit him on the shoulder. *This is for sure his pussy, though. The things he did to it, it's all his.* "Come on and get me home. You ain't slick. Trying to stall so I can say it's too late and have to spend another night."

"Okay, okay, you got me."

They hopped in the car and drove to Ke's house. They made small talk and she loved that they could talk about anything with each other. He made her feel so comfortable and safe and ironically, he felt safe with her as well.

They pulled up to her house and he helped her bring everything into her room. He grabbed her by the waist and said he had to get going. He kissed her and went to pull her dress up.

"Omar, you said you have to go and we just had sex earlier today!"

"I know. I ain't giving you no more days off."

"Nigga, you only gave me one day off," she laughed.

He pulled her dress off, unsnapped her bra, and ripped her panties off. He laid her down on the bed and started sucking on her clit just the way she liked it until she came. He flipped her onto her stomach and pushed his dick inside of her tight, fleshy walls. She spread her legs so he could get in deep and he interlocked his fingers with hers. He pounded her hard and slow while kissing on her neck and shoulders.

"This how you deserve to be fucked," he said as she hollered from all the stimulation.

Her clit was rubbing against the bed and her pussy was making stirred macaroni noises on his dick. She gripped the sheets while he continued to place hickeys on her neck and whisper in her ear. She was throwing the pussy to him and came all on his dick.

"I love you, Ke. I'ma make you so happy. I promise," with those words, he came all in her pussy.

She had no fucking words. Omar slid out of her, went to get his bearings in order, and got the signal from Trae that they were about to leave for their drop.

"Don't act like you ain't hear what I said either. I'ma call you when I can. I don't have much time to address it now. But I meant it," he said directly to her. "What you got planned for this week."

"Well, I'm going to call my doctor first thing in the morning and schedule an appointment for birth control options," she stated with her arms folded and not trying to address the, 'I love you.' "Because one minute you know how to pull out and the next minute you don't. I told you I am not ready for another pregnancy."

She started getting aggravated that she kept allowing him to run up in her raw. They were exclusive now but still, she just wasn't ready for any kids.

"You right. It ain't no excuse. I'ma start pulling out or I'll start strapping up. Your pussy be strangling my dick and it's hard for me to get out of it. But no excuses. You said I need to start taking blame, right?" He motioned for her to get up and come downstairs.

"Yeah. Whatever. I'm not playing with you," she scolded as she grabbed her robe and went downstairs with him. He gave her an envelope filled with fifteen thousand dollars and the key to his house. *Geesh, as if he couldn't overwhelm me anymore.*

"Use some of that money to take care of what you need to do this week and use the rest towards your car, rent and savings," he instructed. "This is my house key, well, your key now. Give me a write out of all your bills so I can give you the money for them, too. Let me know how much all that is or I'll just leave you with one of my cards."

"Omar, I don't need all this money," she stressed. "I already paid my bills for this month and you giving me your house key?" She was sure she looked like a deer caught in the headlights.

"Save the money then. I told you I wanted to take care of you and everything that comes with you. You said you was gon' let me. So let me, okay? No second guessing or overthinking. Let this shit happen," he stated. "And yeah. That's my house key. I'm serious about us so why waste time? You know I don't like wasting my time."

"Okay," she said, hesitating again.

"I'ma call you when I can. Be ready to discuss me saying I love you and all this when I get back. I know having a real nigga is a lot for you to take in," he smiled at her. "Maybe when I get back you will give me your house key," he shot to her as he walked to the door.

"Be safe, Omar," she said, completely unacknowledging everything he said.

CHAPTER
THIRTY-TWO

KE WAS SETTLED back into her routine, but she was feeling a little sad because it had been four days since she heard from Omar. She missed him but felt weird because she didn't want to feel this way about him. She was chilling on her break in the teacher's lounge and then came a special delivery for her, Keisha Harris. A beautiful bouquet of white roses and a fruit arrangement. There was a note on the card that read:

Always thinking bout u, Ke. I meant what I said when I told you to throw away them dildos. You don't need them. You've been takin' the dick just fine. I love how that pussy fit my dick like a glove.

Love, Omar.

S.N: Drink plenty of water. I can't have you passing out anymore when I'm turning that pussy into a tsunami. :).

She was cheesing as she had flashbacks of how much fun she'd been having on that dick. The roses were beautiful, and she was happy to know he was thinking about her. When he got back, she wanted to cook him some pancakes.

She called Jaz and Kyra's pregnant asses over so they could be her taste testers. Kyra and Jaz got there and told Ke how bomb the pancakes were. Then, a delivery man knocked on her door with a large package.

"Keisha Harris?" the delivery guy questioned as he held a clipboard.

"Yes?"

"Sign here. Where do you want this placed?"

"Right here on the floor."

The man left and Ke opened the package with Kyra and Jaz watching. The package consisted of over twenty perfumes and lotions in her favorite Love Spell scent from Victoria Secret. He also remembered her love for candles and picked out over forty candles for her from Bath and Body Works in the scents of Strawberry Pound Cake, Limoncello, and Champagne Toast. There was a gift note and it said:

I love this scent on you. I hope this is enough candles for you, ma. I know how much you love a good smellin' crib. I miss you. Tell me what other fragrances you like when I get back.

Love, Omar.

S.N: *I need you to drink ten bottles of water a day. I'm loving the way you soak my dick when I'm hittin' it. Can't stop thinking about it or U.*

Kyra and Jaz were grinning about the gifts and the note he put.

"Ke, this nigga must be crazy about your mean-ass," spoke Kyra.

"I think he is. He gave me his house key, fifteen grand and told me he wanted to pay every bill I have," Ke chuckled. "Oh, and he said he loves me. My life is literally going in a direction I don't want it to go but I can't control it," she explained.

"I ain't worried about the money because he big time so I know he gonna spend it. But, the house key? And I love you? Already? OMG, he must be ready to put up with your crazy-ass. I'm here for it. I think you need somebody aggressive but patient like him," Jazz stated.

"He was like," What's the wait? I ain't even say anything," Ke confessed.

"He got your key?" Kyra asked and Ke shook her head no. "I'm with Jazz though. You hesitate with your feelings all the time and I think someone like him can really help you get it under control. He's super patient with you and you can really be a handful sometimes. Majority of these niggas would have been gave up."

"I think I may be moving too fast y'all," Ke vented. "I hate when I get to thinking like this," she admitted while acknowledging how "hot" and "cold" she could be with her emotions.

"It's too late to keep saying you're moving fast. Y'all done fucked, the nigga gave you his house key, he's telling you and showing you that he loves you and wants to take care of you," Jaz stated. "You really need to snap out of it, bitch. You ain't no trick-ass bitch and we know you can provide for yourself, but its okay to have a man that wants to assist Ke," Jaz explained. "He clearly wants to put up with that attitude you can get sometimes! You just told us he was your husband over the phone and now you don't know if you want him?"

"Which birth control y'all getting on after y'all have the babies?" Ke deep sighed and tried to change the subject.

They both said they didn't know yet and why.

"Because. We only used protection one time and I need to get on birth control," Ke sounded even more crazy.

"Oh, bitch! Lord, you saying you moving too fast and you letting the nigga slide in raw. You must be feeling him like he is feeling you."

Jaz threw her hands up. *Ke lets her thoughts get the best of her sometimes. Mental stress is really a fucking bitch!* "I know you ain't giving the pussy up to just anybody so If you letting him go in raw after that pussy was on lock then he gotta be doing something right," Jaz stated and they laughed.

"Ke, tell Omar to wear a condom if you're not ready for kids," Kyra added.

"I did tell him. I didn't think I would fall for him so fast and I hate it. This is so aggravating. He tries to pull out and he do it at the last minute or he just ain't doing it at all. I'ma just get on birth control and call it a day. Y'all know my uterus is tilted anyway and I can still get pregnant but it may take a little longer since things aren't fully aligned. I just want to be on a birth control that ain't gon' make me gain too much weight," she said.

"Well, you know what to do. Your ass done fucked around and fell in love just like him. Get ready for this rollercoaster because he ain't gon' play many games with your ass."

They laughed then Jaz and Kyra hugged her before headed out to their cars. Ke still hadn't received a call from Omar. She showered and got ready for her bed. This must be how Omar felt when Ke went a few days without talking to him during her research proposals.

While at work, the school she attended called her and said that she will be able to graduate a semester early due to her impressive portfolios. She tried to call Omar to tell him, but he didn't answer.

She started to over think and get paranoid. Not hearing from him made her think about her trauma and the shit he could be doing. *Is he with another bitch? Is he safe? Did he just want the pussy?* Ke's mind was everywhere, and she went straight to assuming the worst. Being alone with her thoughts was taking its toll on her.

CHAPTER
THIRTY-THREE

THE NEXT DAY, Omar was trying to call Ke because he had a surprise for her but it kept saying her number was not in service. After the fourth phone call, his mouth began to run dry and his heart rate sped up.

"What the fuck, yo." Omar sighed as he once again had no success in reaching Ke.

"You straight?" asked Trae.

Omar nodded his head. He then put his head back and closed his eyes, frustrated as hell.

Two days passed, and he still had no luck in reaching her. He was baffled. He didn't know how to process that. He would handle her when he got back in town.

KE GOT ready for her shift at the club but her mind was still on Omar. She had changed her number because she talked herself into not being ready for a relationship.

"If you see Omar tonight, just don't say anything to him. We are done with him," she gave herself a pep talk in the mirror.

She checked out her work outfit. Tonight, they were hosting a party so the bartenders and waitresses had on pleated skirts, tight fitted tees, and heels. She was pleased with her appearance, grabbed her car keys, and headed to work. She pulled up to her job and the men were whistling and asking for her number. She made it inside the club where she tended the bar with her girl Sarah, and they were killing it as they got all the drinks out.

Sarah explained to Ke that the people were so drunk in there that she had already found five lost phones. Ke told her to put the phones in the "lost phones" box, write the date on a sticky note and stick them in there. So many people get drunk at the club and leave their phones. They place them in a big box and labeled them with the date. Sometimes people come back up there and find their phones but most times it was just a lost cause. Ke was making a drink as Angel walked up.

"Bitch, I know you still don't have an attitude," she joked.

"Yes I do. I changed my number but this nigga still been on mind. I can't do this shit though. I don't know what he's doing when I'm not around. It's not even him. Its me and my fucked up healing," Ke admitted.

"You've known since day one what he does for money. You dead wrong for changing your number when you know he can't get to his phone all the time. Shit, Kaylin just called me after about five or six days. You know Omar is crazy about you," Angel seriously stated.

"I don't even care anymore," Ke shrugged.

"Well, you better get yourself together. They all supposed to be here tonight and you better talk to your man," Angel dropped a bomb on her.

Before Ke could respond, Kaylin and Omar were coming through the crowd and walked up to the bar. Kaylin greeted Ke and then Angel left with him. Ke's heart melted when she made eye contact with Omar. He had on a black Ralph Lauren sweatsuit, his waves were swimming, his goatee was lined up and he kept his gaze on her. She was still aggravated with him. Well, not with him, but she was aggravated with whatever her crazy-ass had come up with in her mind. So, she didn't acknowledge his presence.

"What's up, baby? What's going on with your phone? I been calling you," he directly asked her.

She ignored him and kept tending to her customers. He took this time to check out her outfit and noticed that her ass cheeks were hanging out in her skirt. He did not approve. "You hear me talking to you, Ke?"

"Omar, I hear you but I don't have time for this conversation right now."

"Make time," he demanded. "Matter-of-fact, let me speak to you outside," he stated as he prepared to leave.

Her co-workers were watching the whole thing unfold and couldn't believe Ke was being so standoffish to the man she couldn't stop talking about a few days ago.

"I can't leave the bar."

"Why not? I'm not dealing with this attitude or your slick-ass mouth. I told you that," he stood his ground. "Come outside right now. I'm not telling you again," he firmly said as he got up to walk away.

"Fine." She rolled her eyes. "I'll be out there," she took a deep sigh. "Sarah, you good? I'm taking fifteen."

"Yes, I'm good, we slowed up and everybody is ordering through the waitresses," she explained. "Ke, stop being a bitch to him," Sarah told her as she went back to work.

Ke wiped her hands off and headed toward Omar. He grabbed her hand and walked to her car. He opened her back door and sat down with her standing directly in front of him. Her arms were folded, and her attitude was prevalent.

"What's going on with you? Why am I getting all this attitude and why your phone not working?" He watched her roll her eyes and smack her lips. "Ke, I'm not fucking playing with you. You hear me talking, ma. Fix yo fuckin' attitude," he told her. She scrunched up her eyebrows.

"I told you this relationship is too much. I don't want to do it. I changed my number and just was hoping you would get the hint," she huffed while she stared at the ground, avoiding eye contact with him.

"We just had a good time together all last week. I gave you my house key. What the fuck do you mean you don't want to do it?" he asked with a confused expression. "We're already doin' it."

"I told you already," she deep sighed. "It's me. I get into my head about what could be going on when you're not answering my calls. I'm still trying to get my mental shit in order. You didn't do anything wrong. It's me," she said again. She saw the frustration in his eyes.

"You have to stop comparing what we're doing to what you used to be in. When I'm not answering, it's because I'm working. I ain't doing shit else," he said as he took a deep breath.

He started to think about how he had never been in a real relationship and these emotions were unfamiliar to him. He knew he had to have patience with her though because he did make her fuck with him.

"I know. I just missed you," she blurted out. Omar looked at her ass like she was crazy. *One minute she wants nothing to do with me and now she misses me. This muthafucka is crazy. Women.*

"Meet me halfway with this shit. Cut the attitudes out and the drastic measures, too. You changed your number on a nigga for no reason!" he stated. She chuckled. "I sent you things and always signed my notes saying I was thinking of you. I can't always get to the phone but trust, you always on my mind." He grabbed her hands.

"I just wanted to talk to you. That's all, but I get it. I overreacted. I know you can't get to the phone," she paused and looked at him. She was hesitant to admit it, but this felt right. "I'm sorry for being a bitch."

"I accept your apology," he told her. "Come here."

She walked closer to him. He started rubbing on her ass. "I missed your slick-ass mouth," he told her and she smiled. "My dad says I don't check in with him either, though. I can't promise to call. But, I need you to believe I only want you. I wouldn't be doing all this if I didn't."

With all these suspected snitches around, Omar refused to make calls while he was out in the field.

"I believe you," she told him. He made her kiss him.

"You should've gave me your house key and I wouldn't have had to pull you from work to talk to you," he joked as he gripped the cuff of her ass cheeks. "This how you act when you mad at daddy? Huh? You have your ass hanging out?"

"Omar, stop. We had to wear this today," she moved his hands. "And stop lifting my skirt up! We're outside."

"Ain't nobody out here," he stated and then guided his hands toward the front so he could caress her pussy. She told him to stop again because they were outside. He made her lift her leg up, moved her panties to the side and he started to rub her clit.

"Baby, wait until we get home, please," her voice cracked while trying to push him away but he wasn't listening.

The absolute last thing she needed was a co-worker or a customer seeing her outside getting her pussy played with.

"Come sit on my dick," he demanded, staring her directly in the eyes.

"What? No. I'm scared to fuck outside at my job!" she panicked and tried to put her leg down, but he kept it there and continued to rub her pussy.

"Can't nobody see. It's dark and everyone is inside," he said. She looked at him and saw how serious he was. "Take your panties off, Ke."

She rubbed her hand across her forehead and then did what she was told. She took her panties off and handed them to him. He placed her hand on his dick, lightly grabbed her by her neck and began kissing her.

"You know what to do when you touch my dick," he taunted.

She released it from his pants and started massaging it, loving how hard it was. He guided his hands back between her legs and inserted two fingers inside of her while she coated them in her juices.

"*My pussy* ready for me. Now, come sit on my dick," he told her.

She happily obliged and turned around to straddle him with her back toward his chest and eyes looking out into the parking lot. She slid down on his dick and started moaning as her warmth gripped his pole. He used two fingers to reach around and rub her clit while he thrusted inside of her warm kitty.

"Don't make me squirt out here. Baby, no!" She grabbed his hand and that only made him go harder.

"You gon' get your act together? If you can't tear those walls down you have up, daddy gon' do it for you," he whispered in her ear as he kept pounding inside of her. "You giving me some babies, Ke? Let me keep cummin all in it," he said. He kept rubbing while he felt her pussy contract on his dick, not giving her any time to process anything.

"Omar, you on my spot. Oh shit! I'ma get my act together, daddy," she moaned and some of his dick slid out. "I'll give you however many babies you want. Oh fuck!" she hollered while her orgasm shot out of her. Her body started quivering as her pussy squirted over her back seats, on Omar's dick and some got outside.

"Damn. That shit really driving me crazy. I really ain't got no control when I'm in it," he moaned as the last of his nut released inside of her.

She slid off of him and he helped her step back into her panties then put his dick back inside his pants. She told Omar she was too embarrassed that someone had seen them or heard her so she wasn't going back into work.

"Okay, I'll go tell them you going home."

They had no issue with Ke leaving early and Sarah cracked a smile because clearly Ke stopped being a bitch.

"Okay, my house or yours?" he asked when he got back to the car.

"We can go to mine," she said. He hopped in the driver seat.

"Oh, I have a surprise for you." He reached into his back pocket and pulled out two tickets. "I know you said you really like Patricia Wright and how she advocates for Special Education," he told her as he gave her the tickets. "So I got us tickets to go see her speak on Sunday in D.C. I was thinking we can make it a quick getaway and spend some more time together." Her heart was beating with pure joy.

"Oh my goodness, Omar. Wow. I love Ms. Wright!" she expressed as she watched him drive. "I work tomorrow night at the club but I'm sure they will be fine if I call out. This will be my first call out at that," she went on.

They pulled up to Ke's house and got settled in. Omar motioned for her to sit beside him after she got out of the shower.

"I just want you to know that I am working on my communication skills and want this so bad with you. I need it, honestly. You make me so happy, Ke, but I need you to know that your attitude ain't always ideal and a nigga need a li'l bit more understanding from you."

She nodded her head in agreement. Omar went downstairs for a bottle of water and she called the Ritz Carlton Hotel in D.C. to try to make last minute reservations for their getaway tomorrow. When Omar came back up, he fucked her into another dick coma.

BACK AT THE *CLUB PARKING LOT*

"Any new info on those drug traffickers that work for Don Carlos? We are ready to take these fuckers down!" yelled Officer Gaines from the receiver.

"I told you, I got eyes on some people. They come to this same club all the time. I just saw one of them hop in the car and leave. As soon as I learn their drop schedule, I will give it to y'all. My deal still on the table of no jail time, right?" asked Rayzo's snitching-ass while he watched people leave the club from his car.

"Get me the information I need! I'll be having someone help you on this assignment. These men are dangerous and one of them is already a person of interest on a murder case against his mother's ex-boyfriend. So, pause for a few days until I send an additional informant your way," the officer stated.

"Just please promise me my freedom. Please?" begged Rayzo. He was beginning to have second thoughts.

Click

Just like that, the officer hung up. Rayzo was already in too deep. He sparked his blunt and deep sighed as he started regretting the decision to snitch.

CHAPTER
THIRTY-FOUR

THE NEXT MORNING, Ke was still asleep from the full body orgasms. Omar smiled, smacked her ass and told her they had to get on the road. It was already 10:00 a.m., and he was trying to beat that afternoon traffic going to D.C.

"Okay, let me take a quick shower. I'll be ready in ten minutes."

Her Fridays were so damn busy because she had work at the school and at the club. She quickly showered and decided to wear something more chill for the road. She put on a pink vintage Juicy Couture tracksuit with the Juicy embellishment on the buttocks and on the jacket. She paired it with some gray and pink New Balance because she wanted some comfortable shoes to walk in. Omar also had on a Nike sweat suit with Nikes to match.

"Okay, I'm ready. You look very handsome in this gray sweat suit. It really brings out your skin," she said while hugging him around his waist.

"Wow. Did the woman who changed her number on me just compliment me?" he laughed.

"Whatever. I always compliment you."

"No, you're always talking shit to me," he bent down for a kiss. "You want to drive?"

"I can if you want me too."

"Yeah, drive ma."

"Okay," she replied with a little bit of hesitation.

Normally he drove everywhere they went. He tossed her the keys to his Cadillac truck, and she started it up. She backed out of her driveway and headed for the Jersey Turnpike so she could head to D.C. Once on the interstate she had pretty much a straight shot and they had about two hours of drive time left. Omar decided to taunt her.

"Don't act like you ain't hear what I've been saying to you either," he arrogantly stated.

"What you mean? What you say?"

"Yeah, okay. Stop playing with a nigga."

"I'm not. What you say?"

"I told you that I love you and want you to give me some babies."

He saw her body tense and her eyes widened. She looked over at him and she saw how serious he was.

"Lordy, Omar," she sighed. "Did I hear you? Yes, but I didn't think to respond because I just assumed you were in the moment of, ya know... Busting a nut."

He was always talking that good shit to her when they were fucking, and she didn't think those times were any different.

"I *was* in the middle of bustin' a nut both times, but I was aware of what I was saying. I want you to have my babies. I ain't saying right now, I'm saying one day I would like us to start a family. You got a nigga falling hard, Ke."

"We're having sex right now and that's probably why you think you mean that."

"I know what I want. I ain't just saying shit. I told you, fuck all that sex shit and that I want more with you," he honestly stated. "Pussy is everywhere, ma. You know my past. I told you, a nigga falling," he said while looking at her lips quiver and eyes well with tears.

She was beautiful to him in her most fragile state.

"How you know? You had situations where there were two

potential babies. You fucked them women raw and you fucking me raw, so what makes me, or rather what we doing, different?" She challenged him.

"Because you different, Ke." He took a deep breath. "I knew that those women I used to deal with were just fucks. I was just being irresponsible and reckless when I slipped up one time and didn't use protection. My past ain't that pretty, but I've calmed down for the better," he explained to her. She just listened.

"But ever since we had that heart to heart at the club when you told me your dad committed suicide, I knew I had to have you. You overcame so much shit and how strong you are is so attractive to me. You ain't lazy, you get up everyday and go to work, some days multiple jobs and you are still acing your classes. That shit is sexy how much of a hustla you are. But more importantly, you make me feel special and safe," he smiled. "You make me feel like you enjoy talking to me. Even though you say I talk too much." They both chuckled. "You always telling me to be safe and that week and half you spent at my house just made me want to keep waking up next to you," he went on. "I get so happy when I'm around you. Since I started talking to you a few months ago, you have been the first thing on my mind every day I wake up. Your smile. Your smart-ass mouth. Your work ethic. Your patience. You put me at peace and my once lonely-ass world is now full of so much life because of how vibrant you are. You tug at my heart, and I want you to have it. I love you, Ke, real talk. You got a nigga in love and it feels good," Omar expressed.

"I know we ain't ready for kids. But, I just want you to know that I truly do love you and hope one day we can raise some beautiful li'l chocolate children together. The best gift I could ever give my future kids is a mother like you. You got my heart, Ke," he finished. "I wish you could've met my mother."

"Omar," she trembled as tears filled her eyes. "You can't just lay that shit on me like that," she cried.

She was scared to love again but yet love had found her. "I'm falling for you and I'm really trying not to." She looked at him and he looked back. "I was a complete bitch this past week just because I didn't talk to you but you were out handling shit so I do understand now. But me acting like that let me know how mentally fucked up I still am," she said while trying to focus on driving and keep her tears under control. "I don't want to keep putting my insecurities on to you because everything triggers me, and you don't deserve that."

Omar was shocked. So much good shit had happened between him and Ke yet she seems to focus on the negative things. Was there a misunderstanding about the communication, yes. Did she need to practice controlling her emotions a little, yes. He understood she was speaking from hurt, but he wasn't the nigga who hurt her.

"Ke, look at me."

She did.

"We all got shit we got to work on, baby. But we can do that shit together," he softly spoke to her. "Do you love me, Ke?"

She looked at him and the tears were streaming down her face.

"I do, but I don't want to," she said. "I don't want to have these feelings for you."

That response hurt his feelings.

"Why don't you want to?"

"I don't want to be hurt again. We discussed this," she said through tears. "I don't want to get ahead of myself. I'm already fucking you with no protection and can't control my emotions. I don't want to feel like this," she spoke as the tears continued to drop.

"Just stick it out with me. I promise you I won't do the same shit that a lame ass nigga did to you. Ever. I told you I want to give you the world and this money I make gon' guarantee that. Just trust me," he said pleading. "Let me love you, ma, and stop holding yourself back from me, okay? Let me show you how happy I can make you."

She had to pull over and get herself together. Omar gave her some tissue then she used a face wipe to clean off the dried-up tears and snot. He grabbed her by her shoulder and told her again to trust that he could handle her right.

"I won't disappoint you. Everything about you I want. I love you, ma."

"I love you, too."

"We gon' do this? Together?" he said, hoping for the answer he wanted.

She looked back up at him. Her stomach started to turn.

"Yes. We can do it together. I'll fix my attitude and give you the opportunity to have my trust. It's hard fighting these feelings, but I do love you," she expressed.

Omar was moving fast and he had reason to: he was in love with her. He never felt this way before and he didn't feel the need to wait. Keisha was trying to fight her feelings. It was scary being vulnerable again but with him, it felt destined.

"I won't hurt you, Ke. The only thing I'm goin' to hurt is that pussy. In a good way though," he teased. She just shook her head. "I have something for you." He removed a box from the glove compartment. It was a wide, ten thousand dollar diamond bracelet that glistened in the light. He handed it to her.

"Wow. This is beautiful." She admired the beautiful stones and felt the cold rocks through her fingers.

"The inside is engraved to say, 'strong'. I got it so you can have something to wear over your scars on your wrist. You don't have to hurt yourself anymore. I want you to heal with me. You know that old saying about diamonds being made under pressure?" he asked. She nodded her head.

"So I got diamonds for my little warrior. The pressure was on you for a long time, Ke. You can shine your light now, baby."

She couldn't help but smile. He knew how to make love to her mentally and that was rare. He was so considerate of everything traumatic she had experienced, and she couldn't help but to fall in love with him. He was going to make sure of that. He kissed her and told her to get in the passenger seat. He drove the rest of the way to their hotel room while they made small talk.

CHAPTER
THIRTY-FIVE

THEY FINALLY MADE it to their hotel and checked in. Their room overlooked the D.C. skyline. They got dressed and decided to go to Ellipse Rooftop Bar because she wanted some drinks. They found a table in the corner and of course, it overlooked the city. The weather was great, and Omar began ordering her drinks while he sparked up his blunt.

She was on her third strawberry Patron margarita and they were starting to go straight to her pussy. Ke started whining her hips to the music while seductively staring at Omar.

"You look so good tonight, baby," she purred to him.

She started rubbing on his arms through his shirt. "Give me a kiss, Omar."

She wrapped her arms around his neck, he palmed her ass and they started kissing. She started rubbing on his dick and that's when Omar knew the liquor was taking over. His dick started to get hard and she started smiling. The DJ played the song, Everyone Falls In Love Sometimes.

Ke broke Omar's embrace and headed to the small dance floor. She was swaying her hips and all of the other partygoers were hyping her up. Omar laughed as he looked at Ke turn into the party animal she was. The other guests were loving her, and

offered to buy her more drinks. Omar told them she'd had enough. Ke walked over to Omar once she finished dancing.
"Baby, I'm ready to go. My feet starting to hurt," she said.
"Are you sure you've done enough dancing?" He laughed.
"Yes, that's why my feet hurt!"
They walked out hand in hand, and all the other drunk party goers yelled goodbye to Ke.
"You wanna party some more or you ready to call it a night?" Omar asked as they got in the car.
"I'm ready to get fucked by your big-ass dick. I want to feel them veins against these tight ass walls," her drunk-ass responded.
He stared at her with a smirk. He was actually speechless at her response. She took her stilettos off in the car and when they pulled up to the hotel, she ran out of the car barefoot. They made it in the room and the whole elevator ride, Ke kept touching on Omar's dick. He whispered in her ear that he was going to fuck the shit out of her and she giggled like a horny-ass schoolgirl.
He used his key to open the door and started caressing her ass. She unbuttoned his shirt, and stopped to kiss his chiseled chest while unzipping his pants. She started massaging his dick through his boxers and his hard-on was turning her on. He pulled her panties off while she propped her leg up on the nearby table in their room and pulled his dick out his boxers. His precum oozed out and she rubbed his dick head along the slit of her pussy. His breathing started to increase as she teased him with her warmth.
"You ready to be fucked?" He started kissing her neck.
She circled his dick over her clit and then the two started kissing.
"Mmmhmm. Fuck me, Omar."
She moaned as she wrapped her arms around his neck so she could suck on his lips. He lifted her up and each of her legs rested in the crook of his arm. He placed her pussy right on the head of his dick and her wetness allowed more of his pole to

slide in. He pinned her up to their hotel door and thrusted deep inside of her.

"Fuck," he moaned. She grabbed onto his shoulders and started matching his strokes while her pussy made slooshing noises on his dick. She started nibbling on his ear and that made him quicken his pace.

"Shit! I'm about to cum!" Ke screamed as he hit her G-spot.

His dick was hitting the bottom of her stomach, making her legs tremble. She came hard and her juices leaked down to his balls. Once they caught their breath, Omar slid her off and she dropped down to her knees.

"I wanna put your dick down my throat. Can I do that?" she said while looking him dead in his eyes.

He was silent. *This damn Patron got her on demon time,* he thought. She started sucking on the head and then she licked all of her juices off the sides of his dick. She stared face to face with his huge dick and opened her mouth wide as she guided it in her mouth. He felt her take his entire nine and a half inches down her throat. His toes started tingling and he felt like he was losing feeling in his hands.

"Agh, fuck, Ke! You got my dick down your throat, damn!"

She took it out of her mouth and used both hands to stroke his wet dick up and down while simultaneously sucking her remaining juicing off his balls. Omar closed his eyes, leaned his head back, and his dick seemed to have doubled in size. She used the excess spit from her mouth and dropped it on his shaft.

She slid his dick back down her throat and caused him to tense up when she clenched her throat muscles around his tip. Her eyes started watering and she started making gagging noises because of his dick hitting the back of her throat but she didn't care, she kept going. If she died while choking on the dick, then oh well. Sucking dick is a messy sport. Omar couldn't turn away from the sight of her making his dick disappear, her eyes dripping tears, the gagging noises, and how hungry she was being on his dick.

She cupped his balls, and he started moaning her name. He

grabbed her head and started fucking her throat. His dick was jumping, and he felt himself about to cum. She kept the head in her mouth while she twisted both hands up and down his dick and this move caused him to blow. She felt the pulsating in his veins, pulled his dick out her mouth and he shot his load all over face.

"Agh, shit, baby," he moaned.

She held her mouth open, while his seeds dripped down her face and slapped his dick on her tongue. She started rubbing his dick across her face and he couldn't turn his attention away from her. Then she started slowly sucking the head as the last of his nut dropped out.

"Oh, shit, Ke. What the fuck!"

The feeling of her sucking his head after he came was indescribable. His toes were still curling and Omar was tapping on the door to signal that he had tapped out. She just snatched his soul.

"You gotta warn a nigga that you gon' put a mouth-piece on him like that," she giggled at his statement. "You keep trying to fool me saying you're scared of the dick, but you just had it down your throat. The liquor did that," he teased.

"Liquor makes me horny and hungry. I wanted to eat a big, Black dick. Your dick to be exact: is that a problem?"

"Hell no, it ain't a problem. You sucked my dick clean," he said. She was blushing while cleaning his seeds from off her face. "Did your pussy juices taste good to you like they taste to me?" he asked as he wrapped his hands around her waist.

"It did. I see why you can't get enough of me," she smirked as she kissed him.

"You took a cum shot, swallowed some of my nut and spit on it. I love it messy just like that ma," he said to her. "We got a new rule too," he told her as they headed to the showers.

She looked at him to show her interest.

"The rule is: the only time you can cry is when my dick hitting the back of that throat. I saw your eyes running and that's the only time I'ma make tears come down," he told her as he turned the shower water on.

"Omar, shut up," she said as he helped her into the shower. "You always have to go too far," she said while laughing.

Omar made her cum another two more times in the shower. They washed up, lotion down and got in the bed in each other's arms. Ke fell asleep first as usual, and Omar checked his messages. He had a message from this dude at the hospital in Rhode Island. He was checking on the status of Sincere. It ain't sit right with him that this snitch nigga was free. He looked over at Ke. *How the fuck can a nigga wanna abuse a soul so beautiful?* he thought to himself. The voicemail explained that Sincere was expected to be discharged soon. Omar hung up and cuddled up next to his baby. Slowly feeling peace come over him, he was sleep within minutes.

The next day, they went to see the guest speaker advocating for special needs and children with disabilities at the Museum of History and Technology. There was also a speaker by the name of Loretta Lee who came and gave her take on gentrification, the process of changing the demographics of a neighborhood by adding wealthy residents. Omar was interested in this topic because he was planning on investing in real-estate and he wanted all people to have comfortable living, not just the wealthy.

After they saw the presenters, they went sightseeing. They saw the Washington Monument, The Lincoln Memorial and The Martin Luther King Tribute statues. They also saw the Thomas Jefferson Memorial, the Franklin Roosevelt Memorial and the fallen World War II Veterans Memorial where Ke found her grandfather's name.

Omar loved seeing Ke in her element. She was detailing so many historical facts and could tell she had a real passion for learning and teaching. It was sexy watching how excited she got viewing each of the memorial sites. The one that stuck out the most was The Martin Luther King, Jr. Memorial.

Dr. King stood for peace and Omar wanted to know why that

was so hard for folks to agree to, damn. That night, they ate Oohs and Aahs soul food. Ke let him taste what a real turkey wing was like and he had to agree, New York ain't got shit on the real southern soul food. They went back to their hotel room, showered and went to sleep. All that walking had both of them beat.

They packed up and went back home the next day. They enjoyed each other's company once again and Omar kept telling her how happy she made him and how he adored everything about her.

"You're only saying that because I had your dick and balls in my mouth," she teased.

"I was telling you that before you ate all my dick up," he shot back and she laughed. Once they pulled back to Ke's house her phone rang. It was her mother.

"Keisha, are you home? Don't forget we have to go to your brother's basketball tournament in Rhode Island tomorrow. We're leaving tonight though so he can check in with his team," her mother reminded her.

"I completely forgot," Ke said as she deep sighed. "But you know I'm going to be there. I wouldn't miss anything they have going on," she said to her mother. They made plans to meet up later that night so that they could leave together.

"Everything good? You straight?" Omar asked her as she opened her door to get out.

"Yes, I have to pack another bag because my brother has a basketball game in Rhode Island," she said to him and waited for his response.

"Okay. You need me to do anything?" He didn't think she was worried about Sincere so he didn't bring up the issue of Sincere being in Rhode Island.

"No. We're leaving tonight though. I just have to pack another bag," she said while she opened the door to her house.

"Okay. I would come with you to see him play but I'll be tied up later," he said as he placed his debit card on the kitchen table.

"Take care of whatever y'all need for his tournament. I love you. Be safe. I'll call you later."

"I love you too, baby. You be safe," she shot back at him.

"You make sure to be at my house when you get back. I want you in the bed, waiting for me. You got a house key that you scared to use," he kissed her neck.

"Oh, whatever. I'm not scared. I been ripping and running and haven't had time to use it nigga," she giggled.

"When you gone make time and give me your house key? We in too deep for you to still be on this hesitant shit with me." He looked at her and she took a deep breath.

"I know. I don't have any spare keys but I'm going to get you one. Okay? So you can stop acting like a baby."

He told her he had to go and she got ready to leave the house again to go with her family.

CHAPTER
THIRTY-SIX

"LOOK, Rhode Island was too dangerous for me and this FBI informant shit almost lost me my life," complained Sincere as he looked at Officer Parker from his chair.

He had stitches in his forehead and was holding his cracked ribs.

"Well maybe you should've thought about that before you agreed to be an informant!" yelled the officer as he bit his donut. "You want to go back to jail and have the fools in there tear you apart?" the officer challenged as he called his bluff.

"This is not what I signed up for," stated Sincere as reality sunk in about the decision to be a snitch. "You said if I tell on a few people then you wouldn't hold jail time over my head. You didn't say I had to go undercover. Them dudes could have killed me!" Sincere yelled slamming down his hospital discharge papers.

"Oh well. Didn't you beat the shit out of that woman to the point she was in the hospital? Maybe you should use some of those licks you did on her to defend yourself," stated the officer while he threw Sincere a bag of cocaine and a packet with a New York informant in it. "This is your next assignment. You will be working with another rat. His name is Rayzo. The New York Department will give you more information. Be prepared to travel there next week," he showed Sincere Rayzo's picture and the people he has snitched on.

"I don't want to go back to New York," complained Sincere.

He scammed so many muthafuckas, had babies that he didn't take care of, and people who he had robbed there.

"Oh well," the officer stated as he walked away.

Sincere stood up, took a deep breath and headed to his car. He cut up a line of coke and snorted it. He had to ease his mind and relax because going back to New York was not in his plans. His body started floating and he pumped himself up for whatever New York would bring.

CHAPTER
THIRTY-SEVEN

"MY BOY GOT twenty-six points and had the buzzer beater!" yelled Ke as her younger brother Travon met up with them after his game.

"You know I had to show off. Today is Dad's birthday so this was for him." Travon beamed, and his mother and siblings smiled.

"I'm so proud of you. I love you," Ke said as she hugged him.

"I love you too," he told them all and they headed out to their car for their last night in Rhode Island.

They stopped at the gas station and everyone went in for snacks and drinks. Ke spotted a souvenir station that customized keys. She went to the attendant, gave them her housekey, and explained to them how she wanted it customized for her man. Her mother also got herself a spare key made just because older people always needed extra of some shit.

"Here," Ke said as she handed Travon a box of condoms when she returned to the car. Brielle and Denise were cracking up.

"Mama must've told you," he said as he took the condoms and laughed.

"She sure did. You know she tells everything. Better protect yourself. Mama got four kids. So we fertile around here," she joked.

"She too nosey," Travon said and they laughed.

Their mother walked back up carrying the customized keys. Everyone buckled up and they got on the road heading back home. Mrs. Harris pulled out the keys and read the customizations.

"Ummm, Keisha, why does this key say, "Big Dick?" asked Mrs. Harris as she flashed her the black house key for Omar with the red lettering.

"Oh my gosh, Mama! Can you stop being so nosey!" Ke yelled, snatched the key and threw it in her purse. Her siblings were in the back seat snickering.

"So that's why your hips are spreading? Hmmm. I'm happy you finally got laid and we're all ready to meet this Mr. Big-"

"Mama, please!" Ke cut her off.

"I'm just saying! We're ready to meet him. So dinner within the next month and no excuses," she said.

Ke shook her head. She was not ready for them to meet him.

"And another thing, the mouths on all of you are crazy. Y'all get that from your father. One is addressing a man as Big Dick. One says she loves eating pussy, one is sneaky as hell, and one just now starting to have sex and doesn't want to use protection. You kids are going to send me to an early grave!" she vented. The kids chuckled.

"No, you just to nosey, Ma. No one told you to be all in our business," joked Brielle.

"I will be in y'all business until the day I take my last breath! So all of y'all shut up," she told them.

CHAPTER
THIRTY-EIGHT

THE NEXT DAY, Ke was expected to be back in town and Omar had just left from counting product. He couldn't wait to get home because he told her to be there waiting for him after her trip. When he pulled up, his home was empty. So, he called her.

"Ke, why you not here?" he asked.

"I'm home in my bed, baby."

"I told you to be at my house though, ma. You got the key. I knew I was going to be out late, so I wanted you to be there waiting for me," he stated.

He hadn't seen her or barely heard from in two days. He missed her. All he wanted was his baby to be in his bed after a long night of hustlin'.

"I know, baby. I'm sorry," she felt bad. "I just been ripping and running for the past couple of days and was ready to be home," she explained.

She was getting back into that mood where she wanted to fall back from him because... Well shit, she didn't know why. She was just scared about a lot. *This love shit is so fucking annoying*, she thought. Omar did literally nothing to make her feel this way but once again, her negative thoughts and feelings got the best of her.

"My home is your home. But I'm on the way over," he replied. "Stay up so you can come to the door," he went on while he shook his head.

He was in disbelief that he was letting her get away with this housekey bull shit. What makes it even worse was that he had been putting his all into this shit and one minute she wanted it, the next minute she didn't. He was frustrated with her hesitation.

"Baby it is 2:30 in the morning," she whined.

"I don't care. You know you dead wrong. Let me had did this to you though," he vented. "I'm ten minutes away," he said before hanging up.

"Ugh, Omar."

She got herself out of bed and went downstairs to wait for Omar to pull up. He came within ten minutes and she opened the door. He sensed her attitude as she walked away up the stairs back to her bedroom.

"Well hello to you too," he sarcastically stated.

"Hey baby," she mustered as she got back in her bed.

"I told you that last time was going to be my last time discussing this attitude issue with you Ma. Lose it!"

"I don't have an attitude," she said, getting aggravated. "Who you know wants to be up right now? I'm cranky but don't have an attitude."

"This wouldn't be an issue if you would have used your house key you have to my spot or gave me your house key. C'mon, ma. Don't be like this."

Ke rolled her eyes and got her composure together because once again he was right.

"Fine, Omar. This isn't necessary, baby. You're right. I'm sorry," she climbed off her bed and embraced him.

"Meet me halfway, that's all I'm saying, ma."

"Okay. I will."

He took his shoes and clothes off and prepared for a shower. She got back under the covers and tried to go back to sleep. Once he got out of the shower, he slid the covers back and began reaching under her nightgown to pull her panties off.

"I have to be up in the next three hours!" she said as she watched him drop her panties on the floor.

"You ain't fell asleep yet so you must not be tired," he said.

He went back to reaching under her nightgown and found her clit. He rubbed and pressed on it until she wet his fingers up. He put his head between her legs and started eating her pussy. He was licking and sucking on her clit with gentle motions.

"Make me cum, baby," she purred, throwing her pussy to his face.

That's when he placed two fingers inside her and licked her clit at the same time. He slooshed them in and out and had her hollering as she came. She then climbed on his dick and their eyes locked. He put both hands around her neck while she grinded on his dick. She placed her hands on his chest while she bounced and he gripped her booty, spreading her cheeks so he could go deeper. He felt her pussy choke his dick, signaling her orgasm.

"Oh, shit!" Ke hollered while she started cumming on his dick. He lifted her up a little so she could release all her juices.

"I thought you was tired," he said as he lifted his head up and lightly bit on her nipples. "That pussy know what to do when it see daddy." He talked his shit as he guided her to bend over so he could hit it from the back.

"Whatever," she moaned as she arched her back and he entered her.

"Next time I say be at my house waiting for me, what that mean, Ke?" he taunted as he pounded her tight walls and pulled on her hair.

"Ugh ugh, oh shit, baby!" she screamed. He slapped her on her ass and repeated the question.

"It mean…. Mmm… Whatever you say!" she moaned.

"This my pussy?" He placed a hand around her neck and stroked deeper inside of her.

"Yes! It's your pussy!" she moaned as she came.

"Put your head down and keep that ass up."

He slid his hard dick out of her, spread her ass cheeks, and dropped some spit in her ass. His tongue made its way to her asshole and he darted it in and out of her. His nose was at the top of her ass crack as he slowly twirled his tongue inside of her ass.

"Stop all that hot and cold shit. You hear me?" he stated as he kept pleasuring her. "Go ahead and rub your clit. I'm ready for you to cum again," he demanded.

"Fuck!" Ke cried out as she bit down on the sheets and started rubbing on her swollen clit while he ate her ass. "I hear you. I'ma listen!" she hollered.

He stopped eating her ass, grabbed her hips and inserted his dick back inside her warm, gushy pussy. He stroked her while she reached between her legs and started playing with his balls. She felt his breathing quicken and his body started trembling as he dropped his load inside of her. He collapsed on top of her and she turned her head so she could get a kiss. She told him how big and good his dick was. He told her he was not playing with her about that attitude.

Omar woke up the next morning and saw she'd left for work. He went downstairs and saw the engraved black key with a note beside it. This made his heart smile.

Hopefully this will make you stop being a big baby about a housekey. This was custom made for you. You handling me right, you loving me right, and you're doing everything you said you were going to do. I have no complaints... YET. :) I love you. I hope this makes your day.

-Love, Ke.

That for sure made his damn day.

CHAPTER
THIRTY-NINE

"POPS," Omar beamed as he walked into his father's two-story home. His father looked up while Michelle got up to embrace Omar.

"Boy, is your phone broke? I've been calling you for the past three days. I told you about this Omar," his father scolded.

"I know, I know. I'm good, Pops. I told you that, but I know we got a promise." Omar broke into a big smile. "I have to tell you both something."

"Please don't let it be another damn baby that you don't know is yours," Carl begged as he put his newspaper down.

"I want you to meet my woman. Her name is Keisha. She's perfect. I love her pops," he explained while his gone-ass went on and on about her.

His father was stunned. Omar had never wanted to introduce someone to him.

"Well, by the way you're talking, I'm sure she's incredible. I mean look at you, your mouth has been running a mile a minute. I'd love to meet this young woman," smiled Carl.

Omar told Ke and she told him that coincidentally, her family was ready to meet him, too. They agreed for both parties to meet at Ke's mother's house for dinner.

KEELY

THREE WEEKS LATER, they were getting ready to leave for their family dinner and Omar was waiting for Ke who was stuck trying to find an outfit. She was getting annoyed that all of her pants were entirely too tight. She had gained a solid thirteen pounds since dealing with Omar and it went directly to her thighs and ass.

"I can't find anything that fits," Ke fumed, tossing another pair of jeans on the ground. "I've gained so much weight and I know my mom is going to notice," she started to become insecure as she looked at herself in the mirror. "You know Black people love to make comments when a person gets bigger or smaller."

"The only thing that's widened out are your ass and hips. It looks great by the way. All your curves with that little waist makes me want to stick my tongue in that ass," he teased as he slapped her booty and it jiggled.

He stood up behind her and looked at their reflection in the full body mirror. He rubbed on her breasts and his hands traveled down her hourglass figure. "You're a hundred and forty pounds, soaking wet. The weight is perfect on you, baby. I love it."

Ke cracked a smile. She opted to wear an Adidas track suit that gave her a little more wiggle room. It still looked painted on but fuck it. They left and pulled up to her mother's house. His father and Michelle were ecstatic to meet Ke. They enjoyed seeing Omar come alive around her.

"Omar, I'm just glad I'm not the only man anymore. My sisters are annoying," stated Travon as they passed the food around the kitchen table family style.

"Ke annoying to you?" Omar asked.

"Sometimes. She always got something smart to say."

"I tell her all the time that her mouth is ridiculous," Omar said as they chuckled.

Ke's family absolutely adored him. Her mother enjoyed seeing her date again and she called her into the kitchen.

"Keisha, you two are in love," Mrs. Harris stated as she started to clean the kitchen. "What does he do?" she inquired because she noticed all of his jewelry and Ke's new jewelry.

"Mama, please," Ke deep sighed and put her head down.

"Don't start, Keisha! Don't you lie to me."

"Mama, okay. What do you think he does?"

"Are you sure you're ready for that again? I have no problem with him at all, but Keisha, is your mental health ready for that type of relationship again?"

Ke wanted to tell her mama so bad, *Let him lick your asshole and turn your pussy into a running faucet and you tell me are you ready for the relationship?* But she opted to be a little more respectful.

"At times, I fight with myself, but I love him. He makes me happy. Before we even started being intimate, we took the time to just talk. I'm really happy, mama," Ke expressed to her.

"Then that's all that matters baby," she said. "So with the words on the customized key and the way your hips are spreading, I am going to assume that you two are havin' fun in the bedroom."

Ke was speechless. She started thinking about all the fun that they have in the bedroom and bit down on her bottom lip. "Mama, I don't think you want to know about the things we do," she smirked.

"I haven't had any bedroom entertainment since yo daddy passed away. Trust me, I want to know about everything. Give yo nosey mama a lil detail."

"You have to really stop being so embarrassing!"

The women laughed. Omar and Carl helped to take the trash out while the women tackled the kitchen. Everyone promised to have a family style meet up again.

"Drive safe and call me tomorrow, Omar. Check in," Carl reminded him as they headed to the car.

"I'll make sure he calls you a few times a week, Mr. Gaulding! He acts like he too good to open his mouth sometimes," Ke said. Carl chuckled. They all headed home where

Omar made Ke bend her ass over and throw it back on his dick.

CHAPTER FORTY

A MONTH after they met each other's family, she was at her doctor's office getting her uterus evaluated.

"Alright, Ms. Harris, I have great news," expressed the doctor as she gave Ke some documents. "It looks like your uterus is back within normal measurements!" she told her. Ke's face lit up.

"Yes! Yes!" she screamed as she ran over to hug her.

"I told you that sex was going to correct that," the doctor smirked and Ke laughed. Omar was definitely shifting everything around in her guts but more importantly, he was correcting a womb that Sincere almost destroyed. "Now, do you want to explore birth control options?" the doctor pressed on as she looked at the glow Ke had.

"I don't mind birth control, but I'm one of those girls who gain weight too fast," Ke replied as she looked at the papers the doctor gave her and saw how her weight went from a hundred and twenty-seven pounds to one hundred and forty-one pounds in just a few months.

"You're still a nice healthy size. But I can help you monitor your ovulation days if you don't want any hormonal birth control right now."

She smiled at her and then gave Ke details on how to monitor her ovulation.

THE FOLLOWING WEEK, they were getting ready for Omar's cousin Shaheem's get-together, celebrating him earning his GED. Ke was excited because things had been hectic at work and school, and she needed a drink.

"Baby, I know you like to drink and shake your ass, but have it at a minimum tonight. That dress is barely holding your ass in," he stated while watching her put her earrings in.

"I know. I told you none of my clothes fit anymore," she said as she examined herself.

The dress was short but she had no time to change because *everything* was small. "This dress was purchased three weeks ago and its a size up from what I normally wear. I need a diet like yesterday."

"You don't need a diet. You look stunning. You gotta embrace these curves that I done pumped into you. It's happy relationship weight," he teased. "But real shit, don't bend over or your whole ass will be out. Are you ready though? I ain't trying to be out too long. You know I hate being around a lot of people."

"Yes, I'm ready with your antisocial ass," she teased as they headed out.

They arrived at the venue and the party was lit. The liquor was being poured, ass was being shook, and the weed was getting rolled. Shots were being passed around, but Omar declined because he wasn't big on drinking.

Ke on the other hand, was *seven* patron shots in and was tore the fuck up. She was dancing, singing, joking, and having a good time. Things took a left turn when Choppa Style came over the speakers and she climbed on the bar and started shaking her ass.

"Ke, get the fuck down!" Omar yelled as he grabbed her arm

to help her down. "Your ass is out, yo. I told you about that shit when we left the house," he barked as he sat her on the bar stool. "Chill out," he warned.

"Okay."

She slurred her words and ordered two more shots of Patron and downed them.

"Those are your last two shots for the night. You don't need anything else," he demanded. "I'm going back to the section. Control yourself. I'm not in the fucking mood," he warned again and left.

Angel and Tasha walked up to her. "Ooo, bitch, you going to get it," Angel joked as they laughed at Ke who was trying to get her bearings in order.

"No I'm not. He doing too much. All I'm doing is dancing and he's makin' that an issue," Ke mustered.

Then, they heard from the speakers, *Cash Money Records taking over for the 9-9 and the 2000s... O*nce again, Ke found herself on the bar table shaking her ass. *"Back that azz up" is a whole negro spiritual and Ke couldn't help but to twerk her ass to it.*

The minute she popped her ass to the music, her dress flew up and her ass was out. Angel and Tasha tried to pull her dress down, but Omar had already witnessed it unfold.

"Ke, what are you doing? I just told you to control yourself. Come on," he said as he grabbed her hand and led her to the section. "Sit down beside me until they turn the lights on. You're too drunk," he told her and made her sit down.

Ke folded her arms across her chest and flared up her nose. "I don't want to sit down. I'm just dancing Omar!" she yelled as she slurred her words.

"That's not the issue. Your dress is too small and every time you dance, your ass is out. Shut up and sit down for a few minutes." He unscrewed the top off a water bottle. "Drink this to help you sober up." He tried to hand her the water, but she swatted his hand away and some spilled out.

"No. I'm going back to the bar and getting another shot." She tried to get up and walk away. Omar snatched her back down and got in her ear.

"Sit the fuck down. I swear, Ke. You fuckin' trying it." His voice was cold and firm.

She snatched away from him. He was in disbelief that she was acting like this in front of everybody and he was even more embarrassed with all the attention it brought.

"You don't control me," she uttered as she walked toward the bathroom.

Angel and Tasha followed behind her because they saw their girl was really tripping. Once in the bathroom, Ke just stood in the middle of the floor and pouted.

"Ke, what is up with you? You're drunk and being a complete bitch for no reason," said Tasha from the stall.

"No I'm not. He's trying to control everything. I can't dance, I can't drink anymore and he's telling me to sit beside him like I'm a child," Ke vented as she tried to hold her balance from her wobbly legs.

"He is not controlling anything. You're drunk right now so you're being irrational. He doesn't want you dancing because your ass is hanging out. He's not wrong for wanting that new, curvy body to be for his eyes only. Calm down, bitch," explained Angel.

"Ke, you good? Hurry up because we 'bout to leave," Omar spoke from the bathroom's entrance.

"I can't use the bathroom?" she questioned as she rolled her eyes and cocked her neck to the side. "Damn, you don't want me drinking, dancing, and now I can't pee?" she complained with her slick-ass mouth. Tasha and Angel's eyes were wide watching this unfold.

"Keisha. Chill out," he advised her as he came into the women's bathroom.

"No, you chill out. You've been making demands since we left home and I'm overly fucking aggravated with you," she barked.

HEART OF A THUG

Omar was trying to tell her to take it easy with her drinking and her dancing, but Ke was triggered. All she could think about was how Sincere tried to control everything in her life.

"Listen. I've been sparing you all fucking night. You have been pushing this shit with your mouth," he calmly said as he looked her directly in her eyes, which she rolled then smacked her lips. "You got two options for the remainder of the night. Option one, go to the bar with me, wait for your food order, and sit your ass down until they turn the lights on in thirty minutes," he explained while observing her nasty attitude. "Option two, get your ass dragged out this bathroom, dragged down the hallway, and into the car while I stay inside and wait for your food," he kept his eye contact with her and her eyebrows scrunched up.

Her girls were praying her crazy ass made the right decision.

"What's it going to be? Your choice."

Omar was fed up. He wasn't going to play to many fucking games with her and that nasty-ass attitude, because now he was getting triggered by his childhood trauma of seeing how Victor was always drunk and abusing his mother.

"Option three, I do what the fuck I want to do which is go back to the bar and drink. Then I'm going to dance and then I'm going to get my food," she challenged Omar.

Angel's jaw was on the damn floor.

"Ke, stop! You're drunk and he's trying to help you. Stop it right now," Tasha said as she was easing Ke back. She already knew how far her mouth and anger could go.

"Don't tell her shit, Tasha. She love thinking I'm some weak-ass nigga," he responded as he stared at her. "What's your choice? You lucky you g'tting' an option."

"I just told you. Option three. You can't hear? I don't think you a weak-ass nigga at all, but I'm going to do what I want." She stared back at him.

Omar put his phone and keys in his pocket. He then double checked to make sure his gun was nice and tucked inside of his waist band. He snatched Ke by her hair with one hand and her neck with the other hand, dragging her ass out the bathroom as promised. He dragged her with so much force that she came out of one of her stilettos.

"Since you losin' your fucking mind tonight, I'll make the decision for you. Option two it is," he effortlessly dragged her shit-talking behind out the bathroom.

Angel and Tasha were trying to help her, but they knew she made her own bed. She was drunk and it was time for him to take over. He dragged her to a secluded corner in the hallway before her legs gave out.

"Omar, I can barely fucking walk. I have one shoe on! Stop!" she yelled, dragging her words and trying to keep her balance.

"Get your fucking self together!" he yelled as he mushed his fingers at her forehead and she fell to the ground. "You're going to get yo ass up and walk out this building like you got some fucking sense! I don't give a fuck about that shoe! You understand that?" he asked. She nodded her head.

"I have to get my purse," Ke mumbled and tried to head back to the party.

Omar snatched her up again by her neck and caused her to stumble. "Omar, you don't have to grab me. Calm down. Why are you acting like this? You doin' too much," tears welled in her eyes. She was beginning to sober up.

"Yo. Keisha." He paused and took a deep breath. "Stop fuckin' playin' with me! If you say anything else, I'ma punch you in your fucking mouth. Act like you can't fucking hear if you want to. You're a complete mess right now and this ain't you and I'm not in the fuckin' mood for this bullshit!" he yelled.

That scared the shit out of Ke. Her eyes grew wide and she went silent.

"Now, walk out the door right here, go toward our car, and get in the fucking car," he told her.

She did what she was told. He helped her into the car and went back inside to get her food, her other shoe, and her purse.

"You ain't have to drag her out of here, O. She just havin' fun," explained Supreme. Omar shook his head.

"This nigga can't handle having a girl that's the life of the party," said Bo and they cracked up. "You know he a mute," Bo joked. "Let her have fun, Omar."

"It's not her having fun that's the problem. I know this what she does. I want her to have fun. Her dress too small and her ass was out. Then she talking more shit than a little bit," Omar explained to his friends. "Y'all niggas need to mind your business when it come to how I handle my woman," Omar said.

They laughed some more. He got Ke's chicken wing and fry platter with two ginger ales because he was sure she would be hung over tomorrow.

Outside at the car, Tasha and Angel were checking on Ke.

"Don't cry now, bitch. He's been warning you all night to get your act together," joked Tasha while watching Ke dry her tears and blow her nose from the window.

"Fuck y'all. He's so pissed with me. He told me he was going to punch me in my mouth," Ke explained. "I ain't like that shit at all."

"He needs to pop that reckless ass mouth. He gave you two reasonable options and here go your smart ass, 'Option three…' " Tasha mocked and Angel laughed.

"You better stop trying him. Everybody needs to be put in their place every once in a while, and that damn mouth of yours will have anybody ready to knock your ass out!" Angel said and they laughed again. "You need to apologize to him. He has been begging you to sit down and chill out all night. I ain't like how he dragged you, but he knows how to handle you. I see your act is together now," Angel teased.

"Go head and use that mouth in a good way and suck his dick. He deserves it for the stress you gave him tonight." Tasha suggested.

That made Ke smile. "Oh look, and he still went to get your food and something to drink. Mmmhmm, bitch. He cares about your mean-ass," Tasha went on.

Omar came back to the car and gave Ke her food and helped

her put her other shoe on. She ate her food in the parking lot while he sparked up his blunt. Once she was finished, he took her trash and threw it away then headed to her house.

He was so riled up with Ke and her shenanigans that no one noticed Rayzo and Sincere watching them from afar in their car.

CHAPTER
FORTY-ONE

SINCERE'S EYES WERE WIDE, and his heart sank to his toes as he watched Omar give Ke a napkin to wipe her mouth and helped her put her shoe on. *How fuckin dare this bitch move on from me. The fuck!* Sincere was stunned.

"Man, these niggas just at a party. They ain't slangin' shit here," expressed Rayzo.

He looked over at Sincere and saw him focused on Ke and Omar. He was so stuck on them that he didn't blink.

"Yo!" screamed Rayzo to break his trance. Sincere looked at him.

"My fault. Yeah, so we need to find a way to get them in for questioning or something. Have their DNA pop up at a scene or some shit. I don't know. I'm sure the feds wouldn't give a fuck how they got one of them down there but having some evidence or something to plant seems like the easiest way," Sincere explained watching Omar drive off.

"A'ight. I'm with it. I think his bitch is one of the bartenders down at the club. I'ma scope him out and try to use these sticky fingers to snag a drink or somethin'," Rayzo proposed.

Sincere smiled as he pulled some powder out of his pocket and began to cut up some lines to snort.

"Yeah, that's how we gon' take that nigga down," Sincere smirked as he snorted his first line.

"You mean that's how we gon' take all them niggas down?"

Sincere brushed Rayzo off as the high took over him and they headed to go check in with the feds.

CHAPTER FORTY-TWO

"BABY, I'm sorry about tonight. Are you mad at me?" Ke blurted out as they pulled up to her house and got out of the car. He ignored her and unlocked the front door. "Can you please talk to me?"

He brushed her off and headed for the stairs. Ke asked if he was mad at her again when they entered the bedroom.

"I'm beyond mad at you. I'm not in the mood to talk," he said as he went toward the closet.

Keisha gave him his space to collect his thoughts and she took a shower. When she got out of the shower, Omar was sitting on the edge of the bed with a duffle bag by his foot.

"You straight? I'm about to head home," he stood up and grabbed his bag.

"You're not staying with me? Did you want me to get my stuff together to come with you? What's in your bag?" she freaked out. Her mouth and heart rate were moving at a ridiculous speed.

"My clothes. I just came here to make sure you was good. You think I'm trying to control you and that's not what I'm doing. All I've been doing since we got together is love you and try to let you know you can count on me for whatever. I been tryin' to get comfortable expressing myself. Tonight that shit was a slap to the face. You keep thinkin' I'm that punk ass nigga you use to deal with. I'm tired of repeating myself and telling you that I'm not him. If I wanted to play, I could've kept fuckin' on these tricks. So nah, I don't want to talk to you. I'm out. I'm over talking to you for the day. You pissed me off so fucking bad," he laid her ass out as he walked past her and went downstairs. *Damn. Why it gotta hurt so bad when your nigga cuss you out?* Ke thought.

"Omar," she said as she followed him and was in disbelief that this nigga was leaving.

Tears started forming because she knew she fucked up. He unlocked the door and left her there looking stupid. Keisha tried calling him and he didn't answer.

"Oh, hell no! I know this nigga is not this fucking pissed," Keisha said as she threw on some pajama shorts and a tank top.

She put her bedroom shoes on, kept her hair wrapped in her scarf, grabbed her car keys and headed to Omar's house. "This nigga better be at home, too. The fuck!" she yelled to herself as she hopped in her car.

CHAPTER
FORTY-THREE

Omar pulled up home, gained his composure after smoking his blunt, and went to his door. As soon as he unlocked his door, he saw Ke pulling up on two wheels in his driveway. She came to a screeching halt and jumped out. He looked at her little ass like she was fucking crazy.

"KE what the fuck are you doing?" He looked at her approaching him.

"Staying here with you! You can be mad all you want but you need to at least talk to me before you try to ignore me," she twisted the doorknob and walked in, Omar following behind her.

"I don't have to talk about shit. I did enough talking to yo ass. Why you want to be around a nigga who controlling you?" Omar challenged.

"I wasn't saying it like that. I want to apologize. I'm sorry, baby. For everything. I was being a bitch and just doing too much. I was trying to have fun, but I disregarded the fact that I'm in a relationship now and certain shit just ain't appropriate," she explained as she looked at him. "I pushed it to the limit and got back into my head when I need to stop doing that. I love you. I'm sorry. I don't want you mad at me," she said to him as she folded her arms.

"Okay," he said. He was enjoying seeing this side of her.

"Can you stop being mad at me, please," she went toward him and hugged him.

He was still being nonchalant. She started rubbing on his dick and that woke his ass up.

"You don't deserve no dick tonight so stop touching me," he told her and tried to move her hands. She pushed his hands away and kept going. "You don't play fair at all, Keisha. Why I can't be mad at you?" He taunted her.

"I do play fair. I'm sorry, baby. You know how I get off the liquor," she explained as she dropped to her knees.

She stared face to face with his dick and went straight to sucking on his balls, causing him to quiver. She then licked up the length of his dick until she reached the tip then started sucking it slow and seductive. She spit on the head of his dick and stuffed it in her mouth.

"Fuck, Ke!" he moaned as his knees buckled and goosebumps covered his body.

She started gagging as the dick went down her throat and her eyes started to water: two of Omar's favorite things to see and hear from her. She stuffed it further down her throat to create even more tears for him. She took the dick out her mouth and started stroking it up and down.

"I see you know how to talk now," she teased as she wrapped both hands around his shaft and started sucking the head.

She twisted her hands along the shaft and suctioned his head like she was a vacuum. His dick was covered in her saliva and so were her hands.

"Got-damn. Baby, hold up," he begged but Ke kept going.

She put her hands down and began deep throating his dick with no hands. Omar grabbed her by the neck and was thrusting his hips while he fed Ke his dick.

"Keisha," Omar moaned.

Ke felt his dick quivering and in the back of her mind she heard the Mortal Combat game tell her to, *Finish him!* She held her mouth wide open while he shot his load all over her tongue and face. She slowly sucked his balls while completely draining his dick. *I gotta get my girl Tasha a gift for that dick sucking suggestion. This nigga definitely is less tense,* thought Ke. Omar had to sit down in the chair and catch his breath.

"Now. Are you ready to talk?" she asked as she headed to his downstairs bathroom to clean off her face.

Omar chuckled and got ready to talk. He wanted to stay mad at her but how could he. "I guess I'm ready," he said as he continued to laugh. "Okay, first thing's first, I'm not controlling. I just want you to know that you're in a serious relationship right now with a nigga that love you. I don't want you to be out here acting a fool, drunk, and having your body showing. I'ma snap the fuck out if a nigga get out of line or try some shit. We represent each other every time we leave the house, and I can't have you out here looking like that, baby. That's it. Then you got me looking crazy because I'm tryna help you and you talking shit," he told her as he pulled his boxers up. "I got a short tolerance for that drunk shit because of the nigga who killed my moms. I told you, he was a drug addict and an alcoholic, and the shit just gets to me sometimes."

"Baby, you're absolutely right. I can't argue and I won't argue with you about that. You were just trying to help me and I was acting out of line."

"We both have our flaws, but again, meet me halfway. I love the fuck out of you, Ke. But you gotta control that attitude, them negative thoughts, and that mouth,"

"I know. I love you too and I am working on them all for you." She kissed him and they headed upstairs for bed. Ke did beg for her man's forgiveness and came to his house to do what she had to do to ease his attitude.

Keisha wasn't dumb. She knows that Omar is a good one, and that it was fine to show him that she was afraid to lose him. She just wanted to make sure she ate that dick up like she skipped out on dinner first before conversing about the disagreement.

The next morning, Ke woke up to Omar just staring at her.

"You're creepy," she teased him. he smiled.

"I just like looking at you," he said. "You have the worst morning breath, Ke. You could kill a nigga with that shit," he joked.

She cracked up. "Oh, whatever!" she said as she threw a pillow at him.

CHAPTER
FORTY-FOUR

OVER THE NEXT SEVERAL MONTHS, Ke worked on her attitude as promised. She was considerate by thinking before she spoke and was doing her best not to let her trauma get the best of her. She talked about her emotions without being overwhelmed by her feelings. Although homegirl was still rolling her eyes and smacking her lips because the sassy shit was just a part of her. She had been religiously using her key to Omar's house and she spent most of her nights there, even if he wasn't there: his request.

She was at his home preparing stuffed chicken breast, with roasted broccoli and macaroni and cheese. She put Omar's food in the microwave with a sticky note attached.

Thank you for loving me. You really were made perfectly for me. Your dinner is in the microwave. -Love, Keisha.

She also had a gift bag on the table for him with items she picked specifically for him. She took a shower and headed to bed. Omar strolled in around midnight, and smiled when he saw the note and the plate. He loved having her here, waking up to her and spending all his time with her.

He opened up the black gift bag and started pulling out the contents. She got him two Gucci sweaters, an abundance of Ralph Lauren socks, briefs, and T-shirts. The bottom of the bag had a custom collage of pictures with his mom, himself, and his brother. Ke noticed that he didn't have any pictures of them hanging up, so she wanted to give this to him. Omar's heart smiled at the gesture. He loved how thoughtful she was. He ate his food, showered, put his gift items up and got in the bed with Ke.

"I just want you to know that I've noticed your attitude change and I know you really trying to be the best you. I love you, baby. Thank you for the gifts. I appreciate them all," he whispered in her ear and kissed her cheek.

"I love you, too. Thank you for being patient with me. I'm so glad you're the man I'm giving my heart to. You're the best thing that has happened to me in a long time and I'm so grateful for you, Omar," she told him as she turned around to kiss him.

He made his way home in her pussy.

A WEEK LATER, Ke came home after work looking miserable.

"Omar, I think I caught a virus that has been going around at the school. I'm lethargic, have no appetite and my stomach feels queasy."

"I'll go the store for you and see if I can find some things to help you feel better," Omar said, concerned.

He ended up buying her medicine, soups, crackers and ginger ale. She had to take the next few days off of work because of the virus. By day seven, she was feeling a little better and Omar told her she might need some fresh air. He said the guys were meeting up at a new lounge and he told her she should come because she's been cooped up in the bed the last week. She declined, but Omar insisted. She hated going back and forth with him. Even if she said no to something, he always asked why and would convince her to go anyway.

"Can we not stay long? I have to be up early," she said.

"Yeah, we can stay for about an hour or two. A change of scenery will help get your spirits back up."

He sported a throwback jersey, some baggy jeans and his favorite shoes, timbs. She wore a pink mini-dress with matching shoes and the new polka dot Chanel bag Omar bought her. She wore her natural hair in a slick bun and put on her earrings.

"Damn, Ke! You wearing that dress!" he said admiring her widening hips.

He didn't understand why she complained about the happy weight he had given her.

She thanked him and they hopped in his car and headed to the lounge. Once inside they found Kaylin, Angel, Bo, Shanna, Supreme and the chick Supreme was dealing with in the section. They went towards them, and Omar asked Ke if she wanted something to drink. She opted for water because she was feeling light-headed. When Omar came back with her water, three females walked up. Two of the females looked familiar and it dawned on Ke that this was Patrice, Jamie, and someone else.

"Omar, so you gonna act like you haven't seen my calls?"

"Lucille, stop. You know I don't fuck with you!"

"You don't fuck with me!" she screamed. "You weren't saying that when you was sticking dick in me!"

Angel, Ke and everybody else looked on. Ke was boiling on the inside. This was the third time those bitches had come at him and this was the first time Lucille made a physical appearance.

"Oh, so you're ignoring me because you got a new ho?" She pointed her thumb sideways to Ke.

Ke wasn't going to say anything because Omar said he didn't fuck with her and the lady was making a fool of herself. But, she did roll her eyes at Lucille.

"Yeah, bitch. I'm talking to yo ho-ass! What bitch pussy get wet for a nigga who made me get an abortion?" Lucille screamed, directing her energy toward Ke.

Omar was ignoring her. Ke stood up though.

"Bitch, your crazy ass cannot be talking to me," Ke calmly stated. "You right here begging a nigga to speak to you who can't keep his tongue out my ass," everybody gasped. "Then you and yo homegirls been pressin' him for months. Who does that to a nigga who they claim made them get an abortion?"

Lucille's eyes got big and she was on mute. Omar was trying to get Ke to sit back down because he was going to handle Lucille. But once Ke got to talking her shit, there was no stopping her. "So, no, bitch. Direct your energy to somebody else and figure out why you was just a fuck, raggedy-ass, whack-pussy-having-ass bitch!" Ke yelled.

"You think you all that because Omar stuck up your ass? You…" Lucille stated and Ke cut her off.

"You wish you was in my position, don't you, bitch? I get it, you miss the dick," Ke stated matter-of-factly. "But you could never be at my standard and have this nigga the way I got him because for one, my pussy only got one man's nut running through it. What about yours? How many niggas nut you got mixing in that nasty-ass pussy?"

Lucille was turning red.

"Yeah, you the same bitch that's married and didn't know who her baby daddy was. That's the real reason you got an abortion. Ho!" Ke yelled as she added insult to injury.

"Calm down. Come on, we're leaving," Omar said, getting amped up.

He didn't have a problem with Ke talking her shit but he felt like things were escalating.

"Lucille, you gotta kill the delusions. You know that shit been over with between us," he said directly to her.

"Omar, kiss my ass, seriously! I'll whoop you and that bitch ass in here," Lucille snapped.

"What's stopping you? Whoop my ass then, bitch!" Ke yelled.

That's where she drew the line. *Ain't no bitch "finna" be threatening me, especially not about a man that's mine.*

"Ke, no!" Omar barked but he was to late.

Lucille threw a drink and then swung on Ke but missed. Ke snatched her up by her hair and started connecting punches to

Lucille's nose. She was slinging her all over the floor and hammering every part of her face she could get.

"You wanna fight over a nigga that ain't yours, bitch!" Ke snapped as she continued to wear Lucille's ass out.

Lucille's friend Patrice tried to jump in and that's when Angel told her to back the fuck up. Kaylin grabbed Angel while Bo, Supreme and Omar grabbed Ke off Lucille. Omar was pissed that Ke was out here fighting in the club.

"Ke! What the fuck!" he yelled. "Calm the fuck down!" He fumed as he carried her out of the club. Bo was right behind him telling him to keep his cool.

"Don't tell me to calm down when a bitch *been* disrespecting me when it comes to my man!" she warned.

"I handled the shit. She a fucking nobody! You think I want you in the club fighting? That shit was unnecessary and embarrassing as hell!" he shot back.

His hands were shaking and his social anxiety was through the roof as people were staring at them arguing. He liked to handle shit in private and this was causing his blood to boil.

"Unnecessary? Embarrassing? Nigga, she swung on me first. What the fuck you mean! You ain't handle shit!" she yelled and was all in his face.

Lucille and her homegirls came walking past, proud of the shit they just caused. Lucille had a black eye, busted nose, and half her weave was snatched out. Ke whooped that ass but that never stops a person from popping their shit.

"Omar, don't ever call me to suck your dick again!" Lucille screamed, thinking she got the last laugh.

This was a lie. Omar hadn't contacted her since he found out she was married and decided not to deal with her. Of course, Ke wasn't going to believe that shit.

"Oh, you askin' bitches to suck your dick now?" Ke charged at him.

"No! I'm not!" he barked.

This is why he hated when Ke got worked up. No matter

what Lucille would have done or said, she was going to question it.

"That lying-ass bitch just want to start trouble and you letting her. I changed my number for the second time and you know she doesn't have this number," he said.

Angel walked up and saw Ke screaming at Omar and went over to calm her down. When Angel approached them, she saw Ke swing on Omar but missed.

"Really, Keisha? " Omar questioned in disbelief. "Don't fucking swing on me about some bullshit that don't even matter!"

Kaylin was there, trying to calm his mans down.

"Whatever, Omar!" she screamed. Angel took her girl to calm down.

"Ke! Chill. Omar ain't tell them weak-ass bitches to come over there," Angel explained. "You have to stop thinking with anger and just think about the facts for a second!"

She knew her girl had been through it but if anybody knows how weird these bitches could be, Ke knew.

"Angel. The girl said, 'Oh Omar, don't ask me to suck your dick again'," Ke stated, getting more pissed.

"She could be lying, Ke. You whooped her ass, going home with the nigga and exposed her business for having a husband. She had every motive to lie on him." Angel tried to get through to her. Omar told Ke to get in the car so they could go home and she ignored him.

"Ke. Come on, yo! Stop fuckin' playing. Are you really letting this stupid shit get to you?" he fumed. He had eyes only for Ke and was in awe of what transpired.

"Omar, just take me home!"

She got up and went toward the car. He slammed her door shut after she got in and went around to the driver's side. He stared at Ke, and she stared back at him. She wasn't scared nor did she give a fuck that he was mad. She was the one that just fought a bitch.

"That shit back there pissed me the fuck off!" he said with

his nostrils flared up. She ignored him and just focused on the street. "Stop ignoring me, ma." He felt like his body was in hell that's how fucking hot he was.

"That bitch had it coming! This is the third time her and her fucking friends done felt the need to address you in my face!" she yelled. "I let the shit slide and was going to let this shit slide too until she said she was going to beat my ass!"

"I can't stand that fighting in the club shit!" he yelled. "That shit was uncalled for!"

"Okay, well stop fucking bitches from the club and maybe bitches wouldn't have the opportunity to do *uncalled for* shit!" Ke shot back with her slick ass mouth. Omar wanted to snatch her ass up. "If you can't understand that she got her ass beat because she threatened me and disrespected me then just drop this conversation, please!"

Omar couldn't even think straight and her slick-ass comments got under his skin this time.

"Okay and if you can't understand how humiliating that shit is then maybe we need to just end things with this fucking relationship!" he yelled. "Matter-of-fact, yeah let's just call it quits Ma. Ain't like you trying to go all the way with me anyway. I'm done with this shit. You ain't used to a nigga like me and I'm at my fucking breaking point. I swear this shit over! Fuck it. Fuck you. Fuck everything! I don't care no more, yo. I'm done."

"What? Fuck me? What the fuck are you saying, Omar?"

She turned around in her seat to face him. She had to pause because she was about to chew his ass out and leave no fucking crumbs.

"I changed my fucking attitude, I let this bitch get away with addressing you three times, I'm trying to do all I can to prove to you that I want this, but a bitch you use to fuck with get her ass beat and now you wanna end it?" Her breathing increased and she shook her head. "One thing you keep forgetting is that you ain't used to a woman like me. You don't know how to be in a healthy relationship with someone that ain't a fucking ho! You don't understand that this shit is not just about how you feel! It's a partnership. I know at times I battle my fucking feelings but one thing about it, once I got over that, I've done nothing but consider you to make this shit work. I have my flaws but nigga your selfishness is going to cause you to miss out on a bitch like me!" she screamed. He was quiet. "But whatever. I'm done arguing. We done, like you said. A relationship is about making everyone's voice be heard. I'm not going to allow you to keep thinking you can say bullshit when you're mad! First you threaten to punch me in my mouth, and now you saying fuck me because I'm not agreeing with you on this one damn thing? Okay."

Ke wanted to punch him in his damn mouth but decided not to. He couldn't understand where she was coming from and then he tried to make it seem like she didn't want him. She comes over after her busy-ass work days, she cooks, makes his groceries, cleans his fucking house, work on her flaws at his pace, and throws that ass back whenever he wanted it. Yes, her attitude got the best of her, but she had been doing better. He even said it. He was speaking off anger and Ke wasn't about to address it. He wanted to be done- okay.

They were silent for the next fifteen minutes and Omar finally calmed down. He tried taking the exit to his place.

"Omar, take me the fuck home. We're done."

"Ke, stop."

"No, nigga. You stop! I will act a complete fucking fool in this car if you don't take me home!" she warned.

He sighed and took the exit for her place. He knew he said some unnecessary shit to her. Ke knew she was at the top over everybody so why did she have to be fighting a bitch that literally meant nothing. It made no sense to him. They pulled up to her place and she gave Omar his car and house key back.

"Ke," he said while shaking his head. "You going too far, Ma."

"No, I'm not. You said you were done. I ain't use to a nigga like you right? Go find a bitch that is! Oh, and give me *my* house key and spare key to my car," she sat there, waiting for her items.

"No, I'm not giving them to you. I don't even have them on me," he lied.

"Omar. Okay, whatever."

She hopped out of the car and walked to her door. He was on her heels.

"Yo. Can you relax!" he yelled.

"Leave me alone! I'm not going back and forth with no grown-ass man about the shit he says. You *used* to bitches doing that and I'm not the one that's going to feed your raggedy-ass ego," Ke kept laying it on his ass.

"Don't act like you don't say shit you ain't supposed to say when you mad, Ke," he replied.

"Stop talking to me," she firmly stated.

She went to put her key in the lock. He snatched her arm, causing the keys to drop.

"Omar, stop! My fucking neighbors are gonna come out!"

"You this mad? I ain't mean to say what I said."

"You're done with the relationship, right! It's fuck me, right?" she said, hiding her tears. "That's your biggest fucking problem! You think it always has to be your way and you can say what the fuck you want then when you calm down you act like you wasn't being foul! Naw, I'm not doing that shit anymore! Stand on the shit you say or don't say it at all. Ain't that what *real niggas* do?" she challenged. "You single. Bye! Go back and fuck them bitches from the club and leave me the hell alone!"

"Ke, yo stop this shit!" he said as he grabbed her arm again. "You know we not done. That shit was the heat of the moment, ma."

Ke snatched away from him. She got into her house and slammed her door. Omar decided to let things chill out for a few hours because he was partially wrong. He went home and Bo called him, making a joke about Ke being Mike Tyson. Omar wasn't laughing though.

CHAPTER
FORTY-FIVE

AS KE WENT to clock in the next day at work, she realized that she left her purse in Omar's car and her purse had her work badges in it. She had to swallow her fucking pride and dial him.

"I left my purse in your car. Are you able to bring it to me at my job or meet me somewhere?" she stated with her face balled up.

"I'm near the school. I'll be there in ten minutes to bring it to you," he stated.

He wanted to play this carefully. She didn't even give him a proper greeting so that had him tight, but tensions were already thick with them from yesterday. Omar pulled up to the school and saw Ke in her car. He grabbed her purse and approached the car. She mean-mugged him the whole walk over.

"Here's your purse." She went to grab it and he snatched it back. "You still not talking?" He said while staring at her and noticing her eyes were puffy from crying.

"Omar, please. Just give me my purse!"

"I'm not giving you shit until you talk to me."

"Talk to you about what? Are you serious right now? After all the shit you talked last night?" She was annoyed all over again.

"Wasn't you talking your same shit?" he shot back. "I'm

sorry. Okay? We need to at least discuss this before we throw the shit away."

"Now you want to discuss something? After you said fuck me and you were done? You know what, nevermind. I can't deal with your ass right now," she walked up to him and snatched her purse.

He was tempted to yoke her ass up and force her to talk, but again, considering the abuse she went through before, he decided not to. He watched her walk into the school and he hopped back in his car. He called Bo and vented to him but he wasn't giving the answers he wanted. Bo told him to give her a few days but Omar was not with that shit at all.

IT HAD BEEN a week since Ke and Omar spoke to each other. She was at the club bartending when Omar and Bo walked up. Omar ordered a water bottle and she gave it to him. She then proceeded to act like he wasn't there while she carried on with assisting her other customers. Omar took a swig of his water and stared at her frowned lips and flared nose.

"Can I speak with you?" he asked her. She rolled her eyes. He took a deep breath. "Keisha."

She threw her head back, huffing and puffing. Bo told him he was going to the bathroom so the two could have somewhat of a private conversation.

"I don't want to talk to you," she replied as tears began to well up in her eyes.

"I just want to let you know that I'll be out of town for a few days. In case you stop having an attitude and start back caring about a nigga." She gave him no response. "I love you and I'm sorry," he told her and once again was ignored.

He left the club, got in his car, and headed home. His feelings were hurt but he couldn't do shit if she was being stubborn like this.

When Bo came out of the bathroom, he went toward the bar

to see if Omar was still there. He noticed that he left but he saw a dude at the bar trying to seriously get his mack on with Ke.

"I'm Rayzo," the man said. "What's your name?" He flashed Ke a mouth full of gold teeth. He had acne all over his face, beady eyes and he sported cornrows. He had on a Dior shirt, jeans and every piece of jewelry he owned. The nigga was ugly as hell, but he had some funds.

"Are you ordering anything, sir?" Ke asked him.

Another customer asked her for some napkins and she turned around to get them. When she turned around, Rayzo snatched Omar's half-drunk water bottle that he left at the bar.

"Yeah, I'm ordering something. Are you available?"

Ke was so annoyed. "I'm not," she rudely stated.

"Well, let me give you my number just in case you change your mind." Ke declined. "Damn girl, okay. You a tough one. You fine as fuck. I bet a nigga would fall in love fucking that pussy from the back."

Ke was shocked. These niggas get more and more bold as these club nights go on. Rayzo made a phone call and then he headed out. Bo heard the whole conversation but he didn't address Rayzo because his name was buzzing about snitching. Shit, Bo was confused on how this nigga was so comfortable showing his face after all these snitching rumors.

"Nigga prolly got the police in here watching him," Bo looked around and then headed out to his car.

He knew Omar was going to fucking snap when he mentioned how Rayzo was trying to press Ke.

CHAPTER
FORTY-SIX

"YO, O!" Bo shouted.

"What?" Omar responded as he went to turn off Musiq's, Teach Me How to Love and plopped back down on his couch. He was emotionally defeated.

"I got some news for you and then I'ma let you get back to your love songs," Bo joked but Omar ain't find shit funny. "Man, how about I'm in the club and caught this nigga Rayzo trying to put the mack down on Ke."

Omar stood up.

"What!"

"I'm at the bar and hear this nigga tryna push up on Ke. Mad disrespectful. Talkin' about some, 'I know whoever hitting that pussy from the back prolly falling in love'. Talkin' about her ass and how he was gone give her his number," Bo stated. "I was going to say something, but you know what they say about his rat-ass and I don't know who he got around him."

"That nigga!" Omar scoffed, shaking his head. "I'ma handle his bitch-ass. How the fuck you tryna push up on mine," Omar said. "What Ke say?"

"She was ignoring him for the most part and she declined his number." Bo smirked. "Don't worry, nigga. She still mad at you but she ain't looking for nobody else." He was full blown laughing now. "You dumped her so why you mad?"

"Nigga, I ain't even dump her. She being dramatic. I told you that I said some shit and when I calmed down she didn't want to talk anymore," Omar vented and took a deep breath.

"Welp, you said you were done so it looks like Rayzo can push up," Bo kept on with his taunting.

"See you muthafuckas think shit a joke but I'm not playing!" he snapped. "She knows better than to give her number up. You saw how long it took me to get it. That nigga Rayzo gon' get dealt with when I see him though."

"You already know I got you, my nigga. You and Ke need to handle this shit though, fa'real. Y'all better than this and need to stop bein' stubborn and talk," Bo sincerely stated.

He felt like Ke and Omar were perfect for each other. Everybody had their flaws, but the character traits she lacked, Omar had and vice-versa.

"I'm trying to talk, nigga. She doesn't wanna talk to me right now. You saw how she ignored me at the bar."

"You'll figure it out, O'!"

CHAPTER
FORTY-SEVEN

IT HAD BEEN two weeks and Ke was still holding a grudge against Omar. She was on the phone with Angel and Tasha and they told her she was being too hard on him.

"No, I'm not being too hard on him. He was the one who said he was done, not me."

She hated how everyone was always saying she did too much. Granted, she did at times. But, Omar was so quiet and seemed so innocent and being that Ke was such a fireball, they always thought he couldn't have been the issue. They didn't see that it was not always her.

"Ke, you know how bad you can piss somebody off with your smart-ass mouth," Angel stated. "He still been trying to make sure your ass is okay."

"Angel, you were right there when everything happened!"

"And I saw Omar telling them bitches to basically go 'head with that bullshit. I saw him trying to calm your ass down. I also saw the bitch swing on you and there was really nothing Omar could do to control that. He cannot control her dumb ass actions," Angel stated trying to get Ke to view the bigger picture.

"When she came outside, I told you the bitch had some other shit to say," Ke explained.

"And you decided to swing on Omar. About some shit that he again can't control. He cannot control if a bitch lie on him, Ke."

Angel was trying to get her girl to see how irritational she was being.

"And Ke, didn't you say he already gave you the rundown on her and another girl. Answer his calls, bitch," Tasha stated. "You know I understand when you gotta whoop a bitch ass, but don't take everything out on him!" Tasha told her.

"Nope. I don't care. Fuck him. We were in the car going at it and he gon' say he swears that he done and he said fuck me. Then he gone make it seem like I ain't used to dealing with a man like him. As if he used to dealing with a real bitch like me! He got me fucked up and I'm fed up with some of his ways."

"You need to really calm down."

She hung up with her girls and got ready to attend her mother's birthday dinner at Sylvia's Soul Food Restaurant. The vibes were great until Omar walked through the door with a gift for Mrs. Harris. He looked so fucking good in his Versace sweat suit and crispy shoes.

But, then Ke became livid. If she was done with a nigga, her family needed to be too. Her friends were trying to get her to talk to him and here her fucking family goes. *Why the hell would my mother invite him here*. They locked eyes and Ke broke their stare and got up to leave. He followed her outside.

"Ke, stop! Why are you acting like this, Ma?" Omar stopped her at her car.

"I don't want to talk to you or see you!" she said as she fumbled with her keys.

"Why? It's been two weeks. When the fuck you plan on talking to me?"

"Never! I'm single!"

Her sister Brielle came out to bring Ke her phone that she'd left on the table. Omar didn't want to argue around her sister, so he let her drive off. He noted that to be the last time he allowed her to leave without discussing them. He wasn't trying to be aggressive with her, but he saw that was the route he would have to take.

She was being an asshole and needed some firmness.

OMAR ENDED up running into Rayzo at the corner store. The men stared at each other, then Omar punched him dead in his mouth and blood flew everywhere.

"You tried to push up on what's mine, nigga?" he barked as he whooped Rayzo's ass.

Rayzo was trying to get away but couldn't handle the punches Omar was laying on him. Omar dragged him outside and before he knew it, he had him over the hood of some car and he put his gun to Rayzo's head. Sincere was in the car, cowardly watching everything.

"Nigga, I'll fucking kill you if you try that shit again!"

Omar hit him with the butt of his gun. Bo came up to him telling him to put the gun away and not to shoot in a public place that had cameras. Bo didn't like how this nigga Rayzo was just walking around like he wasn't a snitch but there was a time and a place for everything.

Omar listened, but knocked Rayzo out before he left. He was still alive but that ass-whooping left a lasting impression.

Ke was still refusing to speak to him, but he had a trick for that.

CHAPTER
FORTY-EIGHT

THREE DAYS LATER, Ke was leaving the university and called her brother.

"Travon, do you still need me to pick you up from practice?" she asked as she started up her car.

"No, I'ma walk home with some friends. Mama already know," he told her as he hung up and gave his attention back to his coach.

"So I have an old player of mine that's here visiting. He was one of my best shooting guards and he wanted to check you guys out," Coach Lucas motioned for Sincere to come in. "This is Sincere Washington, and he was a beast on the court," Coach Lucas boasted.

Travon immediately frowned his face up. He remembered Sincere from when he was with his sister. The only thing that had changed about him was he was extremely thin due to drug use and he now had a low cut.

"S'up! I just wanted to see the team while I was in town," said Sincere and his eyes met with Travon.

"Fellas, make sure you show him your skills! Go ahead and get ready for five on five," Coach demanded. "Sincere, this a good group of boys! Number four, Travon Harris, put up twenty-eight points last night!"

"Oh yeah? Can't wait to see him in action," Sincere smirked.

The athletes came out and began their practice drills. Sincere kept his eyes on Travon the entire time. Two hours later, the boys headed to grab their items and left the practice facility. Travon walked out of the gym with another teammate and Sincere followed closely behind them. Once they hit an alleyway, Sincere yelled to get their attention.

"Travon, what's up. You a beast on the court," said Sincere as he tried to make small-talk but Travon ignored him. "Damn, I see your attitude just like your sister's."

"Nigga, don't fucking mention my sister. She's been doing fine without you. Her new nigga don't hit females," barked Travon.

"Her new nigga may not hit her, but he has done some gruesome shit to multiple people," Sincere admitted as he pulled some pictures of Victor's dismembered body from out his pocket. "Her new nigga.. Omar? Yeah, he was a person of interest for this crazy-ass murder," he added. Travon mushed the pictures away from him. "Yeah, nothing to say? I don't care. I ain't like your little-ass no way! To keep it real with you, your sister got a better chance at the ass-whoopings I use to give her then if her and this nigga was to ever get into it," Sincere mentioned, adding fuel to the fire. "He would be the nigga to really kill her," he smirked.

"Fuck you!" Travon yelled as he spit in Sincere's face.

Sincere pushed him and Travon punched him in the nose, causing Sincere to stumble. Travon then jawed his ass again and busted Sincere's lip.

"You a bitch! Leave my fuckin' sister alone."

When Travon said that, Sincere pulled out a gun. Travon put his hands up. Then, him and his friend turned around to run. Sincere let off four shots, two hitting Travon in the back of his neck and two striking his friend in the head. The two athletes were dead.

"Shit! Fuck. Fuck! What the fuck!" Sincere panicked as he

saw the blood leak from their lifeless bodies. He had never shot a gun before and he did not mean to kill them. "Fuck!"

He looked around to see if there were any cameras or witnesses. He then ran, leaving the two bodies. Once he got to his car, he snorted two lines of coke to calm his nerves. He was fucking terrified about committing those murders and the thought of jail caused his anxiety to shoot up. *What the fuck did I just do.*

CHAPTER
FORTY-NINE

THE SAME NIGHT.

Ke finally pulled up to her home after a long day at work and school. As soon as she got inside her house, she noticed that two candles were lit, two silver platters were on the table, and rose petals everywhere. Jodeci's, Feenin' was lightly bumping through her speakers. She was stuck in her tracks when Omar came from around the corner with a bouquet of flowers.

"I knew I should have gotten my locks changed," Ke sighed as she ruined the mood, unimpressed. "Why are you here? This is literally breaking and entering, Omar," she continued as she put her hand on her hip.

"I have a key. This ain't no damn breakin' and enterin'. It's time for you to stop fuckin' playing and talk, Keisha," he said as he handed her the roses. She threw them on the counter. "Why you acting like this? You want to stay mad forever? I'm sorry. I miss you," he apologized while grabbing her hands and pulling her into him.

"Move, Omar. Get off me," she uttered and tried to push him. He started rubbing his goatee on her neck and made her chuckle. "Can you leave. I don't want to see you," she giggled.

"It's time to talk. Stop being stubborn. At the least I deserve one conversation after all the shit you've talked during this relationship. Right or wrong, I deserve one fuckin' shot, Keisha." She took a deep breath.

"Okay."

They went to sit down at the table, and Omar poured Ke a shot of liquor.

"I am not drinking, Omar," she spoke as she shook her head.

"You still rolling your eyes and flaring your nose. Giving me all this attitude. You need a shot to relax," he joked with her. "Plus, you get extra nasty off the liquor and I know our make-up sex about to go crazy. So stop it and take one shot," he said.

"Nigga, what make-up sex? I'm single and don't fuck with you," she bucked. "I'm here to have dinner and talk so you can leave. This pussy don't belong to you anymore."

"Okay. Let's have dinner then," he smirked.

Ke pulled the top off her platter and it wasn't shit underneath it but a note card that said, air. She looked at Omar and burst out laughing.

"You play too damn much. I swear. You don't know when to stop. Where is the food?"

"I had a feeling you were still going to be talking shit. So, I'm giving you air to eat since you love running your damn mouth. It ain't my pussy and you single, right? Why I need to feed you when you don't fuck with a nigga anymore?' he challenged. She couldn't help but laugh.

He got up and gave her the extra platter that was hidden, and she ate her food. She also decided to take two shots of liquor and it did help her loosen up.

"Let's talk, Keisha. First things first, I love you more than anything and I miss you. I apologize for not understanding where you were coming from and for saying that hurtful shit when I was mad. It was uncalled for but baby, you can't keep ignoring me. This relationship shit is a work in progress for both of us. I want us to work through shit together. You had me sick not hearing from you these three weeks. I'm sorry, baby," he stood up and walk over to her her. "You hear my niggas Jodeci on the bridge to this song, *Lady I'm hooked on you, there's nothing else I'd rather do. Spend my last dime, for a drop of your time. Surely girl without a doubt, you know you got me strung out."*

"You heard them, Ke. I felt like I couldn't breathe without you baby. I need you," he expressed.

"Okay. Fine," she said as she looked at him. "I'm only responding so you can stop with that jacked-up-ass singing," she teased. "But, I'm sorry for being stubborn and not talking to you but Omar, you can't say you're done and you're sick of this shit and expect me to wait around after you cool down every time. You need to watch what you say to me. I know I've been the asshole in a lot of our prior disagreements, but you're not always right, baby. You have to know that in a relationship we both have to consider each other. It's not always Omar's way." He nodded his head in agreement. "I'm going to address my mistakes but, there's two people in this relationship. Both of our opinions matter. Just because that fight was embarrassing to you, you have to understand that I'm always going to speak up and defend myself."

"You know talking just ain't my favorite thing to do, especially about my feelings. I'm working on it though. I mean look at me, I pretty much had to break into your damn house to get you to talk to me," he told her. "You making a nigga feel this shit. I'm sorry and I do understand where you comin' from."

"Mmmhmm. I accept your apology. The last thing I ever want to do is have you embarrassed about something I did. But I'm going to whoop any bitch that swing on me first. Let's be clear on that," she said and he chuckled. "And you need to give me back my key. I'm still single," she taunted.

"This my key. It says Big Dick. That's all me," he told her. "You got all that mouth. You must need to be fed dick next," he taunted.

"You're so aggravating," she shook her head.

"Come release those aggravations out on my dick. Its been three weeks since that pussy was away from me. You were sick one week and then being stubborn the other two weeks. Let me see what its been up to."

He stared at her with the look that had been causing her panties to get wet since day one.

"Nope," she giggled and he told her to take another shot. He grabbed her by her neck and lifted her up.

"Give me a kiss," he said. She obliged.

Their tongues danced and she started sucking on his lips. Omar led her upstairs to the bedroom and he undressed her. "Sit on my face," he commanded as he lay down and guided her to take a seat on his mouth.

She got in the 69 position, placed his dick to her lips and her clit to his lips. He licked and sucked on her swollen clit while she throat fucked his dick.

"You missed yo balls being in my jaws?" She talked her shit as she gently sucked on his balls. She placed his dick in her mouth until it hit her throat and clenched down on it. She started plunging the shaft while moving her head in a circle around his dick.

"I missed this pussy in my face." He spread her legs wider across his face and stuck his tongue in her pussy.

He thrust his tongue inside of her gushy walls and his goatee was covered in her juices. He then stuck his tongue in her asshole while he rubbed on her clit and inserted two fingers inside of her. The sensation of his warm tongue being in her ass, his fingers on her G-spot and him rubbing her sensitive clit made Ke's entire body tense up because what the fuck was he doing to her.

"Omar!" she hollered as she was losing control of her body. "Baby, wait!" she screamed as he pulled his fingers out and she squirted all over his face and it dripped down his cheeks. She was hollering and breathing hard while still trying to eat his dick up.

"I knew that pussy missed me," he responded as he went back to suck on her clit. Ke was done for. He flipped her on her side, lifted her legs up, and inserted his dick inside of her. He placed a hand around her neck and whispered:

"You missed me? Tell me you love me."

He stroked in and out of her creamy pussy. His big dick was enjoying her warmth and her pussy grip that Omar shaped to fit only him. He was stroking slow but hard, gearing up for an intense release.

"I love you daddy. Fuck yo pussy," she told him.

Omar spread one of her legs wider so he could get in even deeper. He was so deep that Ke felt the dick coming out of her throat.

"You mine forever. I ain't never leavin' you, Keisha. I love you," he moaned as he nibbled on her ear.

He was still slightly choking her as he reached down with his other hand to rub on her clit. "Kiss me," he told her. She sucked all over his mouth, tasting her own juices. He put more pressure on her clit and her stomach began to cave in.

"Baby, no. I don't wanna squirt again. Please, Omar, no," Ke begged as her body started quivering and shaking.

"This pussy mine. I make it do what I want it to do. You still single? You missed this dick all in yo stomach," he said as he kept going and tried to take her there.

"Okay baby, okay. I'm not single," she moaned as she felt it coming. "Cum all in yo pussy, daddy. It's all yours," she yelled as she squirted all over his dick.

Omar put in a few more thrusts and came inside of her, just like she told him to do. He turned her on her back and got ready for missionary. He slipped his dick in, and Ke gasped when he threw her legs over his shoulders. He started sucking on her neck while his dick thrusted in and out her walls. His balls were slapping against her ass and they kissed until Ke had a hollering orgasm.

"I love you, ma," he said as they caught their breath.

"I love you too. I'm still single," she teased.

"Stop trying me," he told her as he lifted her up and headed to the bathroom.

They showered and went to bed all cuddled up together. Ke couldn't sleep because her phone kept ringing off the hook. She answered it and it was her mother.

"Keisha!" her mother screamed. "Keisha, Travon is dead! Somebody shot and killed him. I have to go to the hospital," her mother sobbed and struggled to breathe.

Ke felt numb. She couldn't have heard her right. There's no way she heard her right.

CHAPTER FIFTY

"WHAT? MAMA, STOP!" Ke yelled as she felt a panic attack coming on. "Mama, please stop! No!" Ke screamed as she hopped out of the bed and threw some clothes on.

Tears were streaming down her face as she prayed to God this was a mix up.

"What's wrong? Why you crying?" Omar hopped up, alarmed. "Keisha! Calm down, you're shaking. What's wrong!" he barked as he grabbed her to break her out of this state of mind.

"Omar. Travon is dead. My mama said somebody shot and killed him. I have to go to the hospital!" she was frantic as she searched for her purse, shoes, and keys.

"Okay, I'm coming," he said as he put his clothes on. "I'll drive."

Ke was in a state he had never seen her in before. She was hyperventilating, crying, shaking, and an emotional mess. When they arrived at the hospital, her mother gave her the news again and repeated those three words, 'Travon is dead'. Ke could not believe it.

The news hit her in the gut and she threw up everywhere. Her mother couldn't control her breathing and everyone was crying. Omar was trying to soothe Ke and her mother, but her grandmother and other siblings were also hysterical.

"Pops," Omar mumbled as he took a deep breath while on the phone with his father. "I need you to get to the hospital. Ke's little brother just died and I need help consoling them. Please, Pops. It's too much for me," Omar confessed through the phone, feeling very overwhelmed.

"I'm on the way right now. Just keep consoling the family until I get there," Carl told him as he jumped out of bed and threw some clothes on. Once he arrived at the hospital, he found Omar with his arms around Ke, her mother holding her other siblings and her grandmother. He came to give some encouraging words and he checked on his son.

"Omar," Carl called out to his son as he watched him hold Ke tight while she cried.

He mouthed the words, 'thank you', to his father and directed his attention back to his lady. After an hour, they left and Ke spent the night with her mother. Omar didn't want to leave her so he stayed there too.

CHAPTER
FIFTY-ONE

KEISHA'S MOTHER couldn't fathom having to bury her only son. Shit, any child for that matter. Omar paid for all the funeral arrangements and her mother could not thank him enough. Ke was still taking the death hard, though. She refused to eat, sleep, or talk. She was overly emotional. Handling grief was not her strong suit.

Three weeks later, Omar walked into the house.

"Baby, where you at? I bought you some food. You have to try to eat Keisha," he yelled as he walked into the door.

He got her food together and she still hadn't come down. He went to the room to look for her and she wasn't in there, but he saw the light from the bathroom on. He walked toward it and saw the diamond bracelets he had given her to cover her wrists on the ground. He could not fucking believe what he was seeing. His heart was pounding.

"Ke! No! No!" Omar yelled. He saw her with the razor on her wrist and a slit causing a trail of blood to leak from her.

"I don't want to be here! One minute I'm happy and the next minute my baby brother is gone. My daddy is gone. My child that I carried is gone. I don't want to live, Omar," she cried while Omar took the razor and looked for a towel to put over her bleeding wrist.

"You have me. I want you here. I need you here. You're my everything, Ke. Think about all the good things that have happened and that you have overcome. I know we can't bring him back but baby, I know he wouldn't want you doing this," Omar expressed as a lump formed in his throat.

"I don't want to do life. It's too much for me," she sniffled.

Keisha never thought she would have these suicidal tendencies ever again, but shit had been too emotional and overwhelming for her. This relationship was a huge rollercoaster and now her brother gets shot and no one knows who did it. The fuck more can a bitch take.

"It's not too much. You can do this. I know you can. You're strong, you're loved, and you have so much shit to look forward to. Don't dim your light. I love you. Please shake this, baby. You're stronger than this and I won't lose you to this." Omar dropped a tear.

He held Ke while she cried and she held him even tighter. He found some gauze to wrap around her wrist and he talked her into eating. She went to bed and finally got a few hours of rest. Omar was distraught seeing her like that and he knew she needed help. He stared at Ke sleeping on the bed and prayed she overcame this just like she does everything else.

The next day, Omar dialed Ke's mother and explained to her what he saw. Her mother came over and told him they had to admit her to the mental health facility. He also made a visit to Kyra since he was aware that she dealt with the psyche.

"What's up, Kyra?" Omar said as he walked into her home.

"Hey, Omar. Everything okay?" Kyra asked while holding her infant Aisha. She didn't expect this visit.

"I don't know," he looked at her with worry in his eyes. "I saw Ke trying to umm-" he said as he paused. It hurt him to say the shit. "I saw Ke with a razor to her wrist and I don't know what to do," he said as his eyes welled and his palms became sweaty. "Her mom wants the psych ward to get called but Ke told me she never wants to go back there."

"Oh my goodness," Kyra said as she covered her mouth.

"She needs to be admitted because she's not coping well with her emotions, Omar," Kyra advised him. She put her shoes on and got ready to head with him to Ke.

"I can't let her go. She doesn't want to be there," Omar was torn. "I want her to get help, but I also want her to be calm and happy. Are there any other options?"

"No, this is the only option. She's not thinking, Omar. She has to go before she severely hurts herself," Kyra explained as they headed back to Ke's home. Ke's mother called the mental health hospital and they told her the professionals would be pulling up within the next hour.

Ke was unaware of all of this and surprisingly, she was up and in her kitchen making her something to eat. She seemed to be back to her normal self. When Omar walked in the door she greeted him with a kiss. Right behind him were Kyra and the mental health workers standing near the door.

"Ke. Baby," Omar spoke as he watched her sit on the couch and eat her sandwich. "Baby, I don't think you're handling your emotions well and I-" Omar got choked up as Ke looked up and saw the workers behind him. She tensed up. "Me and your mom called the mental health facility so they can help you for a few days," Omar blurted out and that shit tore him up.

"Omar, no. I don't want to go. Please, no. Mama, no," Ke panicked as she looked to her mother and Omar.

She started crying and backed up into a corner while the workers walked up to try to restrain her but she resisted.

"Omar, don't let them take me. Please! I promise I won't try to hurt myself again. I promise. Please, no. I'm not sick," Ke cried and kept pushing and kicking the workers.

They were struggling to calm her down and one of them grabbed her hands. Omar couldn't stand to see the men trying to restrain her so he intervened.

"Yo, get the fuck off her!" Omar barked as he pushed the man and the worker stumbled back. Mrs. Harris tried to calm him down, but she could not get a hold of the situation. Ke went to hug Omar around his waist and clung to him so tight as she cried into his chest. He wrapped his arms around her and allowed her to let it out.

"I don't want to go, baby, please. I'll do better, I promise. I'm sorry, please!" she wept.

"I know you can do better, but they just have to watch you for a few days. Okay? Me and your mom will be up there everyday. You're not coping well and we don't want you to hurt yourself. I promise I'm right here. I'm never leaving you or will allow anything to hurt you," he said as he looked at her.

"Keisha, baby, please. I can't lose you like I lost your brother and father. Please," her mother cried.

Ke looked at them both and went with the workers to be admitted to the mental health facility. A little piece of her knew it was for the better.

CHAPTER
FIFTY-TWO

FOR THE PAST SEVEN DAYS, Ke was monitored at the facility. "Have you had any negative or depressive thoughts today, Ms. Harris?" asked the nurse as she handed Ke her tray of food.

"No, ma'am. I told you yesterday and the day before yesterday that I was fine," Ke replied as she looked at the club sandwich and the yellow bag of Lays chips. Her stomach started rumbling and she was ready to eat.

"Now you know I have to keep asking. Go ahead and enjoy your lunch. I believe your mother and boyfriend are scheduled to visit you in thirty minutes," the nurse stated. She left Ke alone to eat.

A few moments later, Omar and her mother came for their scheduled visit. Her therapist was there with them at the table and had some news for him and her mother.

"Keisha has made significant progress. We have not made a diagnosis because all her tests came back within normal limits. We noted her down as struggling with emotional distress. She feels her emotions and sometimes they become overwhelming. She is not suicidal, but the death of her brother triggered those thoughts," Doctor Trecia explained as she looked through her papers. Her mother was relieved. "We did not administer her any medicine because she is pregnant," she dropped a bomb as she looked at them.

"What!" her mother yelled, overjoyed. "Oh my goodness. I'm going to finally be a grandma!" she excitedly said.

"Yes, her HCG levels in her urine marks her at about eight weeks pregnant. There is no OBGYN in the building, but her urine sample was normal and so was her blood work," explained the doctor.

Omar couldn't help but smile. He was going to be a father. A few minutes later, Ke came out and sat down with them. The therapist made small talk and explained to Ke her emotional distress. Then, she told her about the pregnancy and poor Keisha started crying.

"Omar, why the fuck would you get me pregnant!" Ke said through her tears. Omar laughed "I really didn't want any kids yet," she sobbed.

"Oh, Keisha, please! Don't forget that I saw what was on that customized key!" her mother said as she got Ke together. "If you didn't want any children, why were you willingly having unprotected sex, child?"

"Mrs. Harris, she loves playing like she doesn't know why things happen," he grinned at her and she rolled her eyes. "I'm going to be a daddy. I can't wait," Omar expressed as he went over to kiss her. "You told me to cum all in that pussy and I've been doing that since day one," he whispered in her ear. She pushed him and he chuckled. "You are doing better, and Dr. Trecia said you can leave at the end of next week. Now you have our baby to live for," he said to her. "You know I got y'all forever." Omar kissed her, but she was still being standoffish. "I think the therapist needs to see why the hell you're so mean," he mentioned and she started laughing.

CHAPTER
FIFTY-THREE

IT WAS the end of the following week and Omar was bringing Keisha home from the mental health hospital. Once they opened the doors to her house, all of her family, their friends, and his family were there to welcome her. He wanted her to know that there are people that love her and want to be sure that she doesn't try to hurt herself ever again.

Once everyone left, Omar ran them a hot bath and played Keith Sweat's, I'll Give All My Love to You on her radio. He climbed his sculpted body in the tub first and Ke climbed on top of him.

"Thank you for everything, baby. For paying for the funeral, for loving me, and protecting me. Even from myself. I love you so much. Words could never describe it. It's crazy how you're really my soulmate," she confessed as she laid her head back on his chest.

"I would do it all again. All I need you to do is keep your mind clear and carry my baby. I'll handle everything else. I love y'all," he stated as he rubbed her stomach.

"We love you too," she said and they started kissing.

They washed each other up and Omar led her to the bedroom where he beat his pussy out the frame.

THE NEXT WEEK, Ke was in the kitchen trying to get an appointment scheduled with her OBGYN. Her doctor would be out for the next two weeks, and Ke decided she would wait for her. This had been her doctor since she was eighteen and she knew all of her uterus problems. She didn't want anybody else checking her but this lady. After her phone call, she started preparing dinner for her and Omar.

"Keisha, I think it may be time that you stop working at the club. You're pregnant, hormonal and your emotions are everywhere. I just want you to relax, baby," he sat at the table and prepared for her smart ass to argue back.

"You're probably right. I've been feelin' exhausted," she confessed. "I'ma work at the club this week, and then I'll make next week my last week there," she decided. "My body is tired, and I do need to think about giving up something so I can have extra time to rest."

This decision was for the better. Ke had been going to school, bartending, and working at the school for the past year. It was time to slow down. She worked the club this weekend and Omar went there with her to watch out for her for her entire shift. He was always overprotective of Ke but now that she was pregnant, he didn't want her out of his sight.

CHAPTER
FIFTY-FOUR

THE FOLLOWING WEEKEND CAME, and Saturday was officially her last day bartending until her pregnancy was over. It was bittersweet. They were a family there and Ke loved bartending. Shit, it was where she met Omar. They all gave her money, balloons, and a cupcake. Mr. Jose said he didn't care how big her belly got, that she'd better come visit.

Omar didn't come with her that day. He let her be alone with her bar family while he went to chill with Trae and Shaheem. Rayzo was at the bar again taking shots with a few females. He made a phone call, but got too drunk and left his phone on the counter. Sarah placed his phone in the lost phone box and labeled it with the date like they always did.

"Okay y'all. I'm about to leave. This baby is kickin' my ass already," Ke explained as she grabbed her purse. "I thought I could make it the whole shift but I am beat."

"Want me to walk you out?" asked Sarah as she counted her tips.

"No, I'm good, girl. Get that money for these last forty-five minutes. Love y'all! And I'm goin' to visit! I promise!" she stated as she headed out the door.

She pulled her phone out and tried to call Omar to tell him

that she was on her way but he didn't answer. As Ke walked to her car, a deep voice yelled her name.

"Ke! Turn around!"

She was startled, but turned around. Her eyes were wide from shock.

"Oh, don't act surprised now. You don't remember me?" She was speechless and felt like she couldn't breathe. Sincere was standing there in the fucking flesh. She hadn't seen him since they went to trial over two years ago.

"Sincere?" she questioned.

"Yeah, it's me. I see you done moved on from a nigga, huh?" he barked but Ke ignored him as he walked closer. "Oh, you can't hear, bitch?" Sincere spat.

That's when she snapped out of her trance.

"What the fuck could you possibly want?" she asked.

"I heard you got you another nigga. Omar. You begged me not to sell drugs and yet you fucking on another drug dealer. One moving major major weight at that!"

He was hatin' and he desperately wanted the feds to take Omar down. But Omar moved so quietly and carefully, that it was hard to give the feds a tip on him.

"You must've forgot that you wasn't shit without me and my money."

"Forgot what? Nigga, you can't be serious. Sincere, please get the fuck away from me!"

"I ain't getting away from shit you bitch. You think you gon' just leave me and get pregnant by another nigga?"

Ke gasped.

"Yeah, word out all around that you are so in love and pregnant by dude!" he snapped. "Then he round here telling everybody he gon' be a father. You letting that nigga fuck you raw?" Sincere was fuming mad.

"What's your reasoning behind this, muthafucka!" she yelled. "Yes, I'm in love and pregnant. Clearly we fucking raw if I'm pregnant, right? You stupid-ass bitch. What the fuck is your issue? I haven't dealt with you in over two years!"

"You ain't never leaving me, Ke, that's the issue! You belong to me," he firmly stated. "You think I'ma let another nigga take what I been in first? You were sprung over me and now you telling me you not? Yeah right!" Sincere laughed.

"Sincere, I don't fucking love you! I don't belong to you! You gotta be on some type of drug," she frantically stated.

She started to get scared and wished Omar was there. She tried to pull her phone out but Sincere slapped it on the ground.

"Oh, hell no!" she screamed.

Sincere then proceeded to choke her like he used to do but she wasn't going down without a fight. She kicked him in the nuts and started punching his ass in the nose. He let go of his grip. See Sincere was always a bitch-ass nigga. He would fight a girl, but you see he would have never approached Ke if Omar was around because he knew Omar would have whooped his ass or even worse, killed him. He had barely made it out of the hospital for fighting for his life for snitching and now he thinks he can torment her life because she moved on from him.

Once he let her go, Ke ran to get into her car. Sincere pulled out a gun and pointed it at her. Ke's heart dropped to her fucking feet. Her lips were trembling as her eyes welled with tears. He was aiming the gun directly at her chest and then at her belly. She could not let him kill another one of her kids nor could she let him kill Omar's baby.

"Sincere, what are you doing!" she screamed as her hands guarded her belly.

"You belong to me, bitch. You think I'ma sit and let you have a baby by another nigga?" he questioned.

Ke was scared and prayed to God in her head that he would get her out of this. Prayed to God that Omar would show up. Something! All those times of her thinking to commit suicide were staring her right in her face. "Now you can go visit your dead brother and father. This the same gun I used to kill your cry-baby ass brother, too," Sincere spat and Ke froze.

Sincere pulled the trigger twice, hitting Ke with both shots.

CHAPTER
FIFTY-FIVE

KE IMMEDIATELY FELL to the ground due to the impact. Sincere was standing over her with the gun pointed to her head when Sarah came out screaming. Ke had left her jacket and Sarah was trying to catch her before she left.

Sarah's scream caused him to run and when she got to Ke, she found her covered in blood. Ke had tears in her eyes, sweat beads across her forehead and was coughing badly. She was still breathing for now.

"Oh my gosh, call the ambulance!" Sarah screamed. She looked down at Ke and saw fear in her eyes. "Ke, hold on okay? Hold on help is on the way."

By now a crowd had formed. One of the waitresses grabbed Supreme from out of the back of the club and pointed him toward Ke. Supreme had no words for what he saw. Ke was laying there, in a pool of blood from multiple gunshot wounds. He went over to her and told Ke to hang in there as he grabbed her hand. He pulled out his phone and dialed Omar. He didn't answer.

"Fuck!" Come on, O!"

He dialed Trae. Trae picked up and put it on speaker because they were playing pool.

"Yo, yo! Where Omar!" Supreme yelled.

"He's right here, 'Preme, you on speaker. Why are you yelling?" Trae sensed the alarm in his voice and Omar walked up.

"Man, I'm at the club and Ke just got shot!" He broke the news to Omar.

"Nigga, what!" Omar screamed looking for his car keys.

"She on the ground in a lot of blood. I don't know what happened," Supreme stated after hearing the panic in Omar's voice. "The paramedics just pulled up and loaded her up!" Supreme went to his car and proceeded to follow them.

"Is she still breathing? What the fuck happened?" Omar snapped as the fear set in. Flashbacks of his mother and brother popped up in his head. His heart was beating fast and his mind was racing. *This can't be happening.* He started his car with Shaheem and Trae as his passengers.

"Supreme, is she breathing!" Omar yelled.

"They said she got a weak pulse, dawg," Supreme confessed as he shook his head and sighed.

He didn't want to say that shit at all. How could he tell one of his best friends that his pregnant woman had been shot and it's not looking good.

"Oh fuck! Ke!" Omar screamed. "What the fuck man!" Omar yelled and sped through traffic to get to the hospital.

Trae called Tasha and told her to tell Ke's mom and their other friends.

"I'ma follow the ambulance. O, just get to the hospital. She breathing, man. It's faint but she here," Supreme tried to make it better.

He didn't know what happened and prayed Ke made it out alive. *Damn this is fucked up.*

Omar beat the paramedics to the hospital and in the waiting room were Ke's family, Tasha, Angel, Jaz, Kyra, Marvin, Faheem and Bo and Shanna were pulling up. The ambulance came and they rolled Ke toward the entrance. Omar was stuck in his tracks when he saw her on the gurney. It felt like his heart had been stabbed a million times. He felt the lump forming in his throat and the feeling of devastation overcame him. He couldn't stop his tears. She was covered in blood and he couldn't tell where it was coming from.

"Fuck! Baby!" Omar hollered as he coddled her body.

"Omar," Ke whispered with tears streaming down her face while breathing abnormally. "It hurts so bad, baby."

"Ke, you have to fight. Fight for me and the baby! We need you," he said as the tears came down as he continued to coddle her head. "Baby who did this. Give me a name. Please. Who did this!" he begged for any information concerning the matter but Ke passed out. Omar began to panic.

"Ke, no! Baby, no!"

He was grabbing her by her chin and trying to get her to wake up. He was frantic as he kept screaming.

"Sir, we have to get her into a room to operate on her. She's losing a lot of blood!" the paramedic said as they pushed Ke through.

Her mother started screaming at the sight of her baby in that condition. Omar followed the paramedics all the way to the operating room and he tried to go in behind them.

"Sir, you are not allowed in the room while she is being operated on," explained the security guard. Omar snapped and started strangling the man. Bo, Trae, Mel, Supreme and Kaylin tried to get Omar off of him.

"Nigga, this my pregnant fucking woman! The fuck you mean I can't go back there!" Omar yelled as he continued to choke the man and the security guard's eyes were bulging. Carl came over and tried to calm Omar down.

"Son, come on. You have to give them every second to operate on her," his father pleaded. He placed his hands on top of Omar's hand. "Let him go, son. Let them work."

Omar let the man go and stormed away from the room.

"Everyone, we have to have an opportunity to work on her. She is losing a lot of blood and we need all the time we can get. Please calm down," the doctor pleaded.

Omar started punching the walls and Trae, Kay, Bo, Mel, and Supreme had to calm him down again.

"Omar! Chill, man. She gon' make it. Ke is strong and she a fighter, man. Calm down," they said to him, but he couldn't.

The love of his life was fighting for her life and their baby's life. How the fuck could he calm down when she got shot and he didn't know shit about what happened. He couldn't lose her. He would lose his mind. She was everything to him. Their baby was everything to him. Omar was heartbroken and broke down crying right there with his brothers for life around him. They all embraced him.

"I can't lose her man," he sobbed. "I can't take this fucking pain!"

"I know," Trae said trying to remain positive. He remembered how bad it was when Omar's mother, his aunt, passed away. He took it hard and knew Omar would paint the city red once he found out who did this to Ke. And he had his back every step of the way.

Four hours later, they were still operating on her. Omar was getting even more worried. His hands were covered in blood from when he held Ke. That shit enraged him even more. Her mother, siblings and grandmother were also frantic. Her friends were crying and cried even harder when they saw how Omar was taking it.

Sarah and Mr. Jose walked in. Sarah was who made the call to the ambulance and they had to stay back to talk with the police. She explained to the police that she found Ke laying on the ground from the gunshot wound. That wasn't true but she didn't want to tell the police anything else because she wanted whoever did this to suffer from street justice.

"Hey, if y'all have a minute, I need to show y'all something," said Sarah.

She pulled out a bunch of club photos that people take and never come pick up. "The man that shot Ke looked so familiar and I know I've seen him in the club before," she stated. She thumbed through the pictures and found the one she needed. "It's him! This is the man!" she yelled with tears in her eyes.

Ke was one of her good friends. She couldn't believe this was happening to her and wanted to do all she could to help her.

The men looked at the picture. Angel, Kyra, Tasha, and Jaz gasped and placed their hands over their mouths.

"That's Sincere! Oh god, he did this to her?" stated Kyra as they looked at a picture of Sincere, Rayzo, and two other guys.

"Sincere? What!" Omar grabbed the picture. "This nigga did this shit to her?" Omar was furious. He couldn't wait to get his fucking hands on that piece of shit. "What the fuck! He beats on her, he kills his seed she was carrying, and now he does this shit?" he said. "I'ma body that fucking nigga!' he yelled.

Mr. Jose came forward. Ke was for sure like a daughter to him and he remembered how Ke and Sincere used to fight in the club parking lot years ago. In fact, it was his evidence that helped the lawyers in Ke's case prove she was a battered woman.

"I have footage if you would like to see. I told the detectives that I had no surveillance for that area of the parking lot but, I will show *you*," Mr. Jose stated.

He watched the video and it brought tears to his eyes to see a man shoot Ke in cold blood like that. The nurse waltzed up with her clipboard for updates.

"The bullets were successfully dislodged everyone," she stated. "She was shot twice. Two times in the shoulder approximately an inch away from each other. Due to her iron being low she has lost a lot of blood and the doctor is struggling to stabilize her." Omar's heart dropped. "She is fighting hard though. The heartbeats from the *babies* are also still strong."

"Wait. Babies?" asked Mrs. Harris. Everyone was silent.

"Wait, are we having twins?" Omar questioned.

"No, sir. You're actually having triplets!"

Everyone took a deep gasp. It was like that scene from *Soul Food* when everybody found out Faith fucked the husband. The family was shocked. Triplets. Three babies.

"What! Are you serious!"

That made Omar that much anxious and that much worried about Ke making it out alive. She was carrying three of his children and he needed her there. This was a blessing, but it wouldn't mean shit if Ke didn't survive.

"Yes. We found her heartbeat and three additional heartbeats coming from her uterus. As long as her heartbeat is going, theirs will go. She is about ten weeks pregnant and these are crucial times for miscarriages. She is a fighter though," she reiterated and assured everyone. "A woman petite like her, pregnant with triplets and has an iron deficiency has the odds set up against her if something like a gunshot wound was added to that equation. She is fighting and you all should be proud," the nurse said and left.

"Nigga, you got three babies!" Trae stated.

Everyone was shocked but excited for Omar and Ke. Carl was in tears. Omar was an only child from his father and if Ke made it out alive, there would be three grandchildren. He was overjoyed. Omar went outside and viewed Mr. Jose's camera of the incident. He was starting to second guess a lot of shit.

"Trae, why would this nigga shoot her? Ke better not had been fucking around with him," Omar warned.

On top of that, he started analyzing shit and realized that he and Ke did go about three weeks without speaking to each other. Did she creep with Sincere during that time?

"Why would you think she was creeping with him?" Trae asked, confused as they walked outside.

"Yeah O, you ain't thinking!" explained Kaylin who was the most levelheaded.

"Because. I asked her who did this to her and she passed out. Now the whole time it was an ex?" Omar stated. "Shit ain't making sense, yo!"

"I don't think Ke was on them type of times and especially not with him. The nigga might've just shot her just to do it," Kaylin stated. "Then nigga, she passed out due to blood loss. Her adrenaline pumping, heart beating, blood level going down and her iron low. She had a lot of shit working against her," Kaylin explained and Trae assured him, trying to keep his cousin focused.

"Yeah. Yeah. Let me stop over analyzing this shit," Omar said.

They viewed the camera footage of the incident and heard the audio. The audio got rid of all Omar's insecurities but he was sick to his stomach. He watched as Sincere choked Ke and she fought back. She was really giving his ass a run for his money. Once he pulled the gun out he saw the terror in Ke's face. Omar was boiling hot.

The fuck wrong with niggas not knowing how to treat a female but then refuse to let anyone else treat them right. He was so fed up with domestic violence. He lost his mom to that shit and refused to lose Ke and their three babies to it. Omar's heart really started jumping when he saw Sincere stand over Ke and point the gun to her head. Thank God Sarah stopped that shit right on time.

"Omar! Omar!" Ke's mother screamed. "The doctor is here."

The men ran back inside the hospital for the news.

"Her heart stopped-" said the doctor and Omar blacked out.

CHAPTER
FIFTY-SIX

"SIR! YOU HAVE TO CALM DOWN!" Omar was charging at the staff, throwing chairs, and hearing the doctor say Ke's heart stopped was unbearable.

He felt deranged and felt his body losing control. Security was scared to interfere due to him strangling one of the guards earlier, so the men were left to try and calm down an amped up Omar.

"Her heart stopped beating but we got her pulse back up!" The doctor screamed.

"Oh God!" Her mother and grandmother screamed.

"She is now stabilized. She's stable!" He explained while looking directly at Omar and placing his hand on his shoulder. "She's breathing and the babies are doing well."

The doctor was relieved. If he had any bad news, he was sure that Omar would have killed him.

"She is still asleep from the anesthesia but should be waking up within the next hour. Please give her the necessary rest she needs. This was for sure a miracle."

The doctor looked directly at Omar. "Sir, I will not take your anger personally. I lost my sister to gun violence and this is why I chose to be a trauma doctor. I will do everything in my power to help any gunshot victim. I know how bad those emotions can be," the doctor stated while nodding his head. "Congrats on your triplet babies. That is a rare blessing!"

Omar thanked him for saving Ke and even apologized to the security guard for choking him. He felt like a weight was just lifted from his body.

CHAPTER
FIFTY-SEVEN

THEY MOVED Ke to a bigger room on the upper level. An ultrasound technician would be up there to check on the babies and she would be staying at the hospital for the next week until the doctor felt she was healed enough to be discharged.

Everyone anxiously waited around for the anesthesia to wear off because Ke was unaware that she was carrying triplets and they wanted to see her face when they told her the news. Omar's mind was set on finding where the fuck Sincere was. He was going to make him pay for this shit. He had so many questions for Ke, too. For starters, how could Sincere possibly pick this perfect time to do this to her? Was it luck? Had he been stalking them?

Ke's eyes began to blink, and she tried to lift up on the bed but the pressure she placed on her shoulder was excruciating because of the wounds.

"Ouch!" she screamed and everyone jumped up.

"Oh Keisha!" Her mother ran over to her and kissed on her. "You're here, baby, you're here!" her mother yelled in between tears.

Everyone else followed suit and smothered Ke. They were so relieved she was alive and well. Omar went over to her and hugged her so tight he was choking her.

"You scared the shit out of me!" he said to her as he hugged her even tighter, not wanting to let go.

"I was so scared my damn self," she admitted as tears formed. "I just can't believe this. I felt like death was coming and I was so scared for the baby!" she said as she embraced him back with her healthy arm.

Ke had thought about death many times and she never wanted to experience that again. The nurse came in to check her vitals and her heart rate. The ultrasound technician followed immediately after. Everyone got quiet and Angel pulled out her camera. She had a feeling Ke was going to pass out again when they told her about three babies being inside of her.

"Okay, Ms. Harris, glad to see you! Are you ready to see these little babies?" she asked as she pulled out her ultrasound gel and plugged the machine up.

"What do you mean, 'babies'?" Ke chuckled. "It's one baby."

Ke looked around at everyone and Omar had this big ass Kool-Aid smile plastered across his face. Ke's eyes got big and she froze in fear.

"Wait, why y'all looking like that?!" she questioned. "I'm having twins?" she asked as she got more anxious. "There's no way there's fucking twins in here!" she said as she looked down at her belly and at Omar. "Omar, they said its twins!" she yelled at him and he started laughing.

"Ms. Harris, there's no twins," the ultrasound technician stated. "You're carrying triplets. Three babies!" She smiled at Ke.

"What the fuck! No the fuck it ain't no three babies in here!" she yelled. Everyone was laughing and Ke directed her rage at Omar.

"Omar, what the fuck is so funny? Why would you give me triplets! I agreed on one child, not three. What the hell!"

Her heartbeat started increasing and Omar told her she had to calm down.

"Don't cry now, bitch. You weren't crying when you were getting them babies put in you!" Angel teased.

The best part was that Angel had everything on camera.

"Bitch, you and that damn camera gon' get a beat down when I get up watch!" Ke threatened. "This has to be a joke. Y'all paid her to say it was triplets?" She refused to believe it.

"No baby, it's true. The doctor said they heard three extra heartbeats when you were in surgery," Omar said.

Ke placed her hand over her mouth and the ultrasound technician asked if she was ready to see the babies on the screen. She had to know if they shared a placenta or if the placentas were separate. She lifted up Ke's hospital gown, covered her bottom half with a blanket and placed the gel on her stomach. Everyone looked in amazement as the three babies floated around on the screen, all sharing the same placenta. Ke's eyes watered as she saw her babies on the screen. She saw three sets of little arms sprouting and she even saw her babies' heartbeats. Omar beamed with joy. His three babies had strong hearts just like their mother, he was so proud.

"Baby A is here, Baby B is here and Baby C is right here. These are monochorionic triplets which mean they will be identical and they all share the same placenta," the ultrasound technician went on to explain. "Natural monochorionic triplets are extremely rare and have risks of preterm labor, preeclampsia and transfusion syndrome."

"What is transfusion syndrome?" Ke asked, getting worried.

"It's during a multiple pregnancy. When the babies share a placenta there's a risk that one absorbs most of the nutrients and the other baby or babies are malnourished," she explained. Ke became horrified. "When delivery happens, the malnourished baby can eventually result in a fatality or become permanently handicapped because of not growing well in the womb." Omar absorbed the information and Ke panicked.

"Oh god, no!" Ke sighed and she became flustered. Omar tried to soothe her and assure her that everything would work out.

"Ms. Harris, I know this is scary but that's why prenatal care is extremely important, especially in a rare case like this," the technician stated. "On top of your prenatal visits, they will be recommending you see a specialist to monitor the growth of the babies and to try and prevent any risk factors," she stated. "There are so many women who give birth to absolutely healthy triplets or even quadruplets." She shook her head and rubbed Ke's shoulder. "With all you've been through and the fight you put up, I think you will have a safe pregnancy!" the technician stated as she printed out the photos, packed her machine up and left.

Ke's mother, siblings and grandmother gave her a big hug and everyone began to file out. Omar and Ke were now alone.

"I'm so happy you're here. I don't know what the fuck I would've done if I lost you or my babies," he sincerely stated to Ke.

"I'm so happy to be here. I felt like I saw my life flash," she responded.

She was still shaken up. Ke also heard about what Omar did to the security guard and to the doctor.

"Omar, you know you can't put your hands on people that are trying to help. You had no business charging at the doctor or the security guard," she scolded. "You could have hurt someone, baby or you could have given them less time to do their job,"

"I know, I know, baby. I just couldn't think straight. I got the call that something happened to you and it wasn't looking good," he stated. "They told me I couldn't go back there to be with you and this was after you basically passed out. I felt so disrespected and so fucking distraught!"

"Oh not you feeling disrespected about something and putting your hands on people?" she teased.

He was mad at Ke because she whooped Lucille's ass in the club and he was embarrassed about the club fight. Ke whooped her ass due to feeling disrespected. The irony of it all.

"No baby, yours was different," he laughed. "This was life and death with you! You put your hands on somebody that means absolutely nothing to me."

"Oh whatever. Classic Omar. Can't handle it when it's you," she teased.

"I thought I was gonna lose the love of my life and my child!" he laughed. "Let a nigga slide, Ke."

"Maybe I will. Maybe I won't. But that was unacceptable. You embarrassed all of us with your crazy-ass."

She knew the type of dude Omar was and knew he would handle anybody without a doubt when it came to the people he loved. But the doctors and security guard were only doing their jobs.

"Don't do me like that. I was scared and wasn't thinking," he said as he kissed her.

He was ready to cut to the chase about everything though. He looked at her and asked, "Baby, who did this to you?"

He already knew who did it, but he wanted to see if Ke would tell him the truth. He observed her body language. Her face turned into anger.

"Omar, it was Sincere!" She yelled as flashbacks shot through her mind. "He came up to me when I was leaving, started talking shit, and we started fighting," she explained. "Then once I got him off me and tried to open my car door, he pulled a fucking gun out on me."

Ke was pissed. She hated Sincere.

"All I could think about was you and the baby... Well babies," she honestly stated. "I couldn't let him take away another child from me," she said as she started crying.

Omar felt so bad. His insecurities thought Ke still wanted that nigga. This nigga just thought he would always have access to her and when she showed she can do better he couldn't take it. Typical ain't-shit-ass-nigga.

"I'ma handle that shit baby and he will never be able to do this shit again," Omar said. "If the police come here and ask you about what happened. Say you don't know who did this and can't remember. Don't give them any names."

Omar needed this to remain a mystery for the public. Sincere was a pussy and once his name got over the news, he would disappear and Omar couldn't have that.

"Okay. Okay, baby. I don't want you doing anything that could have you not here with me and our babies. I cannot do this without you and I don't want to." She was scared.

"I won't. I promise," he assured her. "This nigga done did too much harm to you. He can't keep getting away with this shit. And he almost took out my seeds. I told you I would always be there to protect you and mine. I got you. I got us," he stated as he hugged her.

"Ke. Don't judge me for this but I got scared when I caught news that it was Sincere who did this to you." He looked at her. "I thought you was creeping with that nigga."

"Omar," she said, getting annoyed and giving him a nasty facial expression. "Why? Why would you think that? I told you plenty of times I only want you and only need you," she said. "I wouldn't even be keeping these babies if I wasn't in love with you and only you," she honestly stated.

"I know. It just ain't make sense to me why he would come out of nowhere and do this. But shit, I guess the nigga really can't comprehend that you moved on," he stated, "and then he knew you would be at the club alone that night. It was just too much shit happening at once for me to take in but I'm sorry."

"Okay. I forgive you, Omar. I'ma charge that to it was the heat of the moment. But please don't ever fucking think I want anybody other than you! I would just leave you instead of creeping. I don't have time to allow two men to drive me crazy," she teased. Omar wasn't laughing.

"Ke, stop playing with me."

"I'm serious. You think I wanna suck two dicks and give out pussy to two men?" She challenged because she knew she was getting to him. Maybe this will let his ass know to stop thinking she would creep on him.

"Yeah, okay, Ke. There are a lot of things I joke with you about but I ain't joking about what belongs to me," he stated as he looked at her.

"I already told you, I would leave you before I ever decide to cheat. That way we both could be free to do whatever without thinking anything I have belongs to you!" she shot back.

"We ain't never leaving each other," he stated while laughing.

"That sounds good. But if I have to ever leave you, I will. I ain't staying in shit that doesn't make me happy. Love ain't enough no more!"

She loved the shit out of Omar and he made her beyond happy in every aspect of life. But, sometimes love ain't enough to make you stay. She wanted to make sure she is happy and at peace because some niggas will destroy it. Omar gave her no major issues other than his communication sometimes and he was overprotective of her just a tad bit, but everything else was perfect. She was just throwing it out there to him that she wasn't putting up with anything that didn't make her happy.

"Oh, I know. I'm doing everything to make you happy, right? You know you're my everything. I know I can get better at communicating and I know I can ease up on how overprotective I am, but I just don't want shit to happen to you," he stated. "When we ain't together, I do get worried and the fact that you love being alone without anybody to watch your back is scary. I just want you to know I'm here and I care. I love you girl."

"I love you, too. But other than this shooting you know I've pretty much been okay maneuvering my way around everything. I know you got us baby," she said and they kissed.

Her pussy was getting hot. But Omar told her she would have to wait until they got home as he looked at her wound. He promised her once they got home, he would stuff her with so much dick that she was going to be crying tears because of how hard she was going to cum. Her OBGYN visited her and told her everything is normal but her pregnancy is high risk. She said her weight gain is happening at a faster rate and Ke deep sighed because she was not looking forward to that. It was a blessing though. Her and Omar kept saying they landed with triplets because their fallen angels were coming back to them.

CHAPTER
FIFTY-EIGHT

SHE WAS DISCHARGED a week later and Omar was her personal doctor during the entire time she was home. He missed out on some of his drops due to being there for Ke, but Mel and Supreme stepped in for him. He helped bathe her, disinfect her wound, fed her and this nigga was even cleaning. He was washing dishes with a little bit of bleach in the water and bleaching the cabinets after every meal just like Ke liked.

He had been stuffing her with dick as promised. Omar was always extremely touching and affectionate when it came to Ke but since finding out about the pregnancy, he couldn't keep his hands off of her. He was constantly slapping her ass, rubbing her nipples, caressing her hips and trying to give her so much dick.

He kept saying her clit was extra sensitive now and he loved it. He loved licking it, he loved rubbing it and loved tapping his dick on it. *I gotta give a gift to that nigga Trae for putting me on game to that pregnant pussy. Damn!* Omar thought to himself.

Ke was fourteen weeks pregnant and it marked week three of her being discharged from the hospital. Omar was staring at her lotion down after her shower. Her skin was glowing, her belly was poking out, and he was happy he still had her.

"Marry me, Keisha. You are my world. You and my kids are my whole heart. I can't imagine loving anybody else like I love you. Too much near death shit has happened and it ain't no need for us to wait. Marry me," he said as he pulled out a beautiful white gold princess cut diamond engagement ring. He walked toward her and got on one knee.

"Oh my goodness!" she screamed as she looked at him and paused before she gathered her thoughts.

She was butt-ass naked and still holding the lotion bottle. "All the times you've came through for me, I'd want nothing more than to have your last name. Of course I'm going to marry you. You've been my husband," she giggled as they kissed.

"I also got something else for you. You're carrying my babies and it's only right I get y'all somewhere to live that can fit everyone," he told her as he handed her a document while she put her robe on. She was puzzled looking at the papers. "This is our home plan. I purchased two acres of land on the outskirts. You wanted generational wealth and generational curses broken and I told you I was going to do that for you. I'm getting us our home built from the ground up. Tell me everything you want and need in our house. Whatever you want, I'ma get it, baby."

"What? Are you serious?" Keisha said with tears in her eyes. "Omar," she cried. What the fuck did she do to ever deserve a love so sweet. He had his flaws but one thing about it, he was as real as they fucking came.

"Dead serious," he told her. "Sign your name on the deed to our land," he handed her a pen. "Then when you take my last name, we'll just update it. This is how much I love you, girl. I'm getting you your own house built from the ground up and we ain't even legally married yet. You got my heart," he laughed. He started rubbing on her dark nipples and leaned in for a kiss.

"I love you baby," she told him in between kisses.

"How much you love me? You love me enough for my dick to touch that throat," he smirked. "Your throat been neglecting me."

"Nigga, I've literally been healing from a gunshot wound and off pain meds. I didn't have the energy to choke on yo dick," she joked back as he grabbed her hand and placed it on his dick.

"You got the energy now. I want extra spit and extra tears while you chokin' on it. You know what I like," he taunted. Ke started kissing on his neck and planted kisses on his chest while rubbing his dick up and down.

"Yeah. I know what *my husband* likes," she said as she dropped to her knees and talked to his dick. After she finished, he made her pussy cry and put her to sleep.

A FEW HOURS went by and Ke was sleep while Omar was downstairs talking with his crew.

"We got that nigga surrounded O. Should have his ass ready by tomorrow," stated Bo.

Omar was relieved. They finally got Sincere and he couldn't wait to pull his machete out again.

"Good," Omar stated as he rubbed his hands together. "This shit gonna be so satisfying watching this nigga bleed out."

He couldn't wait to stare into the eyes of the nigga who caused all this bullshit to happen to Ke. She came down the stairs and all the fellas gave her a concerned look.

"What's wrong, baby? You need more of your pain meds? The babies okay?" he asked, surveying her.

Her pain meds had been knocking her out, so this was unexpected for her to be up.

"Omar, I want to be the one who gives that nigga the kill shot," Ke stated.

Everyone took a deep breath. She looked at Omar as her eyes welled up and he looked back at her with a crazed confused look.

"No. That's too dangerous!" he snapped. "You're not even fully healed and you're pregnant."

"He tried to take everything from me. I have to do something," she cried.

"I'll handle it. You don't have to do anything. I got us. I told you this," Omar explained as his anxiety rose.

He couldn't have Ke out there committing a murder. Things

could easily go left and turn into an ambush or the police get involved. If anybody was gone go down for this, he would. He would always protect her from anything.

"No Omar, you don't get it!" she yelled. "I lost a baby because of him, he killed my brother, I could have lost my life and other babies because of this same nigga!" she screamed.

Everyone was speechless. Ke broke down crying and Omar hugged her. The men went over to make sure Ke was okay and told Omar they would get at him later.

"Baby. I'm not letting you do that," he firmly stated. She just cried.

She cried so much that her breathing was irregular. Omar was torn. He felt this same way about the man who killed his mother, but he couldn't put Ke in danger like that. She ended up going back to sleep and the next day he gave the fellas the rundown. He got dressed in a black sweatsuit and headed to their abandoned warehouse.

CHAPTER FIFTY-NINE

SINCERE WAS BADLY BEATEN and unconscious while hanging by his arms from the ceiling with blood dripping from his nose and lips. Omar approached him with a bottle of rubbing alcohol and dumped it all over him. He screamed in agony as the alcohol attacked his open cuts.

"We finally meet, nigga," Omar smirked as the two men eyed each other.

Sincere was crying and squirming and Omar was trying to figure out what Ke liked about this lame-ass nigga. But this was just Omar examining his competition. His eyes were diluted like a dope-fiend and Omar got the hint that he dabbled in drugs.

"Nigga gon' kill me over some pussy that I had first? I popped the cherry," Sincere mustered up the nerve to say.

Omar cocked his head to the side and punched Sincere in his jaw, breaking it on impact.

"I'm too much of a real nigga to kill you over some pussy. You gettin' handled because you decided to step in between my pussy and my kids! Two things I ain't fucking playing about," he barked as he talked shit to him. "Didn't you just shoot her because you thought the pussy belonged to you?" Omar questioned as he punched him in the other jaw. "You the same nigga that was tricking in the club but tried to keep her put away so you can do your dirt. Bitch-ass nigga."

Omar punched him again and knocked teeth out of Sincere's mouth, causing him to sob.

"I don't give a fuck about what you slid in first. A real nigga handling that heart and pussy now. And I'm putting babies in it, nigga. Is that why you so upset?" he continued to beat the shit out of Sincere's punk ass. "I popped that cherry for a second time and I love when those tight pussy muscles flex on my dick. I love holding her ankles, too. How you feel 'bout that, bitch?" Omar taunted as he physically and verbally bruised Sincere's ego. The same shit Sincere used to do to Ke. Oh, how the tables had fucking turned.

Sincere felt like the size of an ant and he blurted out, "She ran a car through my door and shot a gun at me!"

When Sincere said that Omar yanked him down from the ceiling and started beating the shit out of him. He was screaming like the bitch he was and trying to crawl away but wasn't quick enough for Omar.

"Nigga, she ran the car through your shit because you killed her fucking baby!" he stated.

Sincere was still crying. Omar headed off to the side and grabbed his handy dandy machete, which was his tool of choice for muthafuckas that didn't know how to stop hitting women. He walked back to Sincere while clutching the machete.

"Please, Omar please," Sincere pleaded as he coughed up blood.

Omar stepped on his hand, raised the machete, and forcefully sliced it through Sincere's trigger finger and his thumb. He screamed to the top of his lungs as blood leaked out his hand.

"What the fuck! My fingers!" Sincere screamed as he stared at Omar who was smirking at him. "I'm sorry, man. Please don't kill me! I'll never bother y'all again!" Sincere wept through swollen lips and a bloody mouth.

His eye was swollen shut and he had vomited everywhere because of all the blood that was in his mouth. He was feeling lightheaded as the blood kept dripping from his body. Omar sat Sincere in a chair and tied him up. He handed the machete off, pulled his gun out and went to the back. The other men pulled their guns out too when Omar came back out with Ke.

"Oh, Ke. Ke." Sincere wept.

His name never came out in the media in regard to the club shooting so he thought he got away with harming her again. Ke was disgusted by his appearance. Omar fucked him up so bad and if he would have taken one more punch, he might have died from being beat to death. Her stomach was hitting somersaults as she saw his fingers on the ground. *What the fuck.*

"I ain't gon' kill you and you need to be lucky because I was gon' tear you limb from limb," Omar stated and then directed his energy to Ke.

"Option one, machete. Option two, .9 mm Glock 19," he showed her the two weapons and Ke looked at his ass like he had lost his mind.

"This is not medieval times," she deep sighed as she shook her head. *The fuck! This nigga is crazy as hell. Why the fuck would I need a damn machete,* Ke thought to herself.

"Now ain't the time for that smart-ass mouth," Omar countered and Ke took a deep breath and grabbed the Glock.

Her nerves were starting to get the best of her and she didn't know if she could pull the trigger. Sincere looked at her and she smelled fear on him.

"Ke, you don't have to do this! Turn the gun and shoot him instead," Sincere pleaded. "I'm sorry about the baby. Please, Ke. I'm sorry for putting my hands on you!"

The other men put their fingers on the trigger and prayed she didn't let this nigga sway her mind about anything.

"Nigga, you can't be serious!" Ke spoke. "I don't give a fuck about what you have to say," Ke said. "You took away my unborn, my brother, and tried to take me out and my other unborns! Sorry could never fix that."

Ke aimed the gun at Sincere's chest and he pissed on himself. Omar helped straighten up her aim a little by placing his hand on the gun and centering it a little more. They had been going to the gun range so he knew Ke was going to hit her target.

"Two in his chest and one in the head, Ke," Omar instructed. "She won't miss this time either!" He looked at Sincere and added insult to the injury.

Ke missed every shot she took when she first shot at Sincere. She did as she was told and let off two bullets in Sincere's chest and one to his head, killing him then and there. Omar went to reach for the gun and Ke kept shooting at Sincere's body. The other men almost started shooting because they were that on edge.

As Ke emptied the clip until it couldn't go anymore, Omar took the gun from her hands and saw this crazy ass look on Ke's face. Trae walked up to Omar and told him that they had it from there and to go make sure Ke was straight. Omar pulled out his other gun and went over to Sincere and shot him three more times in the head: one for each baby.

He took her to the back room and told her to remove everything she had on. He placed her dirty clothes in the furnace in the warehouse and she switched into something else. He also made her scrub her hands and he did the same. He took her to the car and she was quiet.

"Omar. Can you go to therapy with me?" she stated as she stared into space.

She couldn't believe she had just killed someone and it was eating her up. Omar was there every step of the way and tried to change her mind but she had to do this.

"I'll go anywhere with you, Ke. Anywhere you need me to be," he sincerely stated.

He took her home and laid her down. The fellas called and told him all was clear. They began their therapy sessions three days later and after seven sessions, Ke was back to her normal self. She didn't care that Sincere was dead. That sounds harsh, but he didn't care about her life so why care about his.

But killing someone was not what Ke was about. She was not a murderer and all this gun shit really freaked her out.

CHAPTER SIXTY

AT EIGHTEEN WEEKS PREGNANT, Ke was given the opportunity to finally walk that stage and graduate. Omar beamed with pride watching her grab her degree. Everyone was so happy for her and they were even more ecstatic when he surprised her with a trip to Egypt. Egypt had been her dream vacation for years and she was finally able to see one of the seventh wonder of the world, the pyramids.

They boarded the plane bright and early the next day and embarked on their trip. It was absolutely amazing. Omar enjoyed seeing Ke in her education element and they saw the Pyramids of Giza and the Great Sphinx. They took a tour along the Nile River and Ke explained to Omar this was a huge market place during ancient times and that the Nile was so fertile and important to the Egyptians.

Now, Ke always had to do some thrill seeking shit and she signed them up for a tour of King Tut's Tomb. Omar heavily declined, but Ke forced him to. He did not want to see anything about any mummies, and he was honestly creeped out about what those damn tombs could hold. When inside the tomb, it was amazing he had to admit.

Being that close to the boy king was priceless and Ke had tears in her eyes. The pregnancy made her so emotional but being someone who enjoys history, seeing this tomb was magical to her.

Ke also made Omar visit Queen Nefertiti's Tomb and again, being that close to royalty was priceless. They took a picture right in front of the Great Pyramids and someone told them they were empowering and that, 'the universe would bless them for all the years of their entire lives'.

Ke couldn't thank Omar enough for this. They made love as the lights from the city and the Pyramids pierced into their hotel.

TWO WEEKS after they came home from Egypt, Kaylin and Trae finally were released from jail after disappearing, reappearing and the whole shabang that happened in *Every Thugs Need a Lady*. They were heading out to a small engagement party for Kaylin and Angel since Angel's ass loved to throw celebrations.

"Baby, do we have enough time for a quickie," said Omar as he rubbed his dick on Ke's ass and had his hand on her growing five month belly.

"No, we don't. The doctor said no more than two or three times a week for sex since I'm high risk. You've already made me take the dick four times and it's only Wednesday, Omar," she said as she pushed him off her and tried to get out of the bedroom.

"Bend over, Ke," he demanded as he went up her dress to find her pussy.

"Omar, no!" she yelled but he was pressed up against her.

He bent her over the dresser and moved her panties to the side. He pulled his dick out and placed the head to her vaginal opening. He thrusted inside of her and let out a deep breath as her pussy sucked him in.

"Fuck. Ke," he moaned. "I'm about to cum already," he said as he tapped on her spot.

She lifted her leg up, put her head all the way down on the dresser and arched her back.

"Fuck me with that big-ass dick, daddy," she purred and Omar was going crazy as his dick pounded inside of her. "You love this pussy. It's all yours," her legs started to shake and she came all over his dick. Omar came soon after.

"You and my kids, my whole world. I love y'all so much," he said in her ear.

"We love you too, baby," she said as she pushed him out of her pussy and tried to go wash up.

"My dick back hard, Ke," he said as he kissed her neck.

"Omar, I swear this is my last time carrying any more of your kids. You need to really slow down. My hips can't take all this damn movement," she complained as he kissed her on her neck.

"I can't help it," he said as he laughed, laid her on the bed and entered Ke missionary. They were finished fifteen minutes later, took another shower and headed out.

Angel and Kaylin's wedding date was set a year and a half from now. Everyone was having a good time at their engagement party and Omar made a joke that Ke couldn't drink until after her pregnancy. He was serious, too. He had just kissed her when the police barged in with papers.

"Omar Gaulding!" they shouted. He was looking at them. He started to go into a trance because he assumed this Sincere shit caught up to him. "You're under arrest for the murder of Raymond "Rayzo" Latchbark." Omar was confused as the police put the cuffs on him. They received a tip but... that will be revealed in **Thug Series Phase II: Bo.**

Ke looked on in horror and tried to get in the middle. The other men gathered around and were trying to diffuse this.

"Wait, what? Rayzo?" Omar yelled. "I ain't do shit to no fucking Rayzo!" Omar yelled as he tried to resist but his dad told him to stop and just go.

Omar looked at Ke and told her to calm down. She was crying and felt like her heart was coming out of her chest.

"Omar!" she said with tears. "Baby, what's going on?"

"Stop crying, Ke. You can't stress the babies out. I'ma figure this out!" he said as he was being led into the patrol car.

There was five cars with their flashing lights on out there. Ke followed them to the police car and was trying to hold onto Omar, but they moved her and stuffed him into the backseat.

"No, you can't leave me, Omar! No."

She grabbed the door handle and Omar told her to calm down again. Trae and Bo went to get Ke and kept her back and told her they would figure out what's going on. The police had their hands on their holsters and when everyone backed away, they sped off.

"Please, please, Omar."

Ke ran to her car and followed the police. At the station, they explained to them that Omar was held for the murder of Rayzo.

"Yo, what the fuck? I ain't know Rayzo was dead!" Trae screamed. "I know O ain't do this shit."

"Hell naw he didn't!" Bo said, shaking his head.

They drove to Omar's father's house and that's where Ke was. She was at the kitchen table blowing her nose and her girls were gathered around trying to soothe her. Trae and Bo walked over to Ke.

"We gonna figure this out, Ke."

She just stared at them. She wasn't comprehending what was going on. Her phone rang and it was a collect call from Omar. She accepted the charges and heard his voice and tears came down her face.

"Ke, where are you?"

"I'm at your dad's house," she said while crying then put the phone on speaker.

"Baby, I don't know what's going on at the moment but I'm gon' figure this shit out. Before anything happens, I need you to calm down and breathe, okay?" Omar tried to soothe her.

They were charging him with murder, Ke was five months pregnant with the triplets and if she didn't relax she could cause an unnecessary pre-term labor.

"Are the guys there?"

"Yeah, we here, O. I'ma call the lawyer first thing in the morning. You know we got Ke," replied Trae.

"I spoke to my lawyer already. He will be in tomorrow morning. He said he thinks I'm eligible for a bond hearing so we'll see how that goes and see whatever evidence they got."

"Okay, call me tomorrow as soon as the lawyer gets there," Trae stated.

"I will. Ke can you hear me?"

She grabbed the phone and took it off speaker.

"Yes," she sniffled.

"I love you. Stay with your mom or my father tonight. I will call back in a few before these phones turn off."

"Okay. I love you too," Ke said as she felt sick to her stomach.

She didn't want to do anything but be with Omar. She didn't want to stay in anybody else's house. When it was time for bed, she cried herself to sleep while holding her belly. She needed her man there with her. She needed him for this pregnancy. She needed him, period.

CHAPTER SIXTY-ONE

THE FOLLOWING DAY, Omar's name was called to the meeting room because his lawyer, Lewis Shosh was there. He was one of the best defense attorneys New York had to offer. Omar knew he didn't commit the crime, so this had to be a misunderstanding. The guard brought him out with his arms shackled as he directed him to the table.

His attorney was dressed in a black suit and was a Black man who had been practicing law for twenty years. Omar sat down and Mr. Shosh began talking.

"Mr. Gaulding you're being held for the murder of Raymond Latchbart, who was found dead in his home on Saturday, July 12th. He was noted to have been dead for several weeks before his body was discovered. His mother sent the police over for a well visit and they found him shot dead," Mr. Shosh stated and looked at Omar.

"That's insane. How did they think to arrest me?" Omar asked, now even more confused.

He didn't even know where Rayzo laid his head and even though Rayzo tried to push up on Ke, Omar would not have committed a murder this messy. For starters, why didn't whoever did this get rid of the body?

"Well. You and Mr. Rayzo were on surveillance getting into

an altercation," he stated and followed with, "An altercation where you pulled out a gun."

Omar froze. He remembered that day. "Yes, we got into an altercation but he was breathing after that altercation."

"That altercation, according to the surveillance, was several weeks ago," Mr. Shosh explained as he shook his head.

He hated having to see so many Black men on trial for murder. Guilty or innocent, he hated seeing it.

"I didn't commit this crime!" Omar yelled and found himself getting angry.

He hated when he was telling the truth and it appeared to be a lie. He didn't kill Rayzo and based on a fight they were trying to say he did. The hell is up with this justice system.

"Mr. Gaulding, I didn't say you did," he stated while looking at him. "I am going to do all I can to help you. I just had to tell you what the reason was for your arrest," he said. "They are going to deny your bail based on the fact that you pulled your gun out on him prior to him being found dead. I will meet up with you soon. Let me work."

He got up and left. Omar was crushed. He called Trae and told him the news. Trae told him he would keep his ear out to the streets to figure out what the fuck was going on. He then dialed Ke.

"Ke. You okay, baby?"

"I'm doing as best as I can. Are you okay?" Her voice cracked and she felt the tears forming.

"You gotta stop crying, okay? I know this shit is unexpected but it will work out," he responded, trying to be positive.

He always tried to tell her not to let little things get to her and he knew he had to stay in good spirits so her overthinking wouldn't trigger.

"How? I'm pregnant with your three sons. You're not here. You could be gone for a long time. I can't stop crying!" she snapped and felt her emotions taking over.

"I get that, but I don't wanna be in here, Ma. You have to

keep your composure," he shot back. She was silent after that. "When is your next doctor's appointment to check on the boys?"

"Why? You won't make it so why do you need to know?" she rudely replied.

She didn't want to say that but she was so annoyed. How could he let himself get caught up behind some bull shit like this. She was gonna ride for him with no questions but damn, she had to feel her emotions.

"Ke. Don't fucking start!" he barked between clenched teeth. "I know you're upset but look at my situation. Don't start with that slick-ass attitude shit," he warned.

"Okay. Okay," she said between sniffles.

She hated when she couldn't control her mouth. She ended up getting herself together and she told him about her appointment. Omar told her about why they were holding him and she said she believed he didn't do it. That was a relief to him.

He went back to his cell after the call ended and thought about what could possibly be going on. He knew for a fact he didn't do this crime but who did and why did they want Omar to take the fall.

CHAPTER
SIXTY-TWO

OMAR HAD BEEN in jail for four weeks and was missing Ke something serious. She was coming to visit today. His lawyer also came to visit him, but he had bad news. There was a water bottle present at the scene that had Omar's DNA on it.

"What! No way!" Omar yelled as he pounded the table.

His lawyer showed him a picture of the water bottle and a paper confirmation of Omar's DNA matching. This places him at the scene.

"Man, this some bull shit!" Omar yelled.

His lawyer just stared at him thinking something did seem off.

"Mr. Gaulding, you have to calm down." He took his glasses off and rubbed his forehead. "You have to tell me everything. Give me the information so I can help you," the lawyer stated.

"I told you about the altercation and that was it."

"Why did the altercation happen?"

Omar had to be careful with his words. He did not want Ke involved in this shit at all.

"He disrespected me and I chose to react that way," he replied and Mr. Shosh looked at him. That response made him feel a way. He thought to himself, *How convenient is it that a water bottle with his DNA was placed there?*

"Listen. You're my client and I will represent you. We'll talk in a few days," he stated as he packed up.

He didn't want to tell Omar too much or get his hopes up too high, but he planned on digging further into this case. Some things were just too convenient. Omar left the meeting boiling hot with his face screwed up.

About an hour later, Ke came down to visit. When he saw her he smiled. Her belly was huge and her small frame was still managing to carry the triplets. Her brown skin was glowing. He noticed how juicy her ass was and how wide her hips were getting. Besides the big belly, she still had it going on.

"Baby!" She jumped into his strong arms and he gripped her ass. They kissed and it felt so good to be in his arms after four weeks. They were sick without each other.

"Look at my babies!" he said as he rubbed her protruding belly. "I miss y'all so much!" he said as he hugged her around the waist.

They sat down and Ke got emotional about how defeated Omar was looking. She had been staying with her mother as a direct order from him and she hadn't returned to work at the school yet because he didn't want her doing that while he was locked up and no one to really patrol her.

"What's wrong, baby?" she asked as she grabbed his hands. He was trying to be strong but Ke knew him.

"It ain't looking good, Ke." The minute he said that she started crying. "They found my DNA at the scene." Ke gasped and it felt like she was having a heart attack.

"Omar," she sighed. "Wh… what? How?" she asked, confused.

"I don't know," he admitted, getting frustrated as she kept crying. "Baby, I told you, you gotta calm down. You can't keep crying and stressing out the babies," he firmly stated.

"Omar… this shit is stressing me out!" she cried. "I told you, I cannot do this without you." She was full blown crying and heaving at this point. "I've been getting all your affairs in order, keeping up with your money, rescheduling meetings for your real estate investment, cleaning my place and yours, going to four doctor visits every week and you're making me sleep at someone else's house and you keep telling me not to cry," she went on. "I'm literally overwhelmed with everything that is going on," she sobbed. "Then the babies can technically be born any day now and who knows when you will be home. I need you!" she vented as she looked at him.

"I have you staying places so you won't be alone with your thoughts and be like this all day," he stated.

"Be like what, Omar? Feeling my emotions?" she challenged.

"Yeah. Feeling your emotions. It's a lot to take in, Ke, but.. Nevermind," he said, shaking his head. "Look," he said as he took a deep breath. "You have to calm down and understand I'm telling you this shit for you and the babies sake, Ke."

"Telling me what? You haven't told me anything but bad news and the arrangements I need to make as far as where I'm living."

"Ke. Stop. Stop," he glared at her and she stopped.

Things were getting heated and it wasn't the time for that.

"I may be facing a lot of time but no matter what, I need you here and for my kids to come see me on a daily basis." He followed with, "That's why I need you to stay put like you are so I can keep an eye on you and eventually the kids from my father's or your mother's house and then you bring them to the jail to see me. This gotta be done my way."

"I have no problem coming to see you. I told you I was doing this with you," she sincerely stated. "But I will not be toting three newborn babies up here on a daily basis who could potentially have health issues because they will be born a little early."

That was the truth. Triplet pregnancies don't go full term and he can't possibly expect her to come up here every visiting opportunity with three car seats, three diaper bags and three fresh babies.

"As soon as their immunity is up, I'll figure out the best way to consistently have them come here," she responded and made eye contact with him.

"What the fuck do you mean? I will be a part of my kids' life so you *will* bring them up here. It ain't no debate Keisha. You bringing my kids to wherever I'ma be at, like I just told you," he demanded. "As soon as they leave the hospital, seeing me will be the first stop."

"Omar, do you hear yourself right now and how selfish and controlling you're being for literally no reason?" she questioned while she frowned her lips.

His paranoia about the potential outcome of this case caused him to be so damn controlling and say shit that wasn't logical.

"Listen, okay? I have no problem coming to see you, answering your calls and taking care of whatever you need me to on the outside but Omar, how can I possibly check in with three damn newborns?"

"Do you hear your fucking self? You sound crazy as hell, Ke," he snapped. "I'm not waiting for shit when it come to my seeds. So figure out now what needs to happen," he said while he gave her a mean mug. "If I want my kids everyday all fucking day then that's what's going to happen. You trying not to let me be a part of their lives because I'm in here?"

"Calm down. You're creating an issue that's not even here yet! Why would I not let you be a part of their lives? I don't care that you're here. As long as you're breathing, I will make sure your kids are in your life. I understand you're not in the best situation, but I told you I am with you. I'm here, baby. Please understand that I am not bringing our three newborn children into this dirty-ass place being that they are at risk for health issues. They have to get their immunity stronger first."

She went to reach for his hands, and he snatched away.

"Well how about you just stop coming to see me too then, Ke," he bucked. "Yeah. I'll remove you from my visiting list. I'm over this bullshit. The engagement off, too. I don't care. Call my dad when you go into labor," he stated as he got up.

Ke was wide eyed as she watched him. He could be so hurtful with his words sometimes.

"Omar, seriously?" she was in disbelief about his behavior.

"Dead ass."

"I said I would still come and do this bid with you! The kids will come too after they have a stronger immunity. Can you just think and consider someone else's perspective, please! Why are you acting like this?" Her feelings were hurt and Omar had her on the verge of tears. "This the same overreacting bullshit you pulled after I fought that bitch in the club," she explained.

"Keisha, I'll just take you off my visiting list. No more conversation about this. Do whatever you want to do with the ring. I ain't doing this shit. Last thing I want you to do is feel like you are putting my kids in a bad situation by allowing them to come see their father," he said with a nasty attitude as he looked at her and completely twisted everything around. "I am the father, right? They came from my nut sack, right? Or do you have some other shit going on with another nigga that you finally ready to confess about? Is this enough overreacting for you?" Ke's jaw dropped as he gave her a death stare. This muthafucka was really talking crazy.

"Oh, really, Omar? Watch your fucking mouth! I'm not them trifling-ass bitches you used to deal with. Are you the father? Did they come from your nuts? After you've been begging me to have your babies every time we fuck and choosing to cum in me every chance you got, really? Okay. I'm not going back and forth with you," she stated while the tears streamed down her face. "When the babies are born, we can keep everything strictly about them because I told you about watching what you say when you mad! Engagement off? Cool. This what you want. I'm not going to allow you to talk to me like that."

Omar got up and gave Ke his back to view. She left the jail devastated as she cried her heart out in the car.

He can't get his way with this one damn thing and he acts like this. Ke was so hurt. She would never keep him from his kids and the fact he thought that was ridiculous. But, she already told him about watching what he says when he's upset. When it came to the people he loved, he just felt like he knew what was best. He felt like he knew what was best for his parents and he felt like he knew what was best for Ke and their children.

However, Keisha wasn't scared to use her voice and let his ass know that both parties have to be considered. Her feelings were hurt but she knew her nigga and she had a trick to make his mean-ass swallow his words.

Omar went back to his cell and immediately regretted speaking to Ke the way he did. He definitely begged her to keep the babies, kept releasing himself inside of her, he was excited about the pregnancy and he knew she wasn't fucking anybody else. He said that shit to piss her off because he was mad. He was getting paranoid about his case and just wanted to be sure he would still be able to see his kids and be a part of their lives. He was missing the pregnancy and didn't want to miss any parts of their lives. He had to get out of that damn jail.

He rarely got paranoid because that could cost you your life in the streets. But when it came to that muthafuckin' Keisha, he couldn't help but to let the paranoia consume him and then he started saying dumb shit he didn't mean and doing dumb shit he would normally never do.

CHAPTER
SIXTY-THREE

KAYLIN, Bo and Trae came to visit Omar two weeks later. Mel and Supreme kept their ears to the streets. He explained to them the situation with Ke and told them to just make sure she was good. They called him a dumb-ass for even telling her not to come see him and they told him it would be more trouble for her to get all the babies there by herself. Bo told him he can't get mad when the control ain't in his hands when it comes to Ke. He felt like shit, but they did have some uplifting news for him.

"So get this," Kaylin stated. "How about Rayzo was at the club the night Ke got shot." Omar looked towards him. "Word around town is that Rayzo on a lot of niggas paperwork!" Kaylin stated.

"Yeah, remember how the feds got tipped off about our last drop?" Trae whispered. "Well supposedly they got a tip from an informant and the damn informant was Rayzo!" Trae said as the men were in disbelief about what was unfolding.

"But how could Rayzo know?" Omar asked, still confused.

"See now here is where things get tricky," Kaylin paused. "So the night Ke got shot was on camera and the next day was the day detectives say was when Rayzo got killed based on the decomposing stage of his body." Kaylin said. "So we asked Mr. Jose for the camera footage of that night from inside the club."

"Mmmhmm," Omar mumbled, letting Kay know to keep the story going.

"Minutes before Ke got shot, Rayzo made a phone call," Kaylin said.

"Now this can all be a coincidence but remember you said you were wondering how Sincere knew Ke would be alone?" Bo asked. "Sincere and Rayzo are listed on a few niggas paperwork together!" Bo dropped a bomb on Omar. "So we thought to ourselves, no fucking way these niggas are dumb enough be interacting on camera together but seems like they were that dumb," Omar was starting to piece things together.

"We asked Mr. Jose for footage of the club for the past two months and we saw Rayzo make several phone calls toward the end of Ke's shift, but most of the time, you were there O or she walked out with the rest of the bartenders. The time she got shot was when she left out early so she was alone," Bo continued. "The only thing that ain't sitting right with me is how and why these niggas was lurking in the club in the first place. They've been prancing their snitching asses around for weeks. They came out of nowhere," Bo said because he was adamant on finding the answer to that. "And it doesn't make sense how they found you at the engagement party. There's a lot of questions still needing answers," said Bo as he thought about everything.

"We think Rayzo gave Sincere the word that Ke was alone," Kaylin stated. "They were even seen talking to each other in the back of the club one night after you and Ke left. Rayzo was always making a phone call around Ke's shift and this shit was too coincidental!" Kaylin stated. "We think Sincere popped Rayzo, prolly thinking he was going to snitch on him if Ke didn't make it out alive."

Kay had valid points and Omar was speechless. He still had questions though.

"Yo. This shit makes perfect sense but number one, where is Rayzo's phone? Number two, they got my DNA from a water bottle and that's what's tying me to this case!" Omar stated. "I need my lawyer to know that two informants were in cahoots, and one is trying to frame me." The men nodded their heads. "But I can't have Ke's name mentioned in this. They can't know she was shot that night because then they might try to look into Sincere's disappearance then pull up Ke's attempted murder case that she beat against him."

They all agreed. If they mentioned Ke at all then they might be setting Omar free just to have Ke sitting in his place.

"We got you dawg, hang tight, ok? We got you," they said.

They hugged Omar and left. He felt hopeful and it was like a weight had been lifted off his body. He decided to call Ke and apologize but she didn't answer. He was pissed and getting worried. He tried calling her a few moments later but again, she refused to answer. He knew he had been an asshole but damn he wanted to speak to her.

CHAPTER
SIXTY-FOUR

A WEEK LATER, Omar's lawyer came back to visit and explained to him that their trial would be set five weeks from now. He was getting scared because Ke still refused to answer his calls and she would be around thirty-four weeks pregnant on the trial date. Which is around the time her doctor says the triplets will have to be delivered by to avoid labor complications. Omar had to get out of there before then.

His lawyer also had some good news. He explained that he got the officers to issue another warrant to search inside the home of Rayzo. There was a Federal Authority folder hidden. The folder had pictures of every snitch across the east coast but the ones that stuck out to Mr. Shosh were the ones from New Jersey and New York. He gave Omar Sincere's name, Terrel's name, and two other dudes who were named for snitching.

"Mr. Shosh, are you able to get a copy of Rayzo's phone record to add to my case? If someone murdered him at his home, then they most likely had a phone conversation prior, right?" Omar asked, seeing if his lawyer was on the job.

"I tried, Mr. Gaulding. His phone was nowhere to be found," he stated. "But don't worry. I am working. Being that he was an informant can prove that multiple people were after him."

A FEW DAYS LATER, Trae and Kaylin were at the lounge watching Mr. Jose's surveillance video. They couldn't believe what they saw. On the screen was Omar taking a sip of his water bottle while sitting at the bar having a conversation with Ke. He then left the bar and headed toward the exit door. Rayzo swiftly took Omar's water bottle when Ke's back was turned and proceeded to have a conversation with her before he head out to make a phone call.

Omar called Trae and Kaylin to update them on what the lawyer had said. They then updated him about what they saw on the camera. They kept watching the videos while Omar was on the phone and got to the day Ke was shot. Rayzo made a phone call and then Trae noticed that he left his phone at the bar.

"Wait! Omar, you said the lawyer couldn't find his phone right?" Trae asked.

"Yeah, he said they couldn't."

"He left his phone at the club that night! I see it right here on the counter in the video!" Trae said.

"Oh shit! Ask the bartender or ask Ke where they keep that lost phone bin at and see if his is there!"

Omar remembered Ke telling him they have a lost phone bin for drunk customers that leave their phones. This could be the proof he needed. Trae asked Sarah and she found all the phones with that date on them. They found Rayzo's phone because he had a big "R" on his phone case.

They turned the phone on and found voicemails Sincere left, messages from Sincere and a phone call that was placed minutes before Ke got shot. One of the voicemails was Sincere telling Rayzo to not forget to get a DNA sample while he was in the club. There was also a message to Sincere from Rayzo giving him his home address. These had to be the dumbest niggas in the world.

"Oh! we got it nigga!!

"Take it to my lawyer, now!"

By this point, Mr. Jose came out. He told the men that he would call the police and let them know they found his phone so that Trae and Kaylin could avoid getting deeper into this. That seemed like the logical route and he did just that. The police confiscated his phone and allowed the defense and the prosecution to review it. Each side was feeling good about the cases they had to present.

IT HAD BEEN four weeks and Omar had a week before his trial and decided to call Ke. She was thirty-three and a half weeks pregnant and he missed hearing her voice. He tried to avoid missing any time from her pregnancy and it seemed like his actions led to just that, him missing time. She answered the call, shockingly, and accepted the charges.

"Ke. Baby, you good?" he asked. He didn't know what to say because he knew she was still pissed.

"I'm in labor, Omar," she blurted out and tried to hold her composure from the hospital bed but giving birth was terrifying her.

"What? Are they coming today?" Omar asked as his heartbeat rose.

"Sometime tonight. No later than tomorrow. I left my doctor's appointment and they admitted me to the hospital. I'm scared." Her voice dripped with worry. "I thought I would be able to finish this week out."

"Baby, don't be scared. Call my dad and make sure he's there," Omar said as he took a deep breath. "Fuck! I'm sorry for putting us in this shit. I don't wanna miss my seeds take their first breath," he explained and banged on the wall.

"I'll be okay," she mustered, trying to stay positive.

"I'm sorry for everything, Ke. I'm sorry about how I spoke to you and accused you of fucking around. I can't believe I'm not there with you," he told her and a lump formed in his chest. "Everything I tried to avoid is just smacking me in the face anyway. You know I need you though, baby. I miss you. I love you."

"I love you too. Omar, call me back in about twenty minutes. I have to start getting prepped for my C-section,"

Omar didn't want to hang up. He called his father and he told him he was already headed to the hospital. Ke was now under anesthesia for her C-section and she was knocked out. Omar stayed on the phone until they cut them off and the babies were born overnight. He didn't get a chance to hear their first cries and that devastated him. Omar's father was on the phone with him the following morning while he was visiting his grandchildren.

He was overjoyed hearing his sons make baby noises, but it was bittersweet. Ke was filled with all types of emotions. She loved looking at her three baby boys but wished Omar was there in the flesh to share this moment.

"When you see them, you're going to be so happy. They are the spitting image of you already. They even got your chocolate skin and they aren't even a day old yet," Ke said over the phone while she held her babies.

"I can't wait to hold and kiss y'all. Damn. This shit got me fucked up. I can't believe I'm listening to my sons breathe through a jail phone," he vented as he shook his head. "I'm praying this trial rules in my favor and I make it out. I'm feeling good about it,"

They continued to talk and Omar's heart was melting hearing his sons coo through the phone.

CHAPTER
SIXTY-FIVE

SIX DAYS LATER, it was the day of the trial. The judge came out and the lawyers stated their case and evidence. Omar's lawyer presented the phone records and the surveillance tape of Rayzo grabbing Omar's water bottle and then disappearing.

Rayzo grabbed the water bottle at Sincere's request because Sincere told him they needed it to tip the feds off. This information was found in the Federal Informant folder that was hidden at Rayzo's home.

Sincere's plan was to get Omar locked up on drug charges with that DNA but he used it to frame him for murder when he killed Rayzo, assuming Rayzo was going to snitch on him about Ke's shooting. Neither tape that was presented had Ke in them.

Omar's lawyer also had surveillance from the night Rayzo was killed. A car registered to Sincere Washington was on camera pulling up to Rayzo's house and ten minutes later was found speeding off. Omar was so anxious seeing that and they all held their breath as the judge gave his verdict. There were many components to this case but the defense focused on the issue at hand, did Omar murder Rayzo?

"In the case of Omar Gaulding versus The State of New York in the murder case of Raymond Latchbert, the defendant is found NOT GUILTY. Court is adjourned."

Omar was beaming and couldn't wait to be processed out. All his family were there waiting and greeted him with hugs. Omar's mind was focused on Ke and his kids. Once he was processed out, his dad drove him to the hospital and he was overjoyed with emotions as he waited to meet his sons.

CHAPTER SIXTY-SIX

OMAR WAS at the door to Ke's hospital room, and he heard her talking. He had butterflies in his stomach because it had been so long since he last saw her.

"Mama be for real. Are my babies ugly? You can tell me."

Ke surveyed her sons and couldn't believe how some seven day old babies looked just like a grown-ass man. Omar walked through the door and Ke just stared at him. It didn't feel real.

"Am I ugly, Ke? You said the babies look like me, so do you think I'm ugly?" he teased.

Ke wanted to get up and hug him, but she couldn't, all she could do was cry.

"What's the only time you can cry, Ke? My dick is not touching the back of that throat right now so stop with all this crying," he whispered as he watched her hold two babies and searched for the other one. Mrs. Harris then brought baby number three over to the reunited couple.

"Baby!" she yelled while he leaned in for a kiss. "You beat the case? This feels so surreal!"

"I did. I'll tell you all about it later, okay?" She nodded. "I'm so happy right now. Let's enjoy this moment," he told her and relished in the moment of his family being complete.

Omar kept whispering to Ke how much he loved her and

how overjoyed he was. He even kept joking about how he was going to stuff dick so deep in her when she healed that she was going to end up pregnant with another set of triplets. Ke didn't think that was funny at all.

Everyone fell in love with the handsome chocolate baby boys and Tasha and Trae revealed that they were also having multiples, twins. Trae joked that it must be a family thing to produce more than one baby.

Aunt Marva and Nana, Trae's mom, were in tears as they saw the triplets. They told Omar his mother would be in love with them. Aunt Marva and Nana both said that they were coming over to help care for the children and Ke until she could manage. Family and a support system for babies are truly priceless.

The doctor came back in and told Ke that she would have to stay in the hospital for another week and the babies would stay for another month to monitor their progression. This was standard procedure. Omar and Ke were sad to go home without their babies, but they came to the hospital every day. Ke's milk supply was abundant so she was recommended to breastfeed and the boys had an overflow of supply.

When Ke and Omar returned home one day after dropping milk off at the hospital, Omar explained to her all the details of his case and how Sincere tried to frame him. This gave Ke the reassurance she needed for the decision she made to kill Sincere. Even in his afterlife, he was trying to bring her down. Omar also told Ke something she didn't want to hear.

"Baby, our boys won't be home for another three weeks if everything goes well. Our home will be complete within the coming months," he paused and looked at her. He sat her on the chair. "I think it's time I do my final drop so I can be out of the game for good."

Ke was stuck. He had came back from beating a murder charge and now this. It sounded bad but it was best to do it now than to leave her at home with the triplets fresh out of the hospital.

"Omar, are you serious? You think now is the perfect time?"

she said as her incision started to sting and she yelled at him. "You just beat a murder case and now you thinking about risking your freedom again!" she snapped.

"I know, Ke. I know," he replied. "But baby, it's really now or never."

He didn't want to miss the time with the boys when they came into the house and he knew Ke would need him there. Right now, they were still in the hospital, the snitches are all dead and he was tired of this risky life he was living. If everything went as planned, he would be back within four to six weeks, maximum.

"Omar. I don't want to have you missing like Trae and Kaylin were for those months!" she yelled as she remembered how depressed and devastated Angel and Tasha were when their men did their last drop.

"Baby, I told you I got y'all. I gotta wrap this shit up not for me but for you and my kids! This shit has run its course," he explained. She just took a deep sigh. She didn't want to argue. "I leave tonight, Ke."

"Omar, are you fucking serious!" she yelled.

The tears started to come down. She couldn't hold them in.

"Trust me, Ke. Please," she had no choice but to trust the love of her life.

He kissed her and got ready to put this shit to an end. "I'll be back, okay? You can bet your life on that. If you need anything, call Trae, Kay, Mel, Supreme or Bo. They got you until I get back. I love you."

Omar made sure to tell Ke to reschedule his meeting again for his real estate investment firm that he planned on opening up when he returned.

"Omar," she said. "I don't like this at all, but I know it's not much I can do. Just be safe. I love you," Ke stated as she got her mind ready to endure.

Omar went outside and hopped in his car. His thoughts went back to their Egypt trip and how the man told them that a higher power would always be protecting them. He summoned that energy and drove off.

He couldn't keep living this life now that his kids were born and his woman was home. He had to end it. As Omar was almost near crossing state lines, police sirens shined behind him signaling him to stop. His heart sank. This couldn't be happening.

THE END of Part I: Omar's Untold Story

ABOUT THE AUTHOR

Want more info about the author? Follow Keely on:
    Facebook: Keely Minaj
    Instagram: Killaah_Keely

Don't forget to leave a review and talk to me about some of your favorite parts. I welcome them! :). Thank you for reading.

ARE YOU READY TO LAUNCH, WRITE OR BRAND YOUR BOOK?

WCLARKPUBLISHING.COM

CLASSIC STREET LIT SERIES

FROM WAHIDA CLARK PRESENTS INNOVATIVE PUBLISHING

Printed in the USA
CPSIA information can be obtained
at www.ICGtesting.com
LVHW090615111024
793501LV00001B/2

9 781957 954653